Love Finds You™
IN
Branson
MISSOURI

Love Finds You™
IN
Branson
MISSOURI

BY GWEN FORD FAULKENBERRY

summerside
PRESS™

Summerside Press™
Minneapolis 55337
www.summersidepress.com

Love Finds You in Branson, Missouri
© 2011 by Gwen Ford Faulkenberry

ISBN 978-1-93541-191-1

The town depicted in this book is a real place, but all characters are fictional. Any resemblances to actual people or events are purely coincidental.

Cover Design by Garborg Design Works | www.garborgdesign.com

Interior Design by Müllerhaus Publishing Group | www.mullerhaus.net

Photo of Table Rock Lake courtesy of www.OzarkLand.com

The author is represented by MacGregor Literary, Inc., Hillsboro, Oregon.

Scripture taken from the *Amplified Bible*®, copyright © 1954, 1958, 1962, 1964, 1965, 1987 by The Lockman Foundation. Used by permission.

Summerside Press™ is an inspirational publisher offering fresh, irresistible books to uplift the heart and engage the mind.

Printed in USA.

Dedication

....

For Harper Stone Faulkenberry:
fisherman, guitarist, basketball player,
princess rescuer, dragon slayer.
I love you forever!

Acknowledgments
....

The author wishes to thank her wonderful family on the Triple F Ranch for their unfailing love and support through the process of writing this novel. Thanks also to René Ford, for being a great muse; Cheryl Smith, for reading the early draft; Ruston Beecher Smith, for his advice on all things German; Dawn Nevel, for her Branson expertise; Dave Kahn, for his thoughts concerning life in Hermann; Noah Campbell, for his insights about St. Louis; Chip MacGregor, for his guidance; Ramona Tucker, for editing this manuscript with eyes like an eagle and the heart of a dove; and as always, Jason Rovenstine, Rachel Meisel, and the rest of the team at Summerside Press for their confidence and encouragement. The Lord's bountiful blessings on you all!

Branson, Missouri

Nestled in the foothills of the Ozark Mountains not far from the Arkansas border, surrounded by pristine lakes, sits the self-proclaimed "Live Music Show Capital of the World": Branson, Missouri. Immortalized by Harold Bell Wright in his book *The Shepherd of the Hills*, Branson, population 7500, boasts a history as varied as the eight million visitors it hosts each year. It was established more than a century ago, when the first settlers populated the region along the banks of the White River. Then, with the advent of the Missouri-Pacific Railroad's north-south route, Branson became a thriving town supplying lumber to the Ozarks. Though plagued at times by the infamous Baldknobbers, a gang of bandits, Branson soon became a mecca for travelers, workers, and fishermen. In addition, the city—affordable, family-oriented, and uniquely American—became known for its handcrafts and Christian hospitality. Today Branson's history is alive and well in its many shows, attractions, and enduring natural beauty.

Gwen Ford Faulkenberry

This, my story, is a very old story.

In the hills of life there are two trails. One lies along the higher sunlit fields, where those who journey see afar, and the light lingers even when the sun is down; and one leads to the lower ground, where those who travel, as they go, look always over their shoulders with eyes of dread, and gloomy shadows gather long before the day is done....

In the story, it all happened in the Ozark Mountains, many miles from what we of the city call civilization. In life, it has all happened many, many times before, in many, many places. The two trails lead afar. The story, so very old, is still in the telling.

—Harold Bell Wright
Introductory, *The Shepherd of the Hills*

Prologue

....

26 August 1887

My heart within me is sick and sad. I fear—no, it's more than mere fearing—I know I have made the wrong choice. But what else could I do with so many people depending on me? Lives I love hanging in the balance?

Perhaps one day I will believe what Ms. Barrett-Browning says: that it is "better to have loved and lost than never to have loved at all." Heidi tells me so, trying to comfort me, and I want to believe her. But today I cannot see it. Today love is a plague, a curse. For love found me in Branson, Missouri, when I was least expecting it. I wasn't looking. I never dreamed it would come looking for me. Me! A simple hill country girl! And for a brief, shining moment, all the world opened up like a rose. Things I'd never imagined possible, heights of joy I'd never known seemed all within my grasp when I held him in my arms.

I thought that love could last forever. But now, as suddenly as it bloomed, that rose lies dry and dead on the ground. What's worst of all—I cut it down with my own hands. I know it's a sin, but I wish I could die too.

Chapter One

. . . .

"Love Finds You in Branson, Missouri"? Are you kidding me?

Ellie Heinrichs, who was sprawled across the bed with her laptop, hit ENTER and saw her words pop up in the lower right corner of the screen underneath her brother's name. Beecher, five years older than she at twenty-seven and always the overachiever, was an international patent attorney living in Munich. He should be at work right now, Ellie figured, doing the time-change math in her head. It was nine hours later in Germany. But there was the little green dot by his name. No blue crescent moon. She had caught him on Facebook.

> B: *I see you got my e-mail. What do you mean, am I kidding you?*
> E: *I mean, "Love Finds You in Branson." It's a joke, right?*
> B: *Wie kommst Du dazu ahhh… Du unkultiviert Schwein! I am offended. Neither "love" nor "Branson" is a laughing matter.*

Ellie rolled her eyes.

> E: *Well, they're both pretty ridiculous if you ask me.*
> B: *As I remember, I did ask you when I was home. But you were a little preoccupied.*
> E: *Excuse me for graduating from college!*

B: *I'll consider it—if you use the plane tickets I gave you to come see me this summer.*

The thought made her smile.

E: *I'm working on it. Meanwhile, about the marketing campaign…*
B: *Have you come up with something better, O great and powerful little sister?*

Ellie's smile turned to a scowl.

E: *No, but somebody has to try.*
B: *The brochure goes to the printer Friday.*

How did he keep up with all of this stuff? Ellie answered her own question: *Because he's Beecher.*

E: *I know. I just uploaded photos of Branson that I took over the weekend. I got some really good ones. You'll have to look at them and see what we can use.*
B: *Will do.*

There was a pause.

B: *How did the audition go? Did you make the Branson big time?* ☺
E: *Shut up.*
B: *Seriously, how did it go?*
E: *It went fine. I'm still waiting to hear from my agent on something better, you know. This Shepherd of the Hills*

thing is only the backup plan.

B: *Mom's idea?*

E: *Yep.*

B: *Well, it would be convenient, especially with us setting up the new Heinrichs Haus in Branson. Wine-tasting by day, acting by night...*

Ellie snorted.

E: *I thought you opted to become an attorney in Germany rather than a Missouri winemaker—just as I have chosen to become a serious actress.*

B: *Well, like Opa says, you can take the boy out of Missouri, but...*

E: *...you can't take Missouri out of the boy. I know. But this is one girl who's ready to get out of Missouri.*

* * * * *

Sunlight streamed through Ellie's window the next morning when she finally got out of bed. Straightening a brown teddy bear slumped from years at his post on her window seat, she peered out at the view that had greeted her every day since she could remember. Branches of an ancient oak tree waved at her eye level, and down below was the manicured lawn, bordered by a wooden fence arrayed with every color of poppies. Beyond that were three neat rows of Norton grapes planted by her great-great-grandfather and still tended by her family and then the rocky bluff overlooking the Missouri River. Two eagles soared over the vermilion water, scanning for a fresh fish breakfast. A squirrel sat on the oak branch nearest her window and surveyed Ellie with black eyes, whisking his tail.

I need coffee, she thought.

Slowly descending the stairs in gray sweats and a light pink tank top, Ellie breathed in the aroma of caramel-and-chocolate-flavored coffee beans as she heard them being ground to dust in the kitchen. This ritual was an obsession she and her mother shared. From the time the Junction Kaffe Haus opened in Hermann, back when Ellie was in high school, she and her mother recognized their Old-fashioned Country Turtle coffee beans as a gift from God to their small town. They bought them by the pound from Dave, the owner, who scooped them into a brown paper sack, and either Ellie or her mom would grind them fresh and make coffee every morning they were home.

"Morning!" Ellie's mother, Katherine, called without turning from where she was preparing the coffee. A huge island separated her from the bar where Ellie stood.

Ellie sat on a stool at the white granite counter and leaned on her elbows. "Morning."

Katherine poured a clear glass mug half full of steamed milk, then added coffee. She added a dollop of whipped cream, sprinkled it with shaved chocolate from a purple Milka tin, and walked around the island to hand it to her daughter. After perching on a stool by the island, Katherine began to cut biscuits on a floured board.

"Um. Thanks. This is awesome." Ellie held the cup to her face, feeling its steamy warmth caress her skin. Her mother had created a masterpiece, as usual.

"You left your phone down here last night."

Ellie picked it up from a painted Italian tray on the counter and saw that there was already a missed call. It was only eight thirty. There was no message, and she didn't recognize the number. She set it back down in the tray.

"Did you decide on what pictures to use? I chatted with Beecher last night, and he's going to check them out too, but which ones did you like best?"

Katherine looked up from her biscuit dough and smiled at Ellie. "I like the one of the sunset over the lake the best. And the sky shot with the trees on the hillside. Let's use that one, and the one of people toasting glasses at the event we sponsored at Branson Landing. Those good with you?"

"Those are good. But about the slogan Beecher came up with—"

"'Love Finds You at Heinrichs Haus in Branson'?"

"Yeah. Something like that. I'm not comfortable with the whole 'finding love' concept. It's too deep or romantic or something."

"Well, we are trying to emphasize the romantic nature of our product and the beautiful setting at Branson Landing for wedding receptions, anniversary celebrations, etc."

"I know. But I have something better, I think. Something more appropriate." Ellie stirred her coffee. "I stayed up late last night brainstorming. What about 'Taste the Good Life'?"

"At Heinrichs Haus?" Katherine raised an eyebrow, thinking.

"Sure. At Heinrichs Haus Winery's Tasting Room in Branson, Missouri."

"I like it."

Ellie smiled with satisfaction and took a long sip of her coffee. "This is better than anything you can get in St. Louis. You know, Mom, if this carrying-on-the-family-winery thing doesn't work out for you, you could be a coffee barista."

"I'll keep that in mind." Katherine's brow furrowed as she cut out a perfectly round biscuit. "And what if the whole acting thing doesn't work out for you?"

Their eyes met. Under her mother's gaze, Ellie felt like a deer caught in the beaming headlights of an oncoming truck. The vibration of her phone in the tray was a welcome escape.

"Hello?"

"Hello, is this Elise Heinrichs?"

"This is Ellie, yes." She didn't recognize the man's voice. His tone was formal, but he sounded familiar somehow.

"Hi, Ellie. This is Will Howard, director of *The Shepherd of the Hills* in Branson."

"Oh. Hey. How are you?" Ellie glanced at Katherine, who quickly returned her eyes to her work.

"I'm fine, thank you. It's a beautiful morning here in Branson. How are you?"

"Uh, great. Thanks."

"Ellie, I left a message with your agent, but I also thought I'd contact you personally since we're in the same state. I want to offer you the lead role of Sammy Lane for our upcoming season."

For Katherine's benefit, Ellie tried to keep a poker face. "I see." Her thoughts were spinning.

"Is something wrong?"

"No, no." Ellie forced herself to concentrate. "Thank you very much, Mr. Howard. I appreciate the opportunity."

"So, are you accepting this role?" His voice was hesitant now; he sounded a little confused. "We start practice next week."

"Is it okay if I get back with you in a day or two? I really need to talk to my agent."

"Well, sure. I can give you a day."

"I promise I'll call you back tomorrow, Mr. Howard. Thank you again."

"Who was that?" Katherine opened the top oven door to slide her biscuits inside.

Ellie, who was staring at the phone where she'd placed it on the counter, blinked her eyes and shook her head before looking up. "It was the guy from *Shepherd of the Hills*. I got the part."

"That's fantastic!"

"Well, I need to talk to René about it first. I mean, we've got a few other things in the works."

"I know, but wouldn't she have called if there was any news? And this *is* news. This is great news, honey."

Katherine's blue eyes gleamed with an excitement Ellie didn't feel. Instead, for the thousandth time she thought what a paradox her mother was, standing before her with a stylish yellow apron over her crisp white shirt and jeans. Katherine was five-foot-ten with creamy pale skin and short blond hair. Dominating the pastel kitchen the way the sun dominates the sky, she was the strongest person Ellie knew. And yet her eyes were as innocent as a dove's.

"Yeah. It's cool." Ellie grabbed her phone, leaving her coffee on the counter, and went upstairs.

While in the shower, Ellie reflected on the basic plot of *The Shepherd of the Hills*: A mysterious old man comes to the hills of Branson to search for his lost son. After learning to love the people there, he finds out that he himself is the source of many of their sorrows, and that more sorrows are to come before there can be redemption. Then, just as he reconciles with his son, more tragedy strikes. Meanwhile, in a secondary plot, young Sammy Lane becomes a lady and falls in love.

Ellie rolled her eyes. *Definitely a stretch for me.*

She scrubbed her body with a vengeance, letting the water almost burn her skin till she felt some of the tension leave her shoulders. She'd read that Sylvia Plath said there's nothing a good, hot bath won't cure, and stepping out of the shower she concurred, mentally amending the statement to include a good, hot shower. Ellie wrapped her long, dark hair in a towel and made a turban on top of her head. Then she pulled a white chenille robe around her and walked across the room to her window seat, where she sank into the candy-apple-red-colored cushion. She scanned the screen of her phone till she found René's number, and pressed CALL.

"You have reached René Schay of Class Act talent agency. I cannot take your call at this time, but feel free to leave me a message at the tone." *Beep.*

"Hi René, this is Ellie Heinrichs. I need to talk to you today if possible. I've had an offer on a part in Branson. Wanted to hear your thoughts. Thanks."

Ellie hit END and leaned against the bay window, gazing out at the river. What was she going to do? What did she *need* to do—for her career? All of her acting experience so far, and even the things she learned in college, didn't give her much real-world direction. The basic message she'd taken away: it's nearly impossible to make a living in the arts. Of those who do—and Ellie was determined to be one of them—there seems no set formula for success other than hard work plus luck. She could try to work her way up, building a repertoire as best she could in Branson and St. Louis till a big break came, or she could move to New York and—what? Wait tables and hope for a part in something substantial?

She had hoped an agent would be the answer or at least provide expert advice. But so far René had not done much for her. "It's tough in this economy, kid," René had said the last time they talked.

The phone vibrated in Ellie's robe pocket. It was René.

"Ellie, hello. How are you?"

The agent's East Coast accent was not unpleasant, though she sounded a bit distracted. Ellie could hear typing in the background.

"I'm well." Ellie waited, staring out the window and twirling a tendril of hair that had escaped from underneath her turban.

"I got your message just now and wanted to call you back and touch base. Mr. Howard called me yesterday—I didn't talk to him, but he left a message—so I knew about the part in *The Shepherd of the Hills.*"

"What do you think? Should I take it? I mean, where are we with the other options you were working on?"

"Other options?" A pause. "Oh, yes. Well, my contact in LA hasn't gotten back to me, but New York looks like a no-go for this fall. I mean, that's the word right now. Marty Strohmeyer really liked what he saw of your performance in *The Glass Menagerie*—I sent him that clip from the production in St. Louis. He said you were a 'haunting Laura.' Those were his exact words! But he's playing it safe this fall with people he already knows. You know what it's like in this economy. People aren't spending as much money on things like the theater. So companies—directors—aren't taking as many risks on new talent."

Ellie liked the sounds of a "haunting Laura." Tennessee Williams would be proud.

"Do you think I should take this gig in Branson then?"

"Yeah, I do. I think it's your best option right now. That's just this business, Ellie. And you never know what one thing may lead to—what you may find or who may find you in Branson. That Will Howard is bound to have some connections. You know what I mean, sweetie?"

Ellie could hear papers rustling. She thought she knew what René meant. "Okay. I guess we can be in touch about things as they develop?"

"You bet. And there's no fee on this one for me, Ellie. It's practically in your backyard, isn't it? I mean, you got the part all on your own. I wouldn't feel right about taking any money for it."

That was something at least.

* * * * *

By the time Ellie dried her hair and dressed, returning downstairs, her mother had left the kitchen. It was spotless again, as usual. All remnants of coffee were gone from the white granite counter. A pyramid of flaky biscuits adorned an antique blue plate, loosely covered by a napkin of white Battenberg lace. Softened butter and wildflower honey in a crock were neatly set beside the biscuits, and Ellie lathered a biscuit with both before heading out the back door.

She found her Opa in the toolshed, where he was gathering his hoe and shovel. "Headed to the garden?"

"Hello, Sunshine." Extra wrinkles formed around the outer edges of his blue eyes, which were the same color as her mother's. He reached out to hug her. "I'm waging war on some weeds today. Care to join me?"

"There's already a weed problem? It seems like you just put in the garden."

"I did. In fact, I'm still putting it in. But the weeds are already trying to take over. One must be vigilant." He winked.

Ellie considered her grandfather with amusement and suddenly felt twelve years old. The worn overalls, the brown boots, the straw hat, the leather gloves—like the cover of a favorite book.

"Sure, Opa, I'll help. But I need to talk to Mom first. Do you know where she is?"

"I suspect she's in the office."

Ellie jogged down to the foot of the hill, to the entrance of the winery, and entered a quaint building that appeared to belong in Rothenburg-on-the-Tauber. Red geraniums spilled out of window boxes, and fragrant muscadine vines with serrated leaves the color of sage flanked the covered walkway leading up to the wooden door. The building housed a tasting room and gift shop in the front and offices in the back. Waving at Ruth, who was helping a customer with juice in the gift shop, Ellie made her way to the back.

Katherine held up one finger to Ellie. "We really need that piece of legislation to go through," Katherine said into the phone. "It would help Missouri winemakers tremendously." She continued, apparently talking to someone in the state government as Ellie eased into the chair across from her mother's desk.

Growing up, Ellie had been completely uninterested in the discussions of trade laws, tax laws, and liquor laws that always concerned the winery. She'd left that department to Beecher. He was such a natural that he'd even lobbied the Missouri Congress as a teenager—successfully.

Her mother hung up the phone. "So, what's going on?"

"I guess I'm moving to Branson. René thought I should take the part."

"That's wonderful! I'm happy for you, Ellie. And if you can be happy in Branson, it will be nice to have you close by."

Ellie lifted an eyebrow. "It's three hours away."

"I know, but at least it's not Germany or New York. Even though I want you to do what you want to do, go where you want to go—"

"I know, Mom. And 'be who I want to be.' But I don't really want to be Sammy Lane." Ellie was whining, and she knew it. But she didn't care. "I honestly don't know how I'm going to do the part—hillbilly is *so* not me. The whole idea is hokey. Maybe if it were in a serious theater somewhere...but *Branson*? I might as well be in one of those country music shows."

"There are worse plights." Katherine slid a flat cardboard box across the desk toward Ellie. "I've been waiting to give this to you, but it never seems the right time. Maybe this is the time."

Ellie opened the box and pulled out something hard and rectangular, swathed in crinkled brown paper secured with twine. She untied the twine and carefully peeled back the paper to reveal a small book with a tattered black cover. It was embossed with an ornate floral of orange, green, blue, and white. The design had a foreign flavor, and though she was used to such things, this was exotic, like nothing Ellie had seen before. It was clasped by a tiny protective lock, but the lock was rusted on its hinges and broken. Ellie gingerly opened the cover and read in German from the tea-stain-colored page:

Elise Marie Falkenberg
1887

    Ich lebe, doch nun nicht ich, sondern Christus lebt in mir.
Denn was ich jetzt lebe im Fleisch, das lebe ich im Glauben an
den Sohn Gottes, der mich geliebt hat und sich selbst für mich
dahingegeben.

"Great-great-grandmother's diary?"

"Yes. It's hers."

"Where's that verse from?"

"Galatians, I believe."

"Wow. What a cool thing. I didn't even know you had this diary."

"Like I said, I've saved it for you, but the time to give it has never seemed right."

"Thank you, Mom. I mean, it's really special." Ellie ran her finger over the floral pattern. "But it's in German. It's going to be hard for me to read." She grimaced at the thought. She'd almost completely let her second language go by the wayside in the past few years.

"It'll be a good way for you to brush up before visiting Beecher." Katherine smiled. "And perhaps it will help you identify with your inner hillbilly."

Chapter Two

. . . .

I don't have an inner hillbilly, thought Ellie.

She was dressed in a T-shirt Beecher sent her from MIPLC, the Munich Intellectual Property Law Center, and a pair of comfy boxers she'd stolen from his dresser years before. Her dark brown hair was up in a haphazard French twist, secured by a clippie, and since she'd taken her contacts out, she wore "the glasses of an artist," as her Opa had commented when he first saw them. They were thick-rimmed and black with rectangular lenses. Ellie's amber-colored eyes dazzled most people with their brilliance; however, without the aid of contacts or glasses she could hardly see a thing. Both characteristics—the color and relative blindness—she inherited from her father, along with her dark hair. *The only things he ever gave me.*

Her head propped on two pillows, she lay on her back in bed, feeling her body ache all over. She'd spent several hours in the garden with Opa, fighting the battle of the weeds. Then she "did dinner" for her mother by picking up a pound of smoked chicken salad from The Downtown Deli and Custard Shoppe. She served it with crackers and cheese on the back patio. The evening was pleasant enough, with fireflies doing their electric air-dance above the meadow and frogs chirruping in chorus around the pond. But Ellie felt she would gladly trade fireflies for big city lights and frogs for the hum of traffic on Broadway. How was she going to call that Will Howard in the morning and accept her plight as Sammy Lane?

She opened Elise's journal with a freshly calloused hand.

19 January 1887

Today was my sixteenth birthday. It was nothing like the lavish birthdays I remember back in Germany, but I have grown accustomed to our more simple life here, and it was nice nonetheless. At breakfast, there was a package wrapped in crisp brown paper and tied with a string beside my plate. It turned out to be this diary, a gift from Mama and Papa, who said it came all the way from St. Louis. I was very happy to receive it. Heidi gave me a stick of peppermint candy. There was also a peacock feather from Uncle Robert and Aunt Liesel in Branson. Mama allowed me to tuck it into my Sunday hat.

During the greeting time at church I had many well-wishers, including Richard Heinrichs. He walked right up in the middle of a group of ladies to single me out and handed me a pink rose. They all grinned at me and giggled and winked as he walked away in his new gray suit. No doubt they are impressed by his tall, dark form. Mama says he's Hermann's most eligible bachelor, having come from Philadelphia with a sack of money.

I have no idea how he knew it was my birthday. A bigger shock came after church, however, when he asked if I'd like to go for a ride in his new buggy. I shrugged, not really sure I wanted to say yes, so he asked Papa for his permission to take me home and Papa gave it! Just like that! I have to admit, I felt a bit like a mule being traded between them, though that is probably unfair. Richard is an honorable person. Papa is very dear. This is just how things are done.

I sat beside Richard stiff as a board. The buggy was nice, and I do love the horses. He complimented my hat, noticing the new feather. But Richard Heinrichs makes me nervous. He is so grown-up and sophisticated! I am still a schoolgirl. I don't feel ready for my life to change again, even though Mama and Papa say that it will. I suppose it must now that I am growing older.

Placing the diary on her bedside table, Ellie dozed off, exhausted from the day's events and also the mental effort it took to read German. Her dreams that night were fitful and fragmented.

* * * * *

When Ellie woke, she had the distinct mental image of herself in a red calico dress, hair in a bun, with a peacock feather stuck in it. Only she wasn't riding in a horse-drawn carriage on a country trail dotted with wildflowers through the untouched Missouri countryside. She was trapped in a line of bumper-to-bumper traffic on Highway 76, the thoroughfare that cuts a six-mile stretch right through the heart of Branson.

* * * * *

"Mr. Howard?"

"Yes, this is Will."

"This is Ellie Heinrichs. I'm calling to let you know I accept the part of Sammy Lane." Ellie almost choked on the words and hoped he couldn't tell. Though she wanted to get it out of the way, she was beginning to question the wisdom of making the call before having her coffee.

He didn't seem fazed. "Okay, great. We'll see you in the next few days then. Practice starts Monday, but you'll need to pick up a script as soon as you can."

"What time are you in the office? I can come by tomorrow if you'd like."

"I have some PR to do in the morning, but I should be back after lunch. Could you come around two o'clock?"

"Sure. I'll see you then."

"Okay. See you. Be careful driving."

"Thanks."

Be careful driving? This guy sounded like her Opa.

Ellie texted "Branson or Bust" to Beecher, then set her phone on the bedside table next to her great-great-grandmother's diary.

After throwing on a T-shirt and some cutoff jeans and descending the stairs, she was surprised to find her Opa and Katherine sitting at the breakfast table. She poured herself a cup of coffee and joined them.

"What are you guys up to?" She kissed them both on the cheek before sitting down.

"Just going over some paperwork." Katherine handed Ellie a mock-up of the brochure she'd printed and folded.

Ellie studied it intently for a few minutes before handing it back. "I like it."

"That's all we need to know then." Opa grinned at her. "Let's send it on to the printer, Katherine."

Ellie's mother nodded, taking a sip of her coffee. "Okay, that's a wrap."

Ellie took a deep breath. "I have some news for you guys."

They both looked at her expectantly out of identical pairs of eyes.

"I'm moving to Branson tomorrow."

"You accepted the part?" Katherine's eyes widened.

"Yep. And the director wants to meet with me tomorrow afternoon. I figured I'd just move on over—at least some of my stuff. It's not like I have that much, and what I did bring home from St. Louis is all still packed."

"That's convenient." Opa shuffled through the papers in front of him. "And I happen to have an apartment you might be interested in."

Ellie eyed her mother, who simply shrugged.

Opa put on his reading glasses and recited: "Brand-new two-bedroom, two-bath furnished condominium. Lower-level garage. Hardwood floors, granite countertops, stainless-steel appliances, ten-foot ceilings with crown molding throughout. Wrought-iron balcony with view of the White River/Lake Taneycomo. All in a prime location at Branson Landing."

"You bought this?" Ellie said, staring. "What if I had moved to New York City? What about when I do?"

Opa's eyes held a hint of mischief. "I thought it was a good investment, and I made an executive decision. This apartment is for winery purposes. We need it if we're going to expand operations in Branson. It's not *just* for you, Sunshine, although I do hope you like it."

* * * * *

When Ellie pulled her silver BMW into the garage of the new condo, letting the door down quietly behind her with the remote control Opa gave her, she smiled to herself. After a three-hour drive from Hermann, the trek to Branson Landing and her new apartment had been simple and quick—basically one exit and one turn toward the river. Besides the novelty stores of old downtown Branson, there was even a Starbucks on the route, which she eagerly took advantage of, ordering a tall mocha latte with whipped cream.

The condo was situated on the east end of Branson Landing, part of a tiny community tucked neatly between a walking park on the left and the beginning of a row of exclusive shops and restaurants on the right that all backed up to the water. Ellie recognized her unit from Opa's description. Positioned between two stone-and-brick units, the facade of hers was taupe stucco, with black shutters and iron gaslights. The garage door, trimmed in cedar with black hinges, looked like it belonged on a charming old barn in the French countryside.

She got out of her car, slinging a bag of stuff over her shoulder, and unlocked the door that would lead her inside. Immediately in front of her was a small square foyer that shared another door— the door to the outside. Ellie closed the door to the garage behind her, left the other one locked, and turned toward the stairs, sliding her fingers along the smooth oak banister. The taupe-painted wall on the right was bare except for a good-sized cubbyhole trimmed in white—the perfect place for the Murano glass platter she had brought back from Venice. She and Beecher had gone there for a weekend over Christmas break during the two weeks she'd spent with him in Munich, and she'd fallen in love with the colorful platter, its edges scalloped like an oyster. Beecher had bought her the coordinating vase, tall and thin but equally fantastical, and it would be the perfect complement standing to the side and back of the platter.

I'll keep my keys there, Ellie thought. *Mom will be proud.*

She continued up the stairs, admiring the wide crown molding around the ceiling. To the left of the landing, where she set down her bag, a living room began, and in front of her was the kitchen. To the right a short hall led to a bathroom and a tastefully decorated guest bedroom. Ellie loved the open floor plan—the kitchen and living area divided only by a black granite bar housing a row of four iron-and-leather bar stools with fleur-de-lis on their backs. On the other end of the great room, between two windows, was a stone fireplace with gas logs resembling birch and an eye-level rough-hewn mantel of dark wood. High above hung a deer's head, which Ellie hoped was fake.

Beyond the window to the left, catty-cornered, was a mahogany armoire. Ellie opened its doors to reveal a plasma television set. The drawer beneath it was stocked with movies, including some of her favorites: the BBC's *Pride and Prejudice, Hamlet* with Mel Gibson, *Casablanca, Pretty Woman,* and a special edition set of *The Lord of the Rings.* Had Katherine orchestrated this?

To the left of the armoire was a half wall that overlooked the stairs. Positioned comfortably along it was an oversized chair and ottoman with a funky black-and-white floral print. The iron magazine rack beside it stocked current issues of *The New Yorker, Time, People, Entertainment Weekly,* and *Wine Country.* On the opposite side was a wood-topped table with iron legs and a lamp.

Ellie slipped off her shoes and stepped onto the white sheepskin rug in the middle of the room, feeling its cushiony caress. It tied the room together, with the chair and ottoman bordering it on the stair side and a marble-topped coffee table set in front of a red leather couch on the other. Beyond the sofa, which provided a sort of boundary line for the great room, was a long, narrow dining table along the far wall. It seated six, with one distressed black chair on each end and four along the side opposite the wall. Ellie was astonished at the table's beauty; it was like nothing she'd seen before. The base was iron, but the top was a mosaic of broken tiles—black, white, yellow, cobalt, and terra-cotta. Running the length of the table down the center was an infinity pattern, two red strands intertwining with no apparent beginning or end. She traced the windy path of the white grout, feeling its gritty texture against the smoothness of the tiles it held together.

To the right of the table a door opened into the master bedroom that ran the full length of the great room. The light, airy bedroom featured bay windows on the far end and French doors to a balcony on the back side of the condo. Ellie admired the king-sized bed, its blue and gold bedding and mahogany scrollwork, the two mahogany nightstands with gold marble tops, and the huge matching dresser with mirror and armoire. A charming sitting area with love seat, table, and comfy-looking chair nestled into the bay windows. Flanking the balcony on the left side was the master bath, complete with Jacuzzi tub and large walk-in closet.

What interested Ellie most, however, was the balcony. She opened the French doors and stepped out onto the balcony, leaning over the wrought-iron railing to gaze out at the clear water of Lake Taneycomo. Beneath her, and beyond, a couple holding hands strolled along the water's edge, sharing the walking trail with a few Canada geese. A lone kayaker glided past on the smooth-as-glass lake. Ellie sniffed the clean-smelling air and smiled. Maybe Branson wouldn't be so bad, after all. The condo, at least, was beginning to feel like a haven.

Walking out of the bedroom, she explored the kitchen: stainless-steel fridge, a hooded gas stove top with four burners, a dishwasher, double oven, and white granite-topped cabinets. She peeked into the tiny laundry room, equipped with a stackable washer and dryer, a utility closet, and just enough room for a small drying rack.

On the wall opposite the cabinets was a nice-sized—and completely empty—pantry. Tucked into a nook nearby was a desk. An envelope with her name on it in Opa's elegant handwriting caught her eye. She ripped it open.

My dearest Sunshine,

I stocked a few movies and magazines when I came up here to seal the deal but thought I'd better not leave any food. Here is a check so you can buy some groceries to get you started.

Love you forever,
Opa

The check was made out to Elise Heinrichs for one thousand dollars.

Chapter Three

....

At two o'clock Ellie punched Will Howard's number into her phone.

"Hello?"

"Mr. Howard, I'm so sorry I'm not there yet. I thought I had plenty of time, but I'm stuck in traffic."

"Where are you?"

"I'm on seventy-six, and right now I'm inching past...what's it called? The Hollywood Museum. There's a big monkey—King Kong—on the side of the building."

"Oh. You're a good ways off if there's traffic."

"Is it always like this?" Remembering her dream, Ellie began to feel her former aversions to Branson seeping back into her psyche.

"No, not always. But lots of the time." He sighed. "There *are* ways to avoid it. We'll have to get you a map of the alternate routes."

"That would be great. I didn't know such a thing existed."

"If you see the road Gretna coming up on your right, take it. It winds around behind the main drag and then comes back out closer to where we are. When you come back out on seventy-six, take a right and you'll only have about a mile left before you reach the grounds of The Shepherd of the Hills."

"Okay. I'll do that." Ellie bit her lip. "Thank you for your patience. I'm really sorry."

"No worries. See you when you get here."

Ellie ended the call and stared with disgust into the rearview

mirror, then in front of her again. Cars stretched out in either direction like an endless snake's tail, and she felt like a rabbit the snake had
swallowed, slowly being digested in its belly with no hope of escape.
The traffic slithered forward, ever so slightly.

Ellie inched the BMW along, fussing with her hair a bit. It had
looked good—straight and shiny, pulled back on both sides and held
by a tortoise-shell clip at the crown—when she left the condo. Her
magenta sundress with the big bright flower appliquéd below the knee
was now wrinkled. She wore scant makeup, except for a dash of black
mascara to enhance her eyes and a wine-colored lipstick that was
almost completely gone now. Reaching into her bag, she reapplied the
color, smacking her lips as she scowled into the mirror.

Ellie hated being late. Even though she was less than excited
about the part of Sammy Lane, she'd been raised with good manners,
one of the most important being punctuality. It was a blow to her own
personal standards to show up late to any meeting, much less one
with a new director.

Blasted Branson traffic.

* * * * *

At 2:45 Ellie finally spied the campus of The Shepherd of the Hills.
The road leading to it was lined with flags from different countries,
and a giant wooden sign in big yellow letters and a turquoise-colored
tram announced she had arrived in the correct spot. She pulled into
the parking lot and got out, locking the Bimmer. Flip-flops clacking
the pavement, she ran all the way to the main building, where Will
Howard's office was housed.

"Hi, I'm Ellie Heinrichs, and I have an appointment with Mr.
Howard," Ellie announced, a bit out of breath.

The big-haired blond behind the desk turned from her computer screen and peered at Ellie from underneath long eyelashes. "He was expecting you at two o'clock."

"Yes. I got stuck in traffic, but we've spoken on the phone and he said he would be here. Would you tell me where his office is?" Ellie forced a smile.

"Up the stairs and to your right." The woman whose name tag said DONNA busied herself with the computer again.

"Thank you," Ellie murmured, then quickly moved past the front desk and up the stairs.

Will Howard's door was open, and as she stood at the threshold, she could see the outline of his shoulder in a red shirt, and the back of his head above his chair, bent slightly as though he might be reading something. His reddish-blond hair was thick, with just a bit of wave—not long but not short either. He was turned away from his desk, toward the window behind him, and was wearing jeans with cowboy boots. His feet were crossed and propped on the edge of a bookshelf. When Ellie gave a little knock on the door, he dropped his boots to the floor and slowly swiveled.

"Ellie."

He said the word not as a question but a statement. His voice was deep and full-bodied. Something in the way he said her name— or maybe it was his green eyes—made Ellie catch her breath before she stepped through the door, but she recovered swiftly, walked forward, and offered him her hand.

"Mr. Howard, thank you for waiting for me."

He squeezed her hand firmly before letting it go, then motioned to one of the chairs adjacent to the desk. It was absolutely hideous, a wooden rocker with multiple layers of paint partially stripped, or so it appeared.

"You don't like my chair." Again, not a question.

Ellie blushed. "No." Then, realizing what she'd said, she blushed some more. "I mean, that's not what I mean. I love it. It's the ugliest chair I've ever seen!"

Laughter exploded from Will Howard's throat.

"Oh my goodness, I'm sorry." Ellie plopped down, and the rocker nearly flipped over backward. Her bag dropped off her shoulder, her feet went up into the air, and she grabbed onto the armrests for dear life.

"Whoa!" Will rounded the desk and helped set the chair aright. Then he picked up her bag and handed it to her. Luckily, it was zipped, so nothing had spilled out. That was a mercy.

Sitting on the chair's edge, with her feet firmly planted on the ground again, it was Ellie's turn to laugh. "Is this what you do to everyone who shows up late to an appointment?"

"No. Just you." Will sat back against his desk, crossing his feet in front of him.

"Well, I'm honored."

When he studied her for a while without saying anything, Ellie began to wonder if she'd spoken out of turn, been too free and familiar with the last thing she said. They were having fun, and the conversation was easy, but perhaps she'd gone too far. Stepped over the line. After all, he was her director, and this was their first meeting. She smoothed the front of her skirt.

"Ellie, there's something you must never do again."

His voice was serious and she looked up at him wide-eyed, wondering if he was going to lecture her about being late, or worse, about being disrespectful. "You must never, ever call me Mr. Howard."

Ellie breathed deeply, then smiled. "Okay, Will."

"Good." He crossed back around his desk and sat down, opening a drawer from which he removed a packet. He handed it to Ellie. "This is a bunch of general information we give everybody about the history of the property, the play, what we offer here, etc. You'll need to familiarize yourself with it so you can answer questions people may ask you. Sometimes you'll be expected to interact with audience members after performing, and there may be other opportunities you'll participate in to promote *The Shepherd of the Hills*. It's an interesting story, so I hope you won't mind studying up on it a little bit."

Ellie nodded.

"There's also an identification badge for you that you need to wear whenever you come here, and a parking pass, and of course, the script."

"Did you say we start practice Monday?" Ellie accepted the packet he held out.

"Yes. Monday at nine o'clock, down at the stage."

"Would you mind showing me that alternate traffic route you were talking about?" Ellie unzipped her bag and stowed the packet inside.

"Uh, sure. Come over here, and I'll show you."

Will opened the laptop computer on the side of his desk and moved it to the center. "Where will you be driving from?"

"Branson Landing."

With Ellie glancing over his shoulder, Will pulled up a map of Branson, enlarging it to the full size of his screen. "See here?" He pointed out Branson Landing and the back road from there that would take her around the perimeter of Branson so she wouldn't have to drive 76 all the way the next time.

"I live on the total opposite end of Branson!" Ellie moaned.

"You didn't know that?"

"Not exactly. I didn't choose my apartment. It belongs to my family."

Will raised an eyebrow. "Well, Branson Landing is a nice area. And you should be okay once you learn the alternate route. Want me to print this for you?"

"Sure. Thanks." Ellie noticed the scent of leather and something else—rain—that surrounded her as she stood close to Will. Turning toward the window, she heard the printer come to life.

"Here you go, Ellie." Will stood and handed her the map. Her hand brushed against his as she took it from him. Their eyes met for a second. She thought she heard a clock ticking.

Then Will stepped over, bracing himself with his arm against the window frame opposite her, and looked out.

"I like your view," Ellie said, finding her voice.

Will blew out a puff of air and grinned. "You like the tops of trees?"

"Yes, I do, actually."

"It does beat a concrete jungle. I'll give it that."

"My view at home is from a high bluff overlooking the Missouri River. No matter where I go, I carry that view with me. It gives me some sense of peace wherever I am, I suppose, as Yeats said, 'in my deep heart's core.'"

"That sounds a little better than the tops of trees."

Ellie laughed lightly. "It is, but it starts with the tops of trees. You look over the trees and down to the river. I love to watch the water."

"You'd like my place then. I have a cabin on Table Rock Lake. It's surrounded by woods and right on the water."

"How lovely!"

"It's on family land. Perhaps I can show you sometime—" Will ran a hand through his hair, cutting himself off. "I mean, maybe we'll have a cast party out there or something."

"Sure. Sounds like fun."

Ellie's heart throbbed, like the wings of a moth too close to burning heat. She flew back around the desk and stood perfectly still, staring.

Will smiled at her crookedly and extended his hand. "It was great meeting with you. I'll see you Monday?"

Ellie shook his hand. "I'll be here."

Chapter Four

....

The trip back to the condo had gone much smoother, thanks to Will's map. Using it, Ellie even maneuvered a side trip to the red-roofed outlet mall that housed a kitchen store, where she bought a coffee-maker and matching grinder, a good set of knives, and some very cool magnetic spice containers, which she planned to mount on the side of the refrigerator. Passing by an old-fashioned fruit stand, she stopped and got a quart each of strawberries and blueberries, a canta-loupe, and a half bushel of peaches, her favorite. She also found a nice grocery store where she stocked up on everything else she needed, including some glorious-smelling coffee beans and the spices to put in her containers.

After unloading everything, carrying it up the stairs, and putting it all away, Ellie collapsed into the oversized chair. She closed her eyes and didn't awake till she heard her cell phone vibrating against the hardwood at 9:00 p.m. She reached down and fished the phone out of her bag.

"Hello?" she said sleepily.

"Well, how did your meeting go?" It was Beecher.

"Hey, Beech. What time is it there?"

"It's six o'clock a.m."

"Are you working?"

"No, I'm sitting in a Biergarten watching World Cup Soccer."

"No way. Not at six a.m."

"Okay, so that's what I wish I was doing. I'm really at my desk—way too early. But did you hear about France? The Frogs are imploding. Crazy stuff. South Africa is going to take them out, and I'm glad."

"I never did care for the Frogs anyway."

"Me neither. And I'm all about South Africa. Let the rainbow flag fly."

"Olé."

"Olé. So what about the meeting with Mr. Will Howard?"

She blew out a breath. "How did you know his name?"

"I checked out the website."

"You what? What are they paying you for in that office?"

"I did it in my spare time."

Ellie snorted. "You must be bored."

"No, just interested. Doing my big-brotherly duty, if only from afar."

"You are hilarious."

There was a long pause, and Ellie knew Beecher was waiting. She also knew how he hated to wait.

"Will you just answer the stupid question?" he finally blurted.

She smiled to herself and stretched like a cat. "It was fine. Actually, more than fine. I liked him a lot more than I thought I would. And he didn't seem stupid or backwoods or anything, which was a nice surprise."

"Did you not know anything about him before the meeting?"

"No, not really. At auditions he just sat in the stands and watched, along with a team of others. I saw him point at me once."

"As usual, you should do a little more homework."

"What do you mean?"

"Oh, I don't know, maybe that he was up for an Oscar two years ago. If he'd won, he would have been the youngest director in history to receive it."

Ellie sat up straight. "That's impossible! You read that on The Shepherd of the Hills website?"

"Just that he was up for the Oscar. The other is a bit of useless trivia I pulled out of one of the crevices in my brain. I actually remembered it once I read his name."

"What did he direct?"

"It was a film about Jackson Pollock, a sort of biopic."

"I don't remember it."

"No, you wouldn't. It didn't get a lot of coverage amongst the bigger movies that were made that year. But it's an amazing film. I've seen it."

"Wow. I wonder what in the world brought him to Branson?"

"That is the question of the hour, isn't it? The website doesn't really say."

* * * * *

In an hour's time, Ellie knew everything Google had to offer on Will Howard, which wasn't much. From the articles she'd pieced together, he was raised in Chicago, went to a liberal arts college there called Columbia, and then got his master's degree at UCLA. Submitting his master's project to a contest, he won the coveted opportunity to intern with Stephen Spielberg at DreamWorks Studios, where he collaborated on a couple of important projects. He first tried his hand at solo directing on the Pollock movie, which Spielberg produced. There was a picture of Will, one of the few, on the red carpet on the night of the Oscars. He was standing with a stunning blond Ellie didn't recognize as a star—Lynette Rowe—and they seemed to have dated. The details after the Oscar bid were sketchy, but he basically had dropped out of existence and landed in Branson, Missouri, at The Shepherd of the Hills Outdoor Theatre. One writer questioned his sanity. Another bemoaned his loss. They all had this in common: Will was regarded by everyone in the industry as intensely private.

Curling up on the red couch with a bowl of fruit, Ellie spent the rest of the evening direct-streaming *A Beautiful Mess*, Will's movie about Jackson Pollock, through Netflix. By the end of it her eyes were red and her soul spent. She texted Beecher: *Yes. Movie amazing.*

* * * * *

The next morning Ellie decided to do some exploring on foot. She hadn't run in days and could feel it in both her muscles and her mood. Time for some free endorphins. She donned some black Nike running shorts with a matching pink shirt, gathered her hair into a ponytail, and slipped into her running shoes where she'd left them at the bottom of the stairs. Then she stepped out her front door, which was actually on the side of her condo.

For a warm-up she walked the length of Branson Landing, down the promenade of stores and restaurants that began with Belk Department Store, featured Heinrichs Winery's Tasting Room—a work in progress—and ended with The Bass Pro Shop. It was early, so nothing much was open, but Ellie made mental notes of Coldwater Creek, J. Jill, an interesting-looking Mexican cantina, and another inviting place called The Fudgery. Doubling back along the water, where she saw a rustic catfish restaurant, Ellie started to run.

The smell of the lake beside her filled her nostrils. The air felt balmy, but the temperature was nice. The sun, barely up over the hillside, brimmed over the lake in yellow streams like melted butter. A few scattered geese floated along, carried by the light current. Seeing something jump on the far side of the lake—perhaps a fish— Ellie squinted to see if it would come up again, but it didn't. She continued her trek down past the condo and made a loop around the walking park, exchanging "Good morning" with a few retirees who were walking.

Turning left along the outside of Branson Landing, then hanging a right on Main Street at the light, Ellie ran past the beautifully modern Hilton Hotel and convention center. Her thighs and calves burned as she climbed uphill, entering the labyrinth of streets and shops that made up old downtown Branson. Ellie remembered this section of town as the quaint area she and her family once visited on weekend vacation. It was the only vacation she remembered sharing with her father.

The memory came to her all at once as she passed under the red-and-white-striped awning of the Five and Dime. She and Beecher were seated in the middle of an aisle of toys—he examining every plastic dinosaur for its merits and she choosing her favorites from the large selection of paper dolls—while her mother and father stood at the end of the aisle watching them. The details came into focus for Ellie as if through a camera's zoom lens. Her mother was in a white linen dress, with a stylish jacket and matching belt and sandals of woven brown leather. Her silvery blond hair flowed in loose curls past her shoulders, and she wore no jewelry except for a platinum wedding band on her left ring finger. Her father also wore linen, a steel-gray button-down shirt with a loose collar, and washed navy shorts. His dark, midlength hair was pulled back into a neat ponytail. He wore black Birkenstock sandals. Ellie remembered her mother's tears and the faraway look in her father's eyes as they murmured a conversation she was not meant to hear....

"*You and I are fundamentally different people, Katherine.*"

"*I know that, Drew. It's something we used to celebrate, something we used to enjoy about being together. Why does it have to tear us apart now?*"

Her father's mood seemed to darken. "*Well, I don't enjoy it anymore. I don't know that I ever really did.*"

Katherine winced like she'd been slapped. "*What about our dreams? Our family?*" Her voice caught in her throat.

"*When we got together, I was too young to know what I really wanted out of life.*" Drew looked down the aisle at the kids and caught Ellie staring at him. He lowered his voice to a whisper. "*Now, well, I've come to see that I'm not really cut out for the role of family man. I mean, I love you and the kids, but I just can't do it anymore. I've got to do something for myself—for my own future.*"

A tear slid down Katherine's porcelain cheek, and she quickly dabbed it with her hand. "*But these are our babies—our life. They are our future. Look at them, Drew!*"

Ellie's father stared into her eyes for a long minute, then looked away. He shook his head as if to clear his thoughts. "*I can't let my feelings for them ruin my life. I've got to get out of Missouri, Katherine. I'm moving to New York.*"

She reached out to touch his arm. "*We can go with you. I'll leave Missouri too…leave the winery and my family. I'm your wife—I promised to go wherever you go.*"

Drew's amber eyes turned cruel, and he shrugged her hand off his arm. "*Don't you see, Katherine? I don't want you to go. I have to do this alone.*"

* * * * *

By the time Ellie returned to her condo, it was hot. She took a cool shower and then slipped into her robe—a silk kimono style in red that had been a gift from her mother this past Christmas. Tying the blue tasseled sash around her waist, she padded into the kitchen to fix a bowl of yogurt with blueberries and strawberries. She sat down at her desk to eat while she checked e-mail.

There was one from her best friend, Audrey, who was clerking for an attorney in New York during her summer break from law school at NYU.

> *Elliephant,*
>
> *When are you coming to see me? I am so bored. How does the Beech do it every day? Maybe the law is more exotic in Germany. I'm going to have to talk to him about it.*
>
> *So far this summer, it's mostly been paperwork. File this petition, answer that complaint. I did get to visit the jail the other day to talk to one of Ray's clients. A total thug. I can't give details, but let's just say he's guilty and we're trying to get him to confess for his own good. Ray had the bright idea that if I dressed up in my red suit and went to talk to him by myself we might get what we wanted. I told Ray no way—I like him, and he's a good lawyer, but that was a little unprofessional, wouldn't you say?—so we ended up going together and the bum wouldn't budge. As if we're the enemy! Whatever. (Let me tell you, that NYC jail was a trip.)*
>
> *I'm starting to wonder if this is something I want to do my whole life. Not a great feeling after finishing my first year of law school (everybody here calls it one "L" hell). But I'm going to stick it out for now, I guess, at least till God gives me further direction.*
>
> *What about you? Any word from your agent about a part? I'm still praying you'll get something in New York and we can room together. Mi casa es su casa, remember!*
>
> *Write back when you can. I miss you!*
>
> *BFF,*
>
> *Audrey*

Ellie typed a reply, bringing Audrey up to speed, then skimmed through the rest of her e-mails. Not many of them were interesting.

She finished her yogurt and placed the bowl and spoon in the sink. She was in Branson, Missouri, three hours away from home, and she didn't know a soul in town except for Will Howard. She guessed she'd study her script. But then what else was she going to do with the rest of her day?

Chapter Five

....

Will unlaced his boots, stuffing his socks inside, and set them down on the dock. Next he pulled his sweaty white T-shirt over his head and unzipped his Levi's, stripping down to his boxers. He placed his dirty clothes beside his boots. Then, at a run, he dove off the dock into the cool, refreshing water of Table Rock Lake. He swam underwater about ten yards, edging his way upward before his face burst out onto the surface and he took in a gulp of air. Man, it felt good to get wet.

He had worked outside all day, finally having the chance to put some time into the yard around his cabin. His job at The Shepherd of the Hills had demanded so much from him in the past year that many of the projects he planned to do when he moved into the cabin had gotten away from him. But hopefully that was about to change. With the addition of Cheryl, his codirector, Will's intention was to take more time off. After all, like Thoreau, he had come to the woods to live deliberately. And while he had dreams for The Shepherd of the Hills, he also had plans for a simplified life—time to enjoy home and the natural world the Lord created.

Looking around him, Will breathed a prayer of thankfulness. For whatever he had lacked in family relationships growing up, his surprising inheritance—his little patch of heaven—had given him this spot to now call his own. One hundred acres of woods surrounded his cabin, which was situated on a large cove that was part of Branson's huge Table Rock Lake. Much of the lake was commercialized, with resorts, boat rentals, and camping areas, but all of that was forgotten in Will's private corner. Shaded by giant oaks and cedars, his cabin backed up to a dock that jutted out into pristine water containing all types of bream and catfish. He kept a skiff tied to the dock for when he wanted to fish…or simply row.

The sun was setting over the hillside, giving it a burnished hue, when Will pressed his hands against the dock and lifted himself out of the lake, sitting back down on the boards to drip dry. The fading sunlight spilled like liquid gold over the water, melting into a breath-taking deep amber that made a path right up the dock toward Will, as if he might step out on it and walk across the cove, over the hill-side, and up to heaven. Will stared, spellbound, till the light shifted. It flickered like fire on the water, and then as the sun disappeared, the path washed completely away. The air turned purple…twilight…and then it was dark.

Will shivered. Grabbing his clothes, he jogged barefoot up to the porch and entered his house.

After taking a shower, Will put on a navy terry-cloth robe and made himself a bowl of oats. He'd eaten oats every day for so long that the preparation was something of a personal art form. He never had to measure. He poured them into a bowl, added milk, and micro-waved the ingredients for a minute and a half without stirring. The result was a cross between crunchy, raw granola and mush. Yum. And good for the control of high cholesterol, which was apparently a health hazard he inherited from his father. At least that's what the doctor had suggested several years ago when Will had routine blood work done during a physical. His father had died at age fifty from a heart attack. Will hoped to last longer.

Rinsing out his bowl and setting it to dry on a towel on the coun-ter, Will poured himself a mug of hot tea and sat down in his leather recliner, turning on a lamp. He picked up his Bible from the table beside him and opened to the Psalms. Flipping through the first few pages, his eyes came to rest on Psalm 5:7:

But as for me, I will enter Your house through the abundance of Your steadfast love and mercy; I will worship...in reverent fear and awe of You.

Even though Will knew it wasn't what the psalmist necessarily meant, his thoughts turned to the church he would attend in the morning. It was one of the greatest blessings he'd received since moving to Branson—a true spiritual home. And after the road he'd traveled, and the many places he'd tried before he found it, Will knew that it was only through the abundance of God's steadfast love and mercy that he was able to enter. He looked forward to the opportunity for worship.

A thought crept in. *I wonder what Ellie's doing tomorrow...if she stayed in town over the weekend. Would it be appropriate to call?*

He shook his head. *Of course it's appropriate to call someone and invite them to church,* he chided himself. He almost convinced himself that was the only reason he was calling, until he heard her voice.

"Hello?"

"Ellie? Hey, Will Howard." Why did he sound like a bullfrog?

"Oh, hi. How are you?"

He cleared his throat. "I'm good. Good. How is your weekend going?"

"It's been fine, pretty quiet I guess. I've just been settling in."

"Oh. Okay. Cool." He felt like an idiot, suddenly unable to articulate sentences of more than one word. He cleared his throat again. "I was wondering—I mean, I don't want you to feel any pressure or anything, but I'd like to invite you to my church tomorrow. I didn't know if you knew anybody or might have plans."

"No, I don't."

"You don't have plans?"

"I don't know anybody, and I don't have plans." Her light laugh was like wind chimes.

"Great."

"Actually, it's not that great. I've been a little lonely."

Her? Lonely? Will couldn't imagine it, not with that face. "I'm sorry. I didn't mean—"

She laughed again. "I knew what you meant."

Her confidence was disarming, but Will liked it. "Would you like to join me for church?"

"Where is it? I don't know my way around, but I'd like to go. I was thinking of visiting one I saw close by here, when I was running."

"This one might be a little hard to find. Why don't I pick you up?"

"Sure," she answered quickly. "If you want to, that would be great."

* * * * *

On the way to Ellie's condo, Will's thoughts were full of questions. He knew little about Ellie, other than she was from a Hermann winery family, she was beautiful and smart, and she gave an amazing audition. He was attracted to her, that was sure. But he didn't need to get into another relationship that was going nowhere. *I need to slow down. She said she had thought of going to church, but I don't know anything about what she believes.*

He pulled into one of the parking spaces near her front door. Walking up the brick steps, he pressed the doorbell and stood back to wait. Adjacent to the door, in the corner of the stoop, purple and lime-colored sweet potato leaves spilled out of a concrete urn topped with a lively assortment of flowers.

Within seconds the wooden door swung open on its black hinges and Ellie stood there, smiling. She wore a blue and white tropical flower print crinkle skirt, a white gauze T-shirt trimmed in lace, and brown cowboy boots. Her hair, which had been straight the other two times he'd seen her, hung in loose waves past her shoulders.

Will took a long breath and held it, reaching deep for a way to quiet the pounding in his heart.

"Is that your truck?" Ellie pointed to the red 1945 Ford pickup at the curb. Silver bangles jingled on her arm at the motion.

"It is."

She walked over to the vehicle, made a circle around it, and caressed the chrome hood ornament that looked like an angel. "Did you do this? The paint job is perfect."

"I had some help from a friend but yeah." Will held the passenger door open for her. "Do you like it?"

"It's awesome!" Ellie slid into the seat, running her fingers over the dashboard in front of her. "I've never ridden in anything this cool! It's a work of art!"

Will climbed in beside her. "Thanks for saying that. Sometimes people have to acquire the taste for Scarlett's artistic value."

"Scarlett?"

Will patted the dashboard. "Scarlett O'Hara Ford."

They chatted about this and that as they left Branson Landing and made their way into a rougher part of town. The conversation was easy. However, Ellie's expression turned from comfortable to questioning when they pulled into the parking lot of an old, abandoned warehouse. Will parked the truck, dodging a pothole.

"Is this—church?" Ellie asked tentatively.

It was the first time Will had seen her look the least bit nervous. He tried to view the building through her eyes. It was a sickening yellow with crumbling paint. Someone had spray-painted an obscenity in black, which someone else had tried to conceal unsuccessfully with green. A rusted metal frame hung across the length of the front, stripped of any awning, and the sidewalk was broken. Worst of all, a long sideways crack in one of the big front windows was repaired with gray duct tape.

At that moment he realized two things simultaneously. One was how completely he no longer considered the outward appearance of the church building to be an issue of importance, which was perhaps a good thing. And two—a rather bad thing—that perhaps he should have considered it an issue of importance in the case of inviting Ellie. He should have prepared her, rather than assuming she'd be at ease with him in this setting.

He turned his body toward her and touched her shoulder gently with his hand. "Ellie, I'm sorry. I didn't think—"

She narrowed her eyes at him…not angry but suspicious.

"I didn't think about it and I should have. We hardly know each other. I want you to feel safe with me as a director and a friend. This is just my church. It's here as an experiment—an experiment that's working. I love it, and I felt totally right about inviting you. But if you're not comfortable, I understand. I can take you home right now."

"No!" Ellie surprised him with the force of her reply. "It's different from what I'm used to, but I can handle it. Let's go."

She opened her own door and got out. Will lifted Scarlett's seat to remove his guitar, and they joined one another in front of the truck, walking together across the parking lot and along the rough sidewalk. When they reached the door to the warehouse, it was opened by a hulking black man.

"Come in here, Will. Who's this pretty lady with you?"

Will grinned. "This is Ellie Heinrichs."

Ellie stuck out her hand and the man took it gently in his own.

"Ellie, this is Sam Moore."

"I hate to tell you this, Ellie, but somebody lied to you."

Ellie cocked her head to one side and peered at Sam.

"This man, Will Howard, is not rich."

Ellie looked at Will, who made a face at Sam, who broke out in resounding laughter at his own joke. Soon they were all laughing. Sam could put anyone at ease.

When others entered through the door behind them, Will and Ellie broke from Sam, and Will ushered Ellie into the gathering room, where two sections of folding chairs waited, empty, in neat rows. A makeshift platform across the front held only a few chairs and microphones on stands.

"Let's sit up here." Will directed Ellie to a couple of seats on the left side, three rows back. "I've got to get ready to play a little music. Will you be okay here?"

Ellie nodded.

Carrying his guitar, Will headed for the old office he used as a warm-up room. He didn't know exactly what to pray, so he simply said, "Help." He hated that he'd not planned more ahead, given more thought to her needs, perhaps known her better before bringing her here. But what was done was done. It was in the Lord's hands now.

Will closed the door behind him and sat on the edge of the bulky desk, opening his guitar case. As he started playing softly, his fingers articulated the joy, the pain, the hopes he held in his heart. Everything was in the Lord's hands. It had been all along.

Chapter Six

....

"Will you be okay here?"

Who was this guy, anyway? As Ellie sifted through her feelings for Will, she touched upon conflicting textures. There was the Opa-like protectiveness that felt soft and comforting. *"Be safe."* And, *"Will you be okay here?"* A chenille security blanket. But, unlike Opa, there were rough edges to the blanket. Like bringing her here. What was Will thinking? It looked like a good place to get mugged. Definitely not her idea of church.

Then again there was the exotic texture of adventure, rugged and leathery, coupled with a smoothness—the cashmere—of their conversation. It was rare for her to feel so comfortable so quickly with another person, especially a man. And in the truck today being together was as easy as slipping into her favorite jeans. It felt like well-worn denim. Sturdy. Chic. Something that would never lose interest or go out of style.

I'm probably totally overanalyzing everything.

Ellie drew her leather clutch closer to her and scanned the room. It was filling up. *What a motley crew.* The myriad characters making up the congregation were as varied as her feelings about Will. On the row in front of her was a Hispanic family and, beside them, an Indian woman in a purple sari. On the other side of her was a Caucasian couple probably in their sixties—he in a gray suit and tie and she in a navy dress—more the type of people Ellie was used to seeing at church. The woman was in animated conversation with the sari lady, who burst out laughing at something the Caucasian woman said.

Across the aisle was what could have been the Joad family from *The Grapes of Wrath*. Sitting one row behind them, by herself, was a girl who appeared to be about twenty. She was incredibly skinny, had creamy white skin, and wore dark jeans and red Converse sneakers. Her T-shirt was black and depicted some band unrecognizable to Ellie. All down one arm was a tattoo of the ocean, with white-capped waves crashing across her bicep and rolling into a shore lined with tropical flowers. She had a nose ring through her septum—*like a bull,* Ellie thought—and her top lip was pierced. Her hair was maroon and worn in tufts just below her ears, which were pierced with what appeared to be small film canisters. Her large hazel eyes glanced up and caught Ellie staring. Ellie tried to look away but was somehow held in place by the girl's steady gaze and forgiving smile. When an acoustic guitar started to play, the girl turned her eyes toward the stage. Ellie's eyes followed and rested on Will.

He was sitting on one of the folding chairs in the background of the stage. His designer jeans hugged his waist and legs just the right amount and draped loosely at the bottom over chestnut brown cowboy boots. His button-down shirt, a paisley print in orange tones, was the perfect complement to his sandy red hair. His eyes shone like the water of the lake behind her condo.

Will exchanged a smile with the tattooed girl but then fixed his eyes downward. His fingers took on a life of their own, becoming an extension of the guitar…as if the guitar, his fingers, and all of Will were one. He continued playing softly, a tune Ellie didn't recognize.

A man with dreadlocks rolled in a wheelchair down the center aisle and turned to face the crowd. He lifted a microphone from his lap. "I'd like to welcome you all this morning. We are glad you're here." His smile was so genuine Ellie felt almost burned by its warmth. "In a moment Will is going to lead us in some praise and worship time, but first let's pray and dedicate this time to the Lord."

Many people bowed their heads, but Ellie noticed the man leading the prayer neither bowed his head nor closed his eyes. He spoke, as though continuing the conversation he'd already begun: "Father, thank You for this day, for this time, and for this place to gather together. We invite You to come, Holy Spirit, and fill our meeting with peace and purpose. Lead us in truth and let us leave here closer to Jesus than we were before we came."

There was no "amen," at least not from the man in the wheelchair. He merely smiled again and rolled himself back down the aisle to the place where he would sit at the back during the service.

Will stood then and, carrying his guitar, walked to the front of the stage where a microphone was fitted to his height. He looked out at the crowd, briefly making eye contact with Ellie, then said simply, "Worship with me." The words of the songs were projected on the white wall behind him.

> *Open the eyes of my heart, Lord.*
> *Open the eyes of my heart.*
> *I want to see You.*
> *I want to see You.*
> *(Repeat)*

> *To see You high and lifted up,*
> *Shining in the light of Your glory.*
> *Pour out Your power and love*
> *As we sing, "Holy, holy, holy."*

> *(Back to chorus)*
> *Holy, holy, holy.*

Holy, holy, holy.
You are holy, holy, holy.
I want to see You.[1]

Ellie didn't sing. She read the words on the wall and listened to Will and scanned the scene around her. She had never been anywhere like this before. Church for her was a ritual one performed most weeks, a type of penance for wrong done—for the cumulative wrong of human existence. The experience she was familiar with was in a lot prettier setting with stained glass, an organ, and other normal churchy stuff. It was full of normal people, like the couple by the lady in the sari. Will's church was not normal. But that didn't mean Ellie didn't like it. It was merely foreign—like the first time she went to Germany. A completely different country.

"McKenna, come up here and help me out. You know you want to."

Will's speaking voice broke Ellie's reverie. She instinctively turned to the tattooed girl and saw her blush, running a hand through her hair and smiling. She looked tentative, a bit embarrassed.

Then Will said, "Who thinks I need some help? You guys want McKenna to come up here and sing?"

Everybody started clapping and some motioned to the girl, who rose from her seat. In a few strides she reached the makeshift stage and, in a lithe movement, was beside Will. She grabbed a mic from one of the stands. Will changed chords, and Ellie heard a woman's voice ring out a personal invitation so deep and soulful it appeared impossible to come from so small a package. But there she was— waiflike, yet commanding. McKenna seemed to speak directly to Ellie as she sang:

---

1. "Open the Eyes of My Heart" lyrics by Paul Baloche (Integrity Music).

"Come, now is the time to worship.
Come, now is the time to give your heart.
Come, just as you are to worship.
Come, just as you are before your God.
Come."

She repeated, and Will joined her with a tenor part that wrapped around McKenna's voice like half of a double helix. They broke into the bridge:

"One day every tongue will confess You are God,
One day every knee will bow.
Still the greatest treasure remains for those,
Who gladly choose You now."[2]

It was more than just a song. A world of sonic colors opened as the sound enveloped Ellie, as if originating from inside her head, her heart. She felt drenched in the atmosphere of what Will had called *worship*.

Something was happening. Ellie didn't know what, but she could feel a shift in her soul. She'd never thought about God in such personal terms—in fact, doing so embarrassed her. She usually equated such familiarity with the hokeyness that ran rampant in Missouri. On how many road trips between Hermann and St. Louis had she and Beecher amused themselves by poking fun at the slogans of wayside churches?

CH CH: WHAT'S MISSING? UR.

Or the creatively threatening WITHOUT THE BREAD OF LIFE, YOU ARE TOAST.

---

2. "Come, Now Is the Time to Worship" lyrics by Brian Doerksen (EMI Christian Music Publishing).

Then there was the blatant, late-summer scare tactic: IF YOU THINK IT'S HOT HERE, IMAGINE ETERNITY IN HELL.

Their all-time favorite, the one that almost made Beecher wreck the car, was one they saw on an egg-shaped contraption of a church in the middle of a cow pasture: JESUS GOT 'ER DONE.

But what Ellie witnessed now, in this crazy warehouse of all places, was completely different. It could not be laughed off, disdained, or ignored. For the first time she tasted a flavor new and distinct from the religious fare she was used to.

* * * * *

"Ellie?"

The quiet time at the end of the service was over, and Will, finished with the music, took his seat beside her and brushed her hand.

Ellie, still processing her thoughts and feelings about Will's "church," turned to him and smiled. "Sorry. I'm ready, if you are."

He gathered his Bible in one hand. The guitar, in its weathered-looking case, was in the other. Ellie noticed with some amusement that it had a Smokey the Bear sticker on it right next to a peace sign.

"Would you like to get something to eat?"

She rose to her feet. "Sounds good."

They walked out to the truck, Will introducing Ellie as his friend to the few people who lingered. He opened Scarlett's passenger door first. When the guitar was secure under the seat, Ellie climbed in, and Will closed the door behind her. Then he went around to the other side and took his place behind the wheel.

He cocked his head toward her. "Is there something you're in the mood for?"

"I like Olive Garden."

"Then Olive Garden it is."

* * * * *

The wait at Olive Garden was forever. Ellie started to apologize, but Will said it didn't bother him, unless she needed to get back, which she didn't. In fact, the thought of her quiet apartment was a little less than pleasant at the moment. She was glad for more time with Will. They sat together on a bench in their own world, in the middle of a crowded Olive Garden veranda.

"Ah, look at all the hungry people. Where do they all come from?" Will's British accent, coupled with a feckless smile and his reference to the Beatles' classic, cracked Ellie up.

"Church, like us, and Eleanor Rigby, for that matter."

He nodded. "And Father MacKenzie. Let's don't forget about him."

"I love that song." She grinned.

"Me too."

"You want to hear a story about me?"

"I'd like nothing more."

"Well, I don't know how, but I managed to never hear that song until I was in college." Ellie twisted a strand of her hair around her right index finger.

"Really?" His eyebrow quirked in amusement.

"Really. My mom hates the Beatles, so we never had their music around the house. That's a story for another time, but what I wanted to tell you is that 'Eleanor Rigby' was in our literature book for Comp two, my very first semester of college."

"You were in Comp two your first semester? How did that work?"

"I tested out of Comp one."

"Hmm. Cool." Will stretched out his long legs in front of them and crossed his boots. "So 'Eleanor Rigby' was in your textbook. I like it."

"I did too. There was a lot of neat stuff in there—I think it must have been my professor's choosing. But anyway, we were doing the section on poetry, and we started with the theme of isolation. We did several Langston Hughes poems, and then this one called 'Incident,' by Countee Cullen, and 'Richard Cory,' about a guy who commits suicide. Then we got to 'Eleanor Rigby,' and Star, one of my classmates, said she knew how to play it on the guitar and sing it. 'Awesome, do it tomorrow then,' my teacher said. 'Class dismissed.'

"The next day Star brought her guitar to class and sang the song. Turns out she was a lounge singer." Ellie chuckled. "We all started singing with her, me reading the words from the textbook, and the professor used the moment to talk about art as an antidote for isolation. It was one of the greatest moments of my college career."

"That's awesome. I never had anything like that happen to me in an actual class."

Ellie stuck out her lip, mocking him. "Poor Will. I can imagine. It must have been terrible for you studying under Steven Spielberg."

Will's eyes widened. "How did you know about that? Anyway, he wasn't my professor, obviously."

Was he blushing? "I Googled you. Sorry. It was my brother's idea. He's a bit, shall we say, inquisitive. And protective. Takes the big brother role to a whole new level."

"Hmm. Sounds like a good guy."

"He'll do in a pinch." Ellie smiled facetiously.

"Tell me more about your family. What's your father like?"

She paused. "That's not an easy question, Will."

He leaned toward her, looking into her eyes. His voice was a gentle caress. "I'm sorry. I didn't mean to bring up something painful. You don't have to answer."

To her amazement, Ellie found herself wanting to talk to Will about her father—a subject she rarely discussed with anyone. "No, I mean, I wish I knew. He left us when I was a little girl, and I've never seen or heard from him since. It's like he vanished into thin air."

"Wow. That's brutal. It must have been very hard on you, growing up."

"My mom, Katherine, is amazingly strong. She compensated in every way possible, and her father, my Opa, lived with us after that. He became a father figure in my life, I guess. He's wonderful. But nothing can replace your dad. It's kind of like a gaping hole in my life, and my brother's too, though he doesn't admit it."

"Your dad must have been—must be—a jerk."

Ellie didn't know why, but Will's deduction made her feel defensive. She crossed her arms and averted her eyes, not saying anything.

In a few seconds, the buzzer Will was holding lit up and began to vibrate somewhat violently.

"That's us," he said, rising.

Chapter Seven

....

Ellie liked the stucco walls, festive pottery, and strings of bare, clear lightbulbs that were the standard décor of any Olive Garden. The framed pictures of sunny-faced Italians, gathered for meals under market umbrellas on city piazzas or against the backdrop of a terraced vineyard, reminded her of Katherine, Beecher, and Opa. In many ways her life had been so privileged—vacations in California and various European wine centers, where Katherine and Opa researched and networked, and where she and Beecher learned that the world was big—yet the family portrait was always incomplete. At twenty-two, Ellie still missed her daddy. Still struggled to understand. Still wondered if he might be out there...somewhere...missing her too.

Her stream of consciousness was interrupted when Will returned from the men's room. He slid into the booth, on the bench across from her, and leaned his head across the table. He spoke softly, yet with intensity. "Hey. Ellie."

Her eyes met his.

"I'm sorry for calling your dad a jerk. Can you forgive me?"

Will's eyes were pleading, and Ellie's heart turned to mush. She looked back down and started fiddling with her fork.

"There's nothing to forgive, really. It's a bad situation, and your judgment was fair. I've said it myself plenty of times." A tear slipped out of the corner of one of Ellie's eyes and slid down her cheek. She wiped it away quickly with the back of her hand.

Will waited.

"It's just that I still love him. Beecher—my brother—gets angry if he talks about it. But me, I get weepy and stupid like this. That's why I usually avoid the subject."

"I don't think you're stupid." Will's eyes held her in their gaze for a long moment, broken only when the waiter, no bigger than Frodo Baggins, approached their table with salad and breadsticks.

"Freshly grated cheese?" He held the grater at attention over the bowl of salad. Will looked to Ellie, who nodded at the waiter.

"Say when!" The waiter cranked and cranked while Ellie grinned wickedly at Will. After there was a small mountain of cheese shavings on their salad, Ellie held out her hand like a policeman. Frodo appeared very relieved as he exited their table.

"So, how 'bout you tell me about your family? Or is that a loaded question too?" Ellie took a bite of salad.

"It's loaded." Will smiled, revealing a row of white teeth that would have been perfect except one of the two front teeth was slightly crooked. "But not in the same way as yours." He offered her a breadstick. "I was raised in Chicago. Went to a small liberal arts school there called Columbia—some of this you may know from the Internet. My dad was a truck driver, and my mother worked as a teller at the bank. I am an only child, and, in my mother's words, 'an accident.'"

Ellie gasped. "She told you that?"

"Let's just say she's not the motherly type and leave it at that for now." Will tore a breadstick in half. "My dad was kind to me, but he wasn't around very much. I don't know what his life was like on the road. I know he worked hard. He and my mother fought a lot. He died of a heart attack when I was twenty. My mother remarried six months later to an investment banker—an old guy—and they live in Nevada on Lake Tahoe. I don't see them very much."

"I'm so sorry about your dad. How in the world did you end up in Branson?"

"It's a long story, but the short version is that I inherited some land on Table Rock Lake through my dad's side of the family. I didn't have any reason to go back to Chicago, but I was ready for a change after being in California and doing the movie thing. I thought that was my dream, but it turns out it wasn't."

"Wow. That's unbelievable to me."

Will snorted. "Why?"

"Because it's *my* dream. Or something like it. Not movies necessarily, but serious acting on a world stage, like Broadway. I can't imagine being a part of that world and choosing to leave it."

"You don't have to be on Broadway to be a serious actress."

"Will, I didn't mean—"

"Now I understand your hesitation when I first called you about playing Sammy."

Ellie blushed. "I'm thankful for the opportunity to play Sammy. I'm just being honest with you about my dreams."

"Here's to honesty." Will held up his water glass and Ellie clicked it with hers.

"I think toasts are more effective when it's not water in the glass."

Will took a sip of his ice water. "So, tell me about the winery."

"What do you want to know?"

"What's it like? What's the history? Or would you rather I Googled you?"

"Ha-ha. You wouldn't find much if you Googled me, but we do have a website for the winery. It tells a little bit of the history. My great-great-grandfather Richard founded Heinrichs Haus. Actually, he was one of the first to settle Hermann—it was sort of a satellite community from the greater German community in Philadelphia." Ellie tucked a strand of hair behind her ear.

"They were looking for a new place to settle to preserve German culture, so they sent out a group of explorers, who found Hermann.

The setting reminded them of the Rhineland in Germany. Great-great-grandpa Richard moved there from Philadelphia, pioneered our land on the Missouri River, and started the winery. We have grapes in our yard that he planted."

"That's amazing."

"During Prohibition the wine business was really bad, but my family expanded the juice side of the business, cultivating muscadines. It was during that time they created the nonalcoholic juices that are really wonderful. Since Prohibition we've done about equal amounts of both wine and juice. My mother and my Opa run the business, along with my uncle Garry."

Frodo returned with their entrées. Armed with more cheese, he deposited steaming platters before them: Eggplant Parmesan for Ellie—lunch portion—and "Tour of Italy" for Will, which consisted of lasagna, chicken Parmesan, and spaghetti, the latter being substituted for fettuccine alfredo. They thanked him, and then Will reached across the table for her hand. "Would you mind praying with me?"

Before Ellie could answer, a voice shrieked, "Well, well, well."

Ellie unconsciously pulled back her hand.

A blond about Ellie's age suddenly stood over their table. She wore a tight red halter dress and a mocking smile. "Don't do that on account of me." The girl's brown eyes darted back and forth from Will to Ellie. "I already saw you. The deed is done."

"What are you talking about, Cristal?" Will's voice sounded different than it ever had to Ellie. It was controlled but hinted at rage.

"I'm talking about you and your little girlfriend here, Will. Don't think I don't see what's going on."

"What's going on is that we were about to bless our meal, not that it's any of your business."

"Oh, I think it is my business."

"You need to step away from here, Cristal."

She turned on a satin stiletto heel but glanced over her shoulder to narrow her eyes at Ellie. "He didn't choose you for your acting ability, I can promise you that."

"Oh my gosh." Ellie's skin prickled as she watched the girl in the red dress march away.

"Ellie, it seems like all I've done is apologize to you today."

"Who was that?"

"Cristal Dunaway. She's a girl who tried out for the part of Sammy awhile back—I guess she thought she was entitled to the part because she's been in several shows around Branson, and she knows a lot of people."

"Well, she'd make a good villain."

Will laughed, sounding relieved. "True. Were you getting visions of—"

"*The Wizard of Oz*?" Ellie broke in. "Yes!" She stuck out her forefinger, wagging it as she pretended to be Cristal. "Well, well, well!"

Will roared with laughter. Then he chimed in, "I'll get you, my pretty, and your little dog too!"

"It would seem she has—or had—a thing for you."

"I don't think so. I think it's all about the part. And you beat her fair and square."

Ellie shrugged, then changed her accent from wicked witch to Elly May Clampett. "What can I say? I just found my inner hillbilly."

"Your name *is* Ellie, after all."

Chapter Eight
....

By the time they left The Olive Garden, it was three o'clock. Will seemed reluctant to leave, and Ellie was glad, because she was in no hurry to go either. The drive across town felt faster than usual. Soon they were at Branson Landing, and Will pulled Scarlett into a parking spot beside Ellie's condo. He opened the truck door to let her out, then walked with her to the porch.

Standing on the top step, she turned to face him. "Thank you for inviting me to your church and for lunch."

"Thank you for going."

A shimmer of naughtiness passed though her. "I didn't know I'd be risking my life."

"Huh?"

"Both at church and the restaurant."

Will laughed. "I never imagined myself as a dangerous character. But come to think of it—"

She cut him off. "It was worth it."

Her words seemed to please him. His eyes gazed into hers, then swept downward to her lips, lingering there. Suddenly he jerked his head up as if he'd remembered something. "See you tomorrow at practice?"

"Yes. I'll be there."

"Okay then." He ran his hand through his hair.

Ellie turned away to put her key into the lock, and Will waited while she opened the door. She waved at him over her shoulder. "Bye, Will."

"See you." He backed away toward Scarlett.

* * * * *

Shutting the door behind her, Ellie leaned on it and clasped her keys to her chest. Her heart beat like a tom-tom. She smiled to herself as she skipped up the stairs, depositing her keys into the glass bowl along the way.

Going to her bedroom, she flung off her boots and skirt and changed into a pair of gym shorts and a T-shirt. She didn't quite know what to do with herself. Running would be a good outlet, but it was too hot. That would have to wait till evening. There wasn't anybody she wanted to call just now. And she wasn't hungry. Spotting the scruffy cover of her great-great-grandmother's diary on the nightstand, she opened it and read:

7 February 1887

It seems I will not be a schoolgirl for long. Mama and Papa want me to sit for the exam to become a teacher, and if I pass, I can work, possibly even in my old school, as there is a rumor Mr. Bachman may leave. The family needs the income in these hard times. Of course I am more than willing to do it. I just hope I pass.

Richard Heinrichs came by our house the other evening after supper and asked me to go riding again. Papa gave his permission, though I was not even finished with my chores. I quickly washed my face and brushed my hair, changing my dress. Heidi, who lent me her white ribbon, said that, without it, my straight black hair looked just like an Indian's.

Richard let me hold the reins, which was a great thrill. I do love the horses. They are magnificent creatures. We rode through the countryside, bundled in blankets, and Richard pointed out his land. He said he plans to plant vineyards on it. I cannot imagine all of those acres planted in grapes. When I told him so, he laughed and asked me what I would plant. "Flowers, I guess," is what I said, and that made him laugh harder. His laugh was deep and pleasant, like Papa's, and his eyes wrinkle around the edges when he smiles.

Ellie set down the diary after a page of painstaking translation. It had served its purpose of engaging her mind. Though she'd been joking with Will about "connecting to her inner hillbilly," she had to admit her great-great-grandmother's story was interesting.

Her ancestors were legends in the winery lore, well-recited throughout Hermann, but reading this diary made everything so much more personal. It was almost like she was alive and becoming Elise's friend. A real person with real struggles, and surely real dreams. A girl like her, with the same given name, Elise, and the same nickname, Ellie.

She imagined her great-great-grandmother riding through a primitive Hermann in a buggy belonging to the would-be founder of Heinrichs Haus winery. A man ten years her senior, who would become her husband. He had money on his mind and probably a family. She reveled in the fun of driving horses and thought of planting flowers, if she planted anything at all. It was clear to Ellie that her grandmother's parents approved the match. It was also clear that Elise felt a huge sense of responsibility toward her family. Did she love Richard Heinrichs? Not yet, Ellie decided. Elise seemed like a girl who wanted to hold on to her childhood. But it was clear her heart was softening toward Richard, even after these two entries.

Ellie decided to check her e-mail, something she'd neglected in the last day or two. Going to her desk, she opened the silver laptop and brought it to life. There was a new e-mail from Audrey.

Ellievator,

I just had the most gruesome day of my entire law-student existence. This beats the interrogations in Professor Norvell's Property class. It beats the debates. It beats Guzman's tirades in Criminal Law class, with his tanned leather skin and wiry gray chest hairs poking out of his golf shirts. It even beats Professor Brill's totally over-the-top exams. Nothing could have prepared me for this.

Ray sent me to the public health clinic. Supposedly I was set up to interview a client there, although I couldn't find her to save my life. What I did find was appalling. Beyond appalling. The whole place reeked of urine. Blood was spattered on the wall. The lobby, if you can call it that, was packed like a sardine can. Drug addicts with needle scars up and down their arms moaned and howled about God knows what. Obviously battered women, some with children in tow, stood in line to fill out paperwork, seemingly on the point of complete exhaustion. And the poor of every color—so many—with their grimy faces, stained clothes, and shoes with holes, if they had shoes at all, were scattered throughout like forgotten toys. They were there to be immunized, to sign up for WIC programs, to be treated for various and sundry ailments. Runny noses all. I wanted to gather the children like a mother hen and take them all home for a bubble bath. But what then? I left with a headache and a stomachache— and would be in total despair were it not for my faith.

Please tell me your day has been better.

A.

Ellie hit the REPLY button.

Dear Audrey,

You never cease to amaze me, not only with your uncanny ability to morph my name into new words at will (have you ever repeated yourself since you began this practice in sixth grade?), but with your powers of description. In one fell blow, you have put me in a place I've never been (and never want to go, might I add)—a public health clinic in NYC. I can see it, smell it, feel it, hear it, even (ugh!) taste it. If Ray ever sends you back there, be sure you have a bodyguard.

My day has been better. Much, much better. I cannot believe I am saying this, but I think I have a crush on my director! His name is Will Howard, and he invited me to church, which I know is not a date, but then he took me to lunch afterward, which I'm thinking might have been sort of a date. (?)

His church was very, um, interesting. It was in this area called Mt. Branson, across Lake Taneycomo from Branson proper. I guess you wouldn't really call it a bad part of town, as Branson has nothing to compare with parts of New York—the parts that seem to fascinate your employer—but it is much less affluent, more working-class, more gritty than the Branson you or I have ever seen. In fact, I think Will's church could be called downright seedy. It's in an abandoned building, and on the outside it looks completely forlorn. But inside, well, I'm still getting my head around it. There was a warmth I'd never experienced in all of my churchgoing days. I was a little uncomfortable and wished I wasn't. Do you know what I mean? If you're uncomfortable with warmth, does it mean you're cold?

The people were the most eclectic mix you can imagine, especially for Branson, Missouri. The range was straitlaced

Caucasian middle class, to an Indian woman in a sari, to recently immigrated Mexicans, to a Goth girl in her twenties. The latter had eyes that haunted me, and then, minutes later, she got up to sing like an angel. It was a day of surprises, let's just say that. Will was sort of the music leader, and he played the guitar. Very cool.

After church we ate at Olive Garden. We had some pretty deep conversation. You'll be surprised to know I told him about my dad (btw, have you managed any investigation on that point?). Will was such the gentleman; at the very least I think we might become real friends. He seems so very genuine. And he's really cute. Why don't you Google him and see a picture?

One crazy thing happened while we were eating lunch. This rabid blond came to our table and caused a scene. Even interrupted our mealtime prayer! Evidently she wanted the part of Sammy Lane—and maybe more...I sensed she had a thing for Will too. I found it ironic that someone else could want the part so badly when it meant so little to me at the time I tried out. I can't imagine dreaming of being Sammy Lane. That said, I'm beginning to like the idea more now, I think. Rehearsals should tell the tale. They start Monday.

I can't believe I've rambled on and on in this e-mail. My fingers hurt. I should have just called you.

Love and misses,

E.

P.S. Okay, I have to be honest. He walked me to the door. (He's very old-fashioned—does all kinds of stuff like that. It reminds me of Opa. I sort of like it.) I think he thought about kissing me. And I really wanted him to! But I think it's cool that he didn't, in a way. Does that make sense?

Chapter Nine

....

The campus of The Shepherd of the Hills was buzzing with activity when Ellie pulled her BMW into the parking lot Monday morning. The turquoise trams were lined up in neat rows, presumably eager to tote visitors around the property. Men in overalls and blue shirts with straw hats milled about doing various chores, and a hefty lady in maroon calico swept the sidewalk with a straw broom underneath the sign AUNT MOLLIE'S MERCANTILE. Her kind face glistened with sweat. Hanging baskets of flowers dotted the façade of the store at four-foot intervals.

Adjacent to Aunt Mollie's was the main building, a converted two-story painted yellow—Ellie remembered that one of the owners had lived in it at one time—that housed the main ticket desk, a leatherworks shop, knife shop, and various offices, including Will's. To the other side were restrooms, and beyond them, past a weathered split-rail fence, the Pavilion Theatre, a gathering hall for the Chuck Wagon Dinner Show. This featured a singing group called "The Sons of the Pioneers," touted on the sign as a "Grammy-winning National Treasure."

In front of Aunt Mollie's were a couple of raised flower beds, bursting with color. Curious props like tin pails, washtubs, and other pieces of pioneer Americana held red, yellow, purple, and white blooms surrounded in fresh red-cedar mulch and bordered by giant ropes you might find on a ship. In the center of the main bed was a clock on an ornate yellow pedestal—about six feet tall. Apparently the clock didn't work, because the time read exactly the same as when Ellie came for her first meeting with Will: 7:41. Neighboring the beds was a wagon-cart-turned-flower-showcase full of pink and purple petunias and sporting red spoke wheels. Nearby a man in a candy-striped shirt was setting up an umbrella stand and a sign that advertised ITALIAN ICE.

Ellie, prepared for hiking in her ponytail, jean shorts, green polo, and tennis shoes, chose to bypass the main office altogether. Instead she took the paved road to the right. This route took her past the Livery Stable, another tourist shop where a cute miniature pony was tied, looking miserable. She stopped to pet his head for a moment before continuing her descent. Winding down the steep hill, she cut back to the left, passing a forlorn picnic area with mossy playground equipment and a gazebo that must have been part of the Christmas display she'd heard about.

Before long Ellie found herself at the amphitheatre that was to be her stage for the next few months, or however long. Her heart skipped a beat when she spotted Will several tiers of seats below her. He was on the set, standing next to the Shepherd's cabin, which burned every night, probably checking something. She took a deep breath and slowed her pace, walking carefully down the many stairs and taking one of the stadium seats near the front where other cast members were gathering.

In less than a minute, a red-faced girl with bright blue eyes and dark pigtails plopped in the seat beside her. "Hi, I'm Suzy. I play the part of Mandy. And I'm guessing you play the part of Sammy Lane."

"How did you know?"

"Marcus, the guy in the tower who has been here forever, told me a certain kind of person gets the part of Sammy. She has to be tall, thin, and have a look of elegance. I'm thinking you've got it."

Ellie blushed. "I don't know about that, but it's very nice of you to say. I *am* going to play Sammy. My name is Ellie Heinrichs." Ellie stuck out her hand.

Suzy took it, giving it one good pump. "Where are you from?"

"Hermann. What about you?"

"Blue Eye. But I live close by here. I go to the University of the Ozarks in Hollister."

"Does everyone from Blue Eye have blue eyes as lovely as yours?"

It was Suzy's turn to blush. "Nope."

They watched as one of the trams pulled up with a load of what appeared to be the rest of the cast. When it cleared, and the new arrivals were mostly assembled, Will ambled over to where they sat. A pretty redhead with a clipboard joined him, and a few other guys trickled in from various points on the set. When everyone but Will was seated, he addressed the group. It was nine o'clock sharp.

"I'd like to welcome you all to our first practice. Thank you for being on time. I'm Will, as most of you know, and I'm very honored to work with you on this production. I'd like to take some time this morning to introduce everyone, so when it's your turn, if you'd please stand, give your name, where you're from, a bit about yourself, and what part you are playing. We'll start with Cheryl."

The pretty redhead stood and faced the group. She was very petite, well-dressed, and appeared about forty-five. "Cheryl Jech. I'm from Gentry, Arkansas, but have recently moved to Branson. I'm your assistant director." She sat, crossing her legs and holding her clipboard on her lap.

Next was a man who resembled the legendary Santa Claus. He stood, hooking his thumbs in his suspenders. His voice boomed out a deep bass. "I'm Eugene Johnston. I live here in Branson, and I've been doing this for ten years. Sometimes I play Old Matt and the doctor, but this go 'round I'm Doc Howard, the Shepherd." He gave a nod and sat down.

Beside him was a man just as big and burly, but rougher. Not as polished. And his beard was a scraggly gray-brown. "I'm Billy Joe Spicer. I live out at Kimberling City. Same as him, I play other parts, but for your purposes I'm Old Matt." He smiled, winking at the little boy next to him. Ellie liked Billy Joe instantly.

The little boy, James, had deep-set brown eyes, curly dark hair, and a turned-up nose. Ellie fancied him as Huckleberry Finn in his cutoff overalls. He was Billy Joe's grandson, and he was there to play Pete.

The introductions went on like this for several minutes. Some of the people Ellie recognized, or thought she did, from the tryouts. Others she'd never met. It seemed like a nice group of people to work with. They were just about finished when a blue tram pulled in and a guy jumped out before it came to a full stop. *It couldn't be*, Ellie thought, fear fluttering up in her chest. She squinted through her prescription sunglasses for a better look. Brown eyes, shoulder-length black hair, olive skin, large athletic frame. It was.

"Sorry I'm late!" he bellowed, jogging over and hurdling the rail that stood between the cast and the set. He was dressed like a rock star in ripped jeans, a black shirt, and a red leather jacket.

"Well, last but not least, why don't you introduce yourself?" Will forced a smile in the man's direction.

"Seth Young, from St. Louis. I'm here to play Wash Gibbs and— oh, my gosh, is that Ellie Heinrichs?"

Ellie raised her hand in a weak wave.

Will clasped his hands, rubbing them together. "Okay, guys, we're going to start by walking through the whole thing. I know it might seem long, but in my experience that's the best way to do it. Gives everybody an idea of the big picture before we start refining individual scenes. So we'll need everybody who's in scene one down here—bring your scripts—and everyone else stay in the stands and follow along till it's your turn."

"Boss?" It was the guy playing Buck Thompson. "You want me to do my part at the beginning?"

"Most certainly."

* * * * *

Buck's part, as it turned out, was to welcome the audience and tell the most awful jokes Ellie had ever heard. In holey overalls, a red shirt, and boots, he talked about the corns on his feet—there to feed his calves—and pretended to shoot a hole in his sock. Listening to him, Ellie had a flashback of herself and Beecher lying on denim bean-bags, eating popcorn, and watching *The Dukes of Hazzard*, which was their habit after a hard day at Hermann Elementary. Buck's laughter sounded exactly like Rosco P. Coltrane's. Ironically, it was the per-fected mimicking of Rosco's laughter by Beecher that brought about the end of their *Dukes* watching. After that, Katherine found what she called a more "constructive" activity for them both—musical instru-ment practice.

After Buck's soliloquy, if it could be called that, the play got underway. The first scene took place at the mill owned by Old Matt, and introduced most of the main male characters. Ellie watched Sammy's love interest—Young Matt—trying to gauge his voice and movements. He was surprisingly good. Earlier, when he'd intro-duced himself to the group as Young Matt, his demeanor was meek, which seemed almost a paradox when considered with his strong and sturdy—even beefy—appearance. Like many of the other cast members, he worked at The Shepherd of the Hills in capacities other than just the drama, so he was dressed for his part. His chest was as big as a barrel underneath blue overalls, and huge biceps bulged from the sleeves of a ripped red shirt. But his voice and eyes were gentle. On stage he was gracefully commanding. From Ellie's limited understanding of his character, this seemed right on. He was going to be easy to work with. This greatly relieved her, especially since she now had the problem of Seth Young—one of the last people she ever wanted to see again.

However, if she had any question as to why Will would choose Seth Young for the part of Wash Gibbs, it was answered in that first scene when he swaggered onto the set. Brown eyes blazing and black hair shining, even in modern clothes he was the original outlaw. *He doesn't even have to act*, thought Ellie. Her first real and true identification with the play came when Young Matt beat Wash Gibbs in a match of brute strength. She felt the pride and triumph of Sammy well up inside her heart for Young Matt—and her hatred burn for Gibbs. Will was a casting genius.

The practice was long as they read through the whole script. The exercise gave Ellie a better sense of the overall story. She thought she could do a lot with the development of her character under the wise old Shepherd's guidance. He was almost like a father to Sammy. And the scene in which the Shepherd reunited with his estranged son—just before the son's death—had great emotional impact. It was the perfect picture of redemption. Ellie was beginning to realize the play had much deeper spiritual substance than she previously thought, and Will's passion for it started to seem less ridiculous.

They only stopped once for a bathroom and water break. Will didn't do much interfering; he was focused on the big picture and giving the players a sense of it.

"That's a wrap," he said when the last word of the play was spoken. "Thank you, guys, for sticking through this. You did a great reader's theater, and I hope everyone has an idea now, if not before, of the overall play. Tomorrow we'll meet back at the same time and break into smaller groups to start getting more specific. Any questions?"

To Ellie's surprise, there were none. She guessed everyone was as tired and ready to be done as she was. An empty blue tram pulled into view.

"Any of you who'd like to see the play tonight are welcome. Pick up free tickets from Donna at the main desk. Cheryl's company has gotten us off to a great start." Will scanned his clipboard. "All right then, see you tomorrow."

Most of the cast loaded onto the tram, and Ellie was relieved to see that Seth was one of them. Her less-than-friendly acknowledgment of him during break had hopefully discouraged further advances. Suzy hugged her good-bye, chuckling as she declined the hike together up the hill that Ellie offered. A few stragglers stopped to chat with Will and Cheryl. As Ellie rose from where she'd been sitting, planning to walk back up to her car, Will made eye contact with her. She thought she saw his lips form the word *wait*. So wait she did. He was the director after all.

* * * * *

"I'm sorry you had to wait so long."

Warmth, like sunshine, washed over Ellie at the sound of his voice. Even though she'd been with him all day, it was different now that he was coming toward her, speaking to her directly—and not as director. "Want to walk with me?"

"Sure."

They hiked the steep hillside, feet hitting the pavement. They passed the abandoned playground, where they could have stopped to sit, and then the Livery Stable again with the same sad pony. Will didn't say much. Ellie, uncomfortable with his silence, began to wonder if something was wrong.

At the top of the hill, on the backside of the main office, was a pool with a weeping willow tree for shade, and a miniature waterfall that provided a lovely, refreshing sound. The rocks that formed the pool were fake, but it still looked like an inviting place to rest and chat. Instead Will said, "Would you mind coming up to my office?" His voice seemed hoarse.

Donna eyed Ellie up and down over the reading glasses perched on her nose as Will ushered her past the main desk and up the stairs. When he shut the office door behind them, Ellie began to feel frightened. It was like being in the principal's office. What had she done wrong?

Her fear dissipated into desire when Will's hand brushed gently up and down her arm from behind. He laced his fingers through her left hand, turning her toward him. They were less than an inch apart. Her head fit just below his chin, and she could feel his breath on her hair. She inhaled the aromas of rain and cedar and waited.

Without moving, Will whispered, "May I kiss you?"

Turning her face upward, she answered by placing her free hand on the back of his neck and curving his lips down to hers. They kissed slowly and sweetly at first, both of them tentative, and then with growing intensity. Her fingers curled themselves into his hair, caressing its rugged smoothness. His hands found her waist, enveloping her smallness in his strength, pulling her closer to him, and then moving up to her shoulders, the sides of her neck, till they cradled her face. It was several moments before they opened their eyes, and their lips parted.

"Whoa!" Will's green eyes sparkled with the wonder of discovery, as though seeing her for the first time.

Ellie smiled back at him, then snickered, and then broke into a full-fledged laugh. Will started laughing too and hugged her to him. She rested her head against his chest.

"What was that?"

"I don't know, but I liked it." Will stroked her cheek with the back of his hand. "Let's do it again."

Chapter Ten
....

The next morning Ellie's alarm woke her from a funny yet lovely dream. She was sitting on the front porch of Old Matt's cabin in a rocking chair, but she was not exactly herself. She was an older version of herself, dressed in calico and lace. Beside her, in his own rocking chair, was Will, the hair at his temples graying. He was dressed in a plaid work shirt and blue jeans. They were holding hands and rocking in synchronized time.

She hated for the dream to end, but she needed to run. Her plans to run in the evening the day before had been happily trumped by dinner with Will and their covert attendance at *The Shepherd of the Hills*, under Cheryl Jech's direction. It was fun sitting with Will and analyzing the elements of the drama, seeing it through his professional director's eyes. She had to admit that the story was touching, whether or not it was Pulitzer Prize material. It was wholesome. Life-affirming. Her favorite part had not been the actual show, however, but the pre-show.

Before the drama opened, certain cast members directed a bull-frog jumping contest, inviting children from the audience to participate. There were several kids who entered, and it was a hilarious thing to watch. Each child had to reach into a burlap sack and pull out a frog of his or her own. The frogs were enormous, like the ones Ellie was used to seeing around the pond at home. They were the size of small cats, and dark green, with back legs that hung down about twelve inches. Two bulging gold eyes sat like knots on the tops of their heads, and their mouths were set in wide, tight-lipped smiles.

When the children had their frogs, they were instructed to wait in the center of what appeared to be a giant target, painted in white powder—the kind used for Little League baseball fields—on the hard dirt ground. This, in itself, was a scream, as some of the frogs wriggled and squirmed wildly to get free. Standing in that bull's-eye, the children were to release their frogs on the word *go*. The first frog to cross the outer finish line was the winner.

From the beginning Ellie had her eye on two girls who were seated with their parents toward the front. They were obviously sisters, with blond hair and blue eyes. The older one was tall, and her hair a little darker. She appeared to be about ten. The younger one was tiny—perhaps three—and her hair was the color of cotton. They wore matching red sundresses and held hands as they entered the set.

What struck Ellie as unusual—and a bit of a paradox given their adorable appearance—was the apparent comfort the girls felt with the big frogs. Neither girl flinched when picking one out of the sack, and they each cradled their frogs as they held them, like baby dolls. When the little one's frog wiggled, she simply changed positions, never panicking like many of the other kids. She kept a firm grip. They both listened to the announcer intently. It was clear: these girls were here to win.

When the announcer said "go," all of the kids released their frogs. The tiny girl's frog hopped fast and furiously away. However, when the older sister set hers down, it just sat there, still as a stone. She gently prodded it, clapping her hands and cheering. Was it asleep? Just as the tiny girl's frog crossed the finish line, she began to cheer for her sister's. Arising out of its slumber, the frog suddenly got motivated and leapt—in two gigantic hops—across the finish line, finishing second.

The cutest thing of all to Ellie was watching the girls accept their awards. The cast member asked their names, and the older one said "Gracie." Then the younger one answered, in a bold voice that belied her size, "Adelaide."

"Where are you ladies from?"

Gracie answered, "Ozark, Arkansas," and Adelaide, adding her two cents, explained, "We have fwogs like that in our pond."

The crowd erupted in applause. For a fleeting moment Ellie had the sense she was seeing everything that was right with the world, but she swished away the thought like a pesky fly. *Just the sort of silly sentimental thing that can happen to you in Branson.*

The fifteen-hundred-seat theater was nearly full. Vendors walked up and down hawking programs and popcorn. Not many people recognized Ellie, which was good, she thought. She and Will still hadn't figured out the best way to navigate working together while beginning this new and exciting dating relationship.

Her Boden halter dress, with its smart, funky print, seemed to smile at her from its place on the armchair in the corner of her room, where she had tossed it on her way to bed. Will had said he liked it, and he'd noticed the tiny detail on her Børn sandals that made them the perfect match. He had also admired her earrings and the way she wore her hair, naturally straight as a board. It had fallen like a chocolate silk curtain around their faces when they kissed good night on her doorstep.

Ellie rolled out of bed, rubbing sleep from the corners of her eyes. She slipped into a pair of gym shorts, a sports bra and T-shirt, padded running socks and her Asics, and pulled her hair into a ponytail. Without eating or drinking anything—as was her custom before a run—she stepped out the door and walked down to the boardwalk, where she stretched before taking off running.

The morning sunlight spilled out over the greenish water of Lake Taneycomo like golden honey. The air was fresh and pure and drenched in birdsong from the surrounding trees. How good it was to be alive in this place, Ellie thought, then laughed about how much her perspective had changed. A few days ago, moving to Branson had seemed like a death sentence. Yet today her heart throbbed with new life and possibilities she'd never imagined. Her adrenaline surged, making her body tingle all over. She was ready to run.

This morning she was planning to make a wide loop rather than winding through the tree-dotted maze of downtown Branson, just for variation. She turned out of Branson Landing and briefly onto East Main, but then headed south, away from the shopping district. Her route took her down South Sycamore and up South Commercial till she reached Business 65. Crossing West Main onto Veterans Boulevard, she completed the loop by turning right off of 65 onto Oklahoma, which took her past the cemetery. Along the way she saw a few people, a couple cars, but for the most part, the town was just waking up. This was one thing Ellie loved about running early—watching the world come to life.

As she jogged along the sidewalk that bordered the cemetery, a dog squeezed through the wrought-iron bars of the fence and began to follow her. It was a little bulldog-looking creature, scrawny, with short black and white fur, and markings that gave it the appearance of wearing a tattered tuxedo. Afraid it was somebody's pet that could follow her and get lost, Ellie tried to shoo it away. "Go home!" she said in a loud voice. But when she turned on North Commercial toward Branson Landing Boulevard, she could hear the *click, click, click* of the dog's toenails as they hit the sidewalk, and she knew it was still following her. Drat.

Experience told her to go on back to her condo. In her running escapades in college, through certain neighborhoods especially, she'd been followed by dogs before who eventually dropped out and went back home. She didn't like the irresponsibility of the owners—

after all, their pets could have been lost, stolen, or run over—but most of the time she figured they found their way back to where they came from.

Surely this dog would be no different. Yet this was dissimilar from running in a neighborhood. Ellie had no idea where this dog came from, other than the vicinity of the cemetery. "Go home!" she told it again…and still again, more firmly than ever, when she arrived at her condo. But the dog was sitting on her doorstep, considering her with big brown eyes and a scruffy face, when Ellie closed the door behind her and headed up the stairs.

An hour later she had showered, rolled her hair in Velcro rollers the size of orange juice cans to produce a soft, loose-curly effect, and dried it. She decided to wear something new she'd ordered from Neiman Marcus—a paisley-printed rayon georgette and yellow silk blouse with banded blue edges and embroidered floral detail. It was soft, feminine, and a bit exotic. She paired it with white Capri pants and birch-colored Cole Haan sandals that double-buckled on the side. The only piece of jewelry she wore was a wide wooden bracelet Beecher had bought her on a trip he'd taken last year to Kenya.

When she pulled out of her garage, the dog was still on her doorstep. This bothered Ellie, as she feared it was hungry. But she didn't dare feed and water it, which would encourage it to stay. She hoped it would be gone by the time she got home.

* * * * *

That day's practice was different—a lot more intense. Will broke the company up into groups, overseen by himself, Cheryl, and the two veteran actors—Old Matt, or Billy Joe, and Eugene Johnston, who played the Shepherd. Some groups were large, like the sheriff's posse, and the group of Baldknobbers led by Seth, but others consisted of only two or three people. The characters would practice a scene, then switch to practice a new scene with a new group of actors.

Throughout the morning Ellie found herself in small groups. She was paired first with Eugene and Suzy, then George Castleman, who played the hilarious Ollie Stewart. His character formed a sort of love triangle with hers and Young Matt's, as he was the rich city boy she was expected to marry, though her heart belonged to Young Matt. Ellie found it fun to practice with him because his character was so over-the-top silly, and he was perfect for the part. As a foil for Young Matt, and essentially everything good about country values, Ollie came off as prissy, superficial, a flake. George, who was instructed by Will to play up his interaction with the audience, practiced a slap-stick, body-language-based humor that was interesting for Ellie to watch and learn from, especially since she tended so much toward the serious.

For her final segment Ellie ended up in a threesome with Seth, or the villain Wash Gibbs, and the guy who played Young Matt, whose name was Dillon Cody. It was strange, practicing with Seth, and their interaction brought back all of the reasons she'd been attracted to him in the first place back in St. Louis.

"You git over here and give me a proper howdy, Sammy." Seth growled the lines, taking on a backwoods accent as if it were an old coat that fit him perfectly. He seemed to gain too much pleasure in pulling at her arm.

Dillon—as Young Matt—threw himself between them while Cheryl helped with the choreography. They repeated the move, with Ellie/Sammy serving more or less as a prop. Both of them practiced the maneuver, following Cheryl's instructions and striving for authenticity. They reminded Ellie of two bulls fighting over turf.

She and Seth had met her sophomore year during the production of Sophocles' *Oedipus the King,* for which they both landed lead roles.

Of course, his was the true lead—Oedipus—and hers a supporting role as the main female character, Oedipus's wife/mother, Jocasta.

Ellie was a theater major, in the drama club, and involved in everything related to the arts at Saint Louis University. Before tryouts she'd never laid eyes on Seth or heard his name. But after tryouts it was all she heard. He was an overnight sensation among her peers and professors.

She hated to admit it to herself now, but he'd come by his relationship with her just as easily. She'd been swept off her feet by his talent and charm. As Katherine later pointed out, all of Ellie's good sense left her the day Seth walked through the door. Their love affair lasted about six months—and took her a year and a half to get over.

But Ellie was well over it now. Dealing with his presence in this play was a nuisance, but not painful for her. With his gift for drama, his movie-star looks, and his unfortunate narcissism, he was a disaster waiting to happen to someone else.

"I don't like you, Wash Gibbs," she growled back at him over Dillon's hulking shoulder. Other than perhaps the accent, Ellie didn't need any practice to get those lines just right.

* * * * *

After Will dismissed the actors for the day, Ellie noticed that several people stood in line for his attention. Instead of waiting, she boarded the tram with Suzy, who had invited her to share a barbeque lunch in the picnic area. Back up in front of Aunt Mollie's Mercantile, they each paid five dollars for a plate off the Chuck Wagon and commenced eating at a shaded picnic table while tourists walked by.

"That Seth Young is so good-looking!"

Ellie almost choked on her mashed potatoes. "Oh Suzy, be careful."

"That's right! You know him, don't you? I remember his comment now—yesterday when he introduced himself."

"We were in a play together, and we dated for a few months in college." Ellie paused, trying to balance fairness with honesty and discretion. "I can't say what he is like now; that was over three years ago. But back then, well, he was not someone you'd want to be involved with."

Suzy's blue eyes widened to almost cartoon-like proportions. "Do tell." She slurped on her Diet Coke.

"Oh, I don't know." Ellie groaned. "I'd rather leave it buried. I was pretty immature myself. Didn't have a clue. I was sort of carried away with his good looks."

"He's a good actor too."

"That's true. Amazingly talented. That was a big part of my attraction. But our relationship wasn't good. I hope we both have grown into better, wiser human beings than we were then."

"That's very diplomatic of you." Suzy winked.

Ellie decided to change the subject. "What do you think of practice so far?"

"I really enjoyed today, working with you and the Shepherd. I don't have that big of a part, you know, so I can relax as long as I have my little lines down. Gives me a chance to watch everybody else and try to learn something."

Suzy's eyes were so big and round that with her red hair she reminded Ellie of a young Lucille Ball.

"Your lines are so funny when you talk about love. Last night when I watched the play Mandy really got a laugh from the audience on that one."

"I hope I do."

"You will. I have no doubt."

Suzy smiled, revealing deep dimples. Ellie was glad the girl invited her to lunch. She took another bite of her barbecued pork, which was surprisingly good.

After lunch, they decided to visit Aunt Mollie's shop, where the air-conditioning was on and they could browse a bit before saying good-bye. Ellie wanted to look at postcards to send her family and Audrey. While she perused the display on the wall, Suzy chatted with Darcy, the friendly store manager, about her ice-cream selections.

"I'll get this one for Beecher," Ellie said to herself, selecting a postcard with the caption HILLBILLY LIVIN' at the top, and FAMILY PORTRAIT at the bottom. The picture was of five barefoot children—actors—in front of a shack. They were with their parents, and the father looked like most of the guys in *The Shepherd of the Hills* drama, with long hair and a beard and ratty overalls. The mother wore mismatched rags, a sunbonnet, and held the stump of a corncob pipe in her teeth. A dog played at their feet, and an outhouse stood in the background.

For Audrey she picked one with a grammatical error in the caption: YOU KNOW YOUR FROM BRANSON. The list that followed included:

- *IF you think potted meat on a saltine is an hor-dourve.*
- *IF directions to your house include "turn off the paved road."*
- *IF your mother has ever been in a fistfight at a high school sports event.*
- *IF you have a brother named "Bubba," "Junior," or "Jim Bob."*

And, Ellie's personal favorite: *IF you prominently display a gift you bought at Graceland.*

Four out of five isn't bad, thought Ellie, already imagining what she would write to Audrey, who, among other colorful characteristics and eccentricities, was a huge Elvis Presley fan.

The one for Opa and Katherine was tamer. It featured a picture of the Lookout Tower and the quaint white clapboard Lutheran church on The Shepherd of the Hills property.

Ellie was making a few more selections when she felt a familiar presence behind her and caught the scent of cedar in the air. He brushed her ear with his lips and his breath sent a shiver up her spine as he whispered, "Hey there, beautiful."

She turned her head ever so slightly, touching her cheek to his lips. Her knees went weak. She was losing touch with reality, ready to melt into his arms again until she remembered where she was. Remembered Suzy.

She stiffened and turned to face him, creating a little space. "Hello there. I just had lunch with Suzy, and we came in here to cool off a minute."

"And are you feeling cool now? It seems a little hot in here to me." Will's smile was crooked, his green eyes smoldering. He turned his head at just the right moment toward Suzy, who was walking up.

"Oh, hi!" She smiled, apparently a little nervous around the director.

"Hi, Suzy."

"Look at the postcards I found. I'm going to send them to my family—they're hilarious." Ellie held out her treasures to Suzy, to distract her as much as anything.

"These are great."

Will turned back to Ellie. "Yeah, so if you wouldn't mind stopping by my office before you go, we can take care of that."

"Sure." Ellie nodded. "See ya."

"See you ladies."

They watched him walk away. When Will was out of earshot, Suzy elbowed Ellie. "Speaking of good-looking."

"Do you think about anything else?"

* * * * *

The girls parted ways as they left Aunt Mollie's Mercantile. Suzy had to get back to the campus of The School of the Ozarks, where she worked in the kitchen at the lodge to pay for her tuition. Ellie walked through the door of the main office, trying to avoid eye contact with Donna.

"Mr. Howard is expecting me," she said.

"Yes," Donna grumbled in agreement. From the tone of the woman's voice, Ellie thought Donna hoped she might be in trouble.

She climbed the stairs that led to Will's office. They creaked quietly under her feet, and that, coupled with the scent of old wood, reminded her that this was an old house. The door was open and he was standing, looking out his window toward the trees. Though she relished the thought of sneaking up on him sometime, for now she thought better of it.

She gave a little knock at the door. "Mr. Howard?"

But Will was already around the desk and pulling the door shut. He took her in his arms. They stood there together, holding one another for a long moment, and then he kissed her, hard. The muscles of his arms, chest, and abdomen were rigid, defined like chiseled granite against her comparative softness.

"You drive me crazy, you know that?"

"I think I have that effect on a lot of people."

"Every man you meet, I imagine." He scooped her up and carried her behind his desk to his chair, where he sat, plopping her into his lap.

She kept her arms around his neck and smiled up at him. "I don't think so. Just you." She stroked the stubble on his cheek. "I like this five-o'clock shadow."

"You're not going to like what it's done to your face." He frowned.

"You're worth a little chafe, I guess." And then, as if to prove it, she kissed him again.

"I've got to figure something out, Ellie."

"What do you mean?"

"I mean, I'm not very good at being secretive. I don't want to be. It's just not me."

His tone concerned her. Was this his way of breaking up what had hardly gotten started? She loosened her grip on his neck and started to ease out of his lap, but he hugged her to him.

"I don't mean I don't want to be with you—oh, no. I'm not sure I can stop what we've started, even if I wanted to."

She cocked her head to the side, as though sizing up what he was saying.

"Ellie, what I'm trying to say is that I don't want to hide the fact that we're dating. I'm going to talk to my boss about it, if that's okay with you. Of course, I don't know how you feel about people knowing you're dating your director."

Ellie didn't know how she felt about it either. She didn't know anyone before she came here, so it wasn't like she had a lot invested in these relationships. Yet she didn't want anyone thinking she would get preferential treatment as Will's girlfriend. Her work would have to speak for itself.

"In the end, Will, people are going to think what they want to think, just like that Cristal person. She'll eat it up, won't she?"

"Yeah, she will."

Chapter Eleven

....

Dear Beechnut,

It's me, Audrey. How do you do it? Seriously. The most interesting things about my job right now have absolutely nothing to do with the law. What's wrong with this picture? Ray sends me to these crazy places to hand out subpoenas, get summons signed, and things of that nature. And I end up chatting it up with the people and learning all sorts of things about their lives, and coming home and writing it down in my journal, when I should be studying. The stories are about children, food, sickness, jobs, music, 9/11, you name it. Like I said, mostly unlegal matters. And yet, if I keep going in the current direction, that's what my job will be one day—legal matters. Just like you. How did you know it was your calling? 'Cause nothing about it is really speaking to me at present.

Do you love München? What's up with you and Vivienne? Do you plan on staying there? Or doing the double-continent thing forever? Is the law more interesting over there?

I'm going to tell you one of my most fascinating stories. It's about this girl I interviewed, a server at a place Ray loves to go for lunch. He takes the staff—including lowly interns like me—there at least once a week. It's called Pies 'N' Thighs, and it's in Brooklyn, and just let me say it has the best fried chicken I've ever tasted outside of the South, and the catfish is no less successful. They even have biscuits—and lovely pies. Rhubarb in season! But I digress.

The girl's name is Caroline, and she's around twenty. Other than her rather assertive eyewear, she's pretty in a Jennifer Aniston sort of way. Not stunning. More like the girl next door. Anyway, Ray is ready to go over paperwork, as he always seems to be. We're sitting in this barnlike room behind the kitchen, and here she comes with iced tea for us in plastic beakers. She's wearing plaid with a denim skirt.

She's got this winsome sort of way about her and so I, eager to avoid discussion of paperwork, engage her with a question. "Was she in New York on 9/11?"

Even Ray got interested once she started talking. Turns out as a little kid she went to a private school. Her father, who worked in one of the towers, had come to her school for a meeting with her teacher, and the meeting had run late. Because the meeting ran late, he was not in his office when the airplane struck. He was miraculously saved.

The terrible twist is that her big brother, who was an NYU student at the time, had gone to see his father that morning in his office. He was there when the tower was struck, and his body was never found. Such a terrible tragedy!

And this, just one story from one girl in one hole-in-the-wall restaurant. There must be hundreds like it. That is where my interest lies this summer—not in the law, but in stories. Everyone I meet seems to have one. I'm afraid I may be leaning toward a life much less practical than the law, and it scares me. Whatever will I tell my father? I'm praying for wisdom.

Counsel me, counselor.

A.

Audrey,

It is good to hear from you. Your e-mails, like no others except perhaps my sister's, coax me out of the insular world I've created for myself over here. It's a world where I can avoid thinking too much about things like duty and what my place is in the world. I work hard at my job, but life abroad, for me at least, is something of a perpetual vacation.

That said, I need a vacation after the terrible visit I've had with Vivienne. I'm ashamed to admit that I put her through hell, and when I think about it, I feel very selfish, immature, irresponsible...and all of those other curse words normally attributed to my miscreant father.

The end of the matter is that we have called it quits. Because I am genetically predisposed to becoming a bad life-partner, it brings me great relief to know I will not cause her any more damage than has already been done. That was my greatest concern as we planned this trip. I think she came with the expectation of something totally different, however— something like an engagement.

We were quite the pair when I picked her up at the airport— she, shining and fresh like a new penny, and me, the scowling brown toad. I knew as I have known in my gut for months now that we'd never make it as a couple. I was being unfair to her—and finally summoned the courage to tell her so. She was gracious, as you might imagine, which made it even worse. I deserve to be hit over the head with a beer stein. She'll surely thank me one day for doing her a favor. Anyway, there's the answer to one of your questions.

The others are a bit easier to answer, I believe. Yes, I love München. It's a great city. No, I don't plan to stay here forever, but I don't think I'd mind keeping a bit of a double-continent *lifestyle. You know I bore very easily. The law? Are you really asking how I knew it was my calling? Can you ever imagine me doing anything else, you who have known me through all of my various stages of law (life): i.e., political activism from age fetus–present, the relentless stalking of your father in his law office as a teenager, actual enjoyment of law review, obsession with Law and Order, etc., etc., ad infinitum? I've never thought about it as a calling. It's what I'm good at.*

Your waitress's story is fascinating—so much so that a movie has been made about it, give or take a few details. Remember Me, starring some guy named Pattinson. You mean to tell me that after the Twilight craze you and my sister went through that you haven't even heard of this movie?

Not to burst your bubble, though. You are right that everyone has a story, and it takes a special kind of person to be able to hear those stories and then give them voice through writing. You are an amazing writer—has anyone ever told you that? In just a few sentences you have me sitting at Pies 'N' Thighs with you and Ray. I can smell the chicken; I can taste the pie. I can hear the tea beakers clanking. I want to go there the next time I'm in New York! Incidentally, have you considered becoming a food critic?

My advice is not to tell your father anything—yet.

Beecher

Beach comber,

I had to write you back a quick one. OMGoodness about you and Vivienne. Does your sister know? She will be as happy as I am. We've tried to be nice about it, but now that Vivienne's history I can say that we really didn't approve of her. She wasn't the one for you! And it has nothing to do with your "genetically predisposed" nonsense. You don't really believe that, do you? If you did, it would be such a copout...

A.

P.S. Thanks for nothing on the career counseling. How am I going to make money at what you say I'm good at—writing? Believe me, I'll need a better plan than that when/if I tell dear ol' Dad I don't want to be an attorney.

Chapter Twelve
....

Ellie arrived back at her condo in the heat of the day. After their "discussion" in the office, she and Will surreptitiously left The Shepherd of the Hills at separate times in their separate vehicles, and rendezvoused at Red Lobster, where he ate a late lunch. It was not far away from The Shepherd of the Hills, and Will had to get back to work in an hour for meetings. The plan was that after the meetings he was going to talk to his boss about his relationship with Ellie. Later that evening he was going to come over to her place and let her know how everything went. So she had the afternoon to be nervous.

She'd all but forgotten about the dog till she saw it lying on her WELCOME mat. It lifted its head when she opened the garage door, and by the time she stepped out of the car, it was beside her feet. The nub that must have once been a tail was wagging.

"I should not pet you," Ellie said as she stooped to rub the dog behind its large, pointed ears. It rolled its eyes as if in ecstasy. "I do not need to feed and water you, or you'll end up trying to stay here, and I definitely cannot keep you." She pressed the button to make the garage door go down and held open the door to the house. "But I know you must be thirsty."

The dog followed her upstairs, toenails clicking on the hardwood as they had on the sidewalk. It was a friendly sound. Ellie dropped her keys in the glass bowl, then turned on the faucet in the kitchen and filled a ceramic chafing dish. She set it down beside the bar in front of the dog. It looked at the water, then back up at her, then back at the water, and started to drink. It drank every drop in the dish. "My goodness," Ellie said and filled it again.

She got out the phone book that was in the drawer under her computer, making a quick check to affirm that the dog was a female. While the dog sat on the floor and watched her with head cocked to one side, she called the pound, the newspaper, the radio station, and every veterinarian's office in town. No one had reported a missing animal that fit this description. She left her name and number at each place in case someone did. Finally giving up the idea that the dog was going home, she went to the fridge to find some food.

When the dog emptied a salad plate full of shaved, smoked turkey, Ellie decided it was time for a bath. Something about the idea of bathing a dog in her kitchen sink bothered her, so while she changed her clothes into an old T-shirt and shorts, she filled her bathtub with a couple inches of water. She remembered when she and Beecher, as kids, helped Katherine bathe their golden retriever, Sadie, outside in the yard with dish soap. Sadie used to have such a pretty, shiny coat, so Ellie decided to try dish soap on this dog. But when she walked back into the kitchen to get the liquid, the dog was missing from the kitchen rug, where it had lain down after eating.

"Hey—where are you, girlfriend?" she called, making a quick run through the apartment.

There was a clicking noise as Ellie rounded the corner of the kitchen and saw the dog emerge, ears back, from the guest room. Through the open door she could see a big yellow stain on the zebra-print rug. "Aargh!"

The dog watched her apologetically as she scrubbed the rug. Ellie was so thankful she'd bought a can of Resolve when she stocked her cleaning supplies, knowing herself and her tendency to spill whatever she was drinking—especially when she stayed up late watching movies or studying. "No need to take you out now, I suppose."

She turned on the ceiling fan in the room to dry out the rug and put up the Resolve. Depositing dirty washcloths into the washer, she picked up the dog and hauled her into her bathroom. Bending over the Jacuzzi to make sure the water was warm, Ellie placed the dog in the water.

In the bathtub the dog looked more pitiful than ever before. The animal stood there, not fighting much, as Ellie lathered her in soapy water. Noticing scratches on the dog's back legs, Ellie gently wiped them clean with a washcloth. Around the dog's neck grooves were carved into the fur, and skin was exposed in a worn patch. Ellie wondered if the dog might have escaped from a collar or once worn a chain that was too tight.

She'd never seen this kind of dog. The animal didn't look like a mixed breed. She had distinct features: a snuffed-up nose, a painted blaze of white down the middle of her face, and the white collar of fur that melted into a totally black body. The dog's feet, two of which were white, were small and terrier-like—and the body too, size-wise, though she was stocky, like a bulldog.

The animal's eyes were bright. Ellie was afraid to mess with the dog's face but felt she had to wash underneath the eyes, where the fur seemed stained with brown tears. She lifted the washcloth gently to stroke there, and when she did, the dog licked her on the hand. Ellie's heart warmed. "You can't be licking me. I can't make you my dog, because then someone will call, and you'll go home, and I'll be sad. Okay?"

The dog licked her again.

When the dog had been thoroughly rinsed, Ellie wrapped her in an Egyptian cotton towel and carried her to the couch, where she held the animal for a few moments while she shivered. Ellie planned to dry the dog off and then wash the towel, but as Ellie held her, she stopped shivering, snuggled down into the towel, and fell asleep. This was the situation Ellie was in when she saw her phone vibrating where she'd left it on the coffee table.

"Hello?" She did a full yoga stretch to get to the phone from the table without waking the dog.

"Who's that snoring?" It was Will.

"You'll have to see when you get here."

"That sounds interesting."

"It is."

"Are you having a good afternoon?"

"I am—yes, I am." The dog opened her eyes lazily to look up at Ellie, then closed them again. Ellie patted the animal's head. "What about you? How are the meetings?"

"They're going well. I'll tell you about them later. I'm about to go into the last one, though, and my boss will be there. I'm going to pull him aside afterward to tell him about us."

"Well, good luck." Ellie wished she had more to offer than that. The thought of Will talking to his boss about them dating made her stomach churn, though. She had no idea what to expect.

"Ellie? I wanted to ask you something."

"What is it?"

"I want to ask you to pray for me and pray for my boss that he'll give us his favor."

It was a new concept for Ellie. "His favor?"

"Like in the Old Testament, when God granted His people favor before kings."

"Okay. Sure I will."

"Thanks. I'll feel a lot better if I know we're together in prayer on this."

They said good-bye.

She felt stupid, sitting there on the couch holding a dog and addressing God, but Will had asked her and she'd said she would. So Ellie began. "Dear God, I don't know how to pray like this, but if You're listening, please help Will. And please help his boss to grant us favor—approve of us dating—or I don't know what will happen. We might break up, or I might quit being Sammy, which, come to think of it, might not be so bad after all. But then, what else would I do?" She didn't know how else to end a seemingly one-sided conversation, so she said "Amen."

* * * * *

When Will came over later, he was greeted at the door by Dot, the name Ellie had come up with during the two hours she held the dog on the couch. It occurred to her as she studied the dog's fur that there was a small spot on her white collar. A beauty mark, like Cindy Crawford's, or Marilyn Monroe's. A dot. Dot wagged her nub as though she knew Will was a friend and peed all over his boots.

"So this is the little snoozer!"

"That's her first accident since her bath!" Ellie leaned over to help him remove the boots, but he lifted her face to his eye level.

"I'll take care of those." He kissed her gently on the lips. "You smell wonderful."

"Well, I had to have a bath too after cleaning her up."

"What is that? You always smell wonderful." He nuzzled into her neck, taking a deep breath of her hair. "Scarlett smelled like you the other night after the play. On my way home I was driving while intoxicated."

She punched him lightly. "You're silly. It's just lavender. Let's get this cleaned up."

Will took off his boots, and the threesome walked out onto Ellie's stoop, where he turned on the faucet and rinsed the tops of his boots. "I'll just leave these out here to dry."

"Go on and do your business, if you have any more." Ellie pointed to the patch of grass that was her side yard. Dot trotted off the porch, relieved herself a little more, then scampered back to them. Ellie patted her head. "Good girl."

As they entered the house and climbed the stairs together, Ellie told Will about how Dot had followed her home that morning when she ran, and the subsequent details that ended in her becoming Ellie's adopted pet. "I've made peace with the fact that it might be temporary."

"Well, she's sure cute. And Boston terriers are great dogs. I really can't imagine one being a stray, though."

"Is that what she is? How did you know?"

"I used to have one growing up. Name was Buster. He was the best dog ever."

"What happened to him?"

"He lived to the ripe old age of sixteen, and then he just died. Even my mom cried when it happened."

Ellie squeezed his hand. "It's weird that there's so much I don't know about you. Sometimes it feels like we've been together forever." She crossed into the kitchen while Will took a seat at the bar. "Tell me about your talk with the boss while I get our salads."

"It was a blessed time. I basically told him I'd become attracted to you soon after meeting you but had no idea we'd end up dating, yet that's what's happened." Will took the glass of water she offered him. "I told him the relationship was becoming increasingly important to me, and I didn't want to stop dating, but I also didn't want to do it on the sly."

"Wow." Ellie's pulse quickened as she sliced a tomato and drizzled olive oil and vinegar over baby greens.

"Honestly, Ellie, I think he was afraid I might be about to quit, because he said, 'Well, Will, I don't have a problem with it if you don't. We're all adults. It's not like you were dating before you cast her for the part.'"

She placed a salad plate in front of him, where there was already a fork and linen napkin, and took her seat on the bar stool beside him.

"I said, 'That's true, sir. And I hate it that it puts us all in a strange position, but I think the best course is to face it head-on. We don't have anything to be ashamed of. I simply need your blessing to continue as director.' Then he shook my hand and said, 'You've got that.' And it was over. He was on to other things."

"I. Am. Amazed." The knot that had formed in Ellie's stomach loosened. "Do you think prayer made that much of a difference?"

Will took a bite of his salad. "I know prayer changes things. Of course it doesn't always mean things will turn out as well as they did today. We just have to trust God's perfect will. But I sure am thankful His will was to make things easy on us today."

"Me too." Ellie chewed on Will's words as she chewed a bite of tomato.

"I didn't realize it before, but I think a lot of it was the timing today too."

"What do you mean?"

"The other meetings I had were with all of the Branson bigwigs. They're hosting some VIPs here on our opening night, and they wanted to hammer out all of the details and make sure I was ready with the best show possible."

"No pressure!"

Will sniggered. "Nah."

"Sometimes I forget this is Little League for you."

"It's not, really. I take the work seriously. But it's more in perspective now than it once was for me."

The oven timer went off, and Ellie hopped off her bar stool and took out a pan of pesto lasagna, setting it on the counter to cool. "Tell me more about that transformation—I want to understand it."

A cloud passed over Will's brow, and he turned on his stool to touch her arm as she came back around the bar. "Ellie."

Stopping to face him, she searched the depths of his green eyes. "Is it something you don't want to talk about? I mean, it can wait. It's just that I have all of these ambitions—have had for years. They've been a driving force for me. It's hard for me to get my head around why you would throw all of that away and come to Branson."

He laughed, but the sound held no life. His shoulders sagged.

She continued, "Don't get me wrong—I'm glad you're here. I'm even glad *I'm* here, which I thought I'd never say in a million years."

Will straightened his back. "I need to talk to you. Need you to know. But I want it to be the right time for both of us—and maybe it is. Could we go over to the couch and talk, though? I want you to be sure you're ready. It's pretty heavy."

Chapter Thirteen
....

Will and Ellie faced each other on her red leather couch. He took her hands, which were folded in her lap, and with the motion she felt his urgency, his intensity. It scared her a little. His eyes deepened into pools of darker green. They reminded her of Loch Ness in Scotland, where her family once vacationed. She and Beecher were young enough then to still believe in the legend of the monster, and one day they looked for it—afraid but also hoping to see it pop out of the waters while Opa drove their rented boat. She remembered Katherine saying Loch Ness was about seven miles deep. Was that possible? Yet now Ellie wondered, as she stared into Will's eyes, if she would fall in and drown.

"Do you remember that day at The Olive Garden?" Will's voice broke the silence that had settled like a weight between them. "I was kind of flippant when I made a toast to honesty."

Ellie nodded that she remembered.

"Well, I should not have been so glib about it, because you were telling me about your dreams."

"It's no big deal."

"But it is. There's a quote by Yeats: 'Tread softly because you tread on my dreams.' I haven't done that for you. That day I was a little offended at the thought you might want more out of your career than to be in *The Shepherd of the Hills*. That was stupid of me, and selfish, and I apologize."

"So you're not always God's perfect Will." Ellie attempted a pun to lighten the mood a little. "It's okay. There's no need to apologize."

Will was serious again. "Ellie, what I'm getting at is that honesty is not something small to me. It's everything. If we're going to have anything real, I believe in full disclosure between us. Do you? Is that something that matters to you?"

She raised an eyebrow. "I'm the one who asked you about your past, remember?"

"I'm afraid you're going to hate me—or at least not want to be with me." Will breathed deeply. "But you keep asking, even though you don't know what you're asking. You need to know the truth before we get any more involved." He released her hands.

Ellie longed to make this easier for him. To reach out and touch his cheek. Her life hadn't been a fairy tale, either, and she didn't delight in the thought of pouring it all out to him—especially the chapter on Seth Young. But everybody had a past. They weren't all pretty, and that was life. She wanted to tell him that whatever it was, it would be okay. But something in her held back. Could there be something— anything—that would make her not want to be with Will Howard?

He looked at her, then closed his eyes for a moment, as though straining to hear a half-forgotten voice. When he began, his words came out in a steady flow—barely above a whisper.

"As a kid growing up in Chicago, I didn't have a whole lot. We lived in a blue-collar neighborhood, and it was a decent place, but because of a scholarship I went to a private school. I was the poorest kid there. I was in classes with children of senators, city leaders, doctors, university professors. I saw what all of the other kids had, and it made me jealous. I was ashamed to have friends from school over to my house. My parents were nobodies. I decided—really young—that when I grew up, I was going to be rich and, if possible, famous."

Ellie could relate to the famous part, though for different reasons.

"I was lucky to get a scholarship to Columbia, and I worked full-time too. Then I got a fellowship for UCLA, and the internship with Spielberg. That was unbelievable. My dreams were within my grasp—the money and the fame. The life I thought I wanted."

Will cleared his throat. "While I was working on the Pollock movie, I met a model named Lynette. It was a bad deal from the start. I hadn't dated much—didn't have time—but I fell hard for her. She fit the lifestyle and was pretty caught up with me too. We lived together—when I was in town—the whole year I worked on the movie and after it released and got so much attention."

Ellie felt like she'd been punched in the gut. She winced as she remembered the girl in the pictures on the Internet, elegantly dressed, posing beside Will on the red carpet. Her insides burned, but she nodded for him to continue.

"The night of the Oscars, after I didn't win, I didn't feel like going out. We were invited to a lot of high-profile parties; I think Lynette was disappointed. She liked all of that—we both did back then. But she wouldn't go without me."

Here Will seemed so mournful Ellie wanted to cry, to release some of the pain she saw on his face. She knew he was reliving something. Something very bad. It was like he was watching a movie in his head, scanning through images.

Will shook his head. "There's no need for all of the details." He took in a deep breath. "Ellie, we went back to our hotel, got into an argument, and she told me she'd had an abortion the week earlier while I was out of town." His voice faded to nothing, like all of the air going out of a balloon.

Ellie sat there, staring at nothing. For her, the silence seemed punctuated—with question marks, exclamation points, and then, as reality soaked in, a period.

"It doesn't matter," she finally said.

Will jerked his head up and looked at her like she was crazy.

"I mean," she began, "of course it matters, and I am so desperately sorry for your pain." She touched his face carefully. "But it doesn't make me hate you or not want to be with you."

"Really?"

He leaned his cheek into her palm, closing his eyes as though in prayer. She pulled him to her chest and held him there, caressing his sandy hair and the side of his face with the fingers of her free hand. A tear slid down his cheek, and then another, and Ellie tried to wipe them away. But more came until a rivulet formed, and then the dam broke. Will's body was racked with sobs.

Ellie had never seen a grown man cry. Beecher hid most of his emotions, and Opa, though he got teary-eyed over the simplest things, had never shown her the true grief she knew he must have felt from time to time. She sensed that, through his weeping, Will was somehow purging himself of this memory, this death. And though it hurt her too—the truth had cut like a double-edged blade—it honored her to be his witness. As she hugged Will, giving him every ounce of support and care she had to offer, a new sensation swept over her: strength.

After a long while, Will rose. He went to the guest bathroom, washed his face, and returned to kneel beside where she was still sitting on the couch.

"I think I ruined your blouse." He gazed up at her, the clouds gone from his eyes.

"Snot washes out." Ellie laughed.

Will laughed too. "Want to go change while I take Dot outside?"

"That's a marvelous idea."

She started to get up, but Will stopped her. "Wait a moment. Would you—would you pray with me?"

He remained kneeling, holding her hand. Ellie bowed her head.

"Father, thank You for Your infinite love and mercy, and for Your healing. I thank You, also, for this friend You have given me. I pray to be worthy of her and worthy of You, through Jesus. Amen."

This time it was Ellie whose cheeks were wet. She squeezed Will's hand and went toward her bedroom, closing the door behind her.

* * * * *

When Ellie emerged, she was wearing a powder-blue tie-neck tunic with three-quarter sleeves over her white Capris from earlier in the day. Having taken off her shoes earlier around the house, she dug out a pair of white lattice thong sandals with a wedge heel and put them on. She thought she might ask Will to go for a walk after they ate the lasagna, if he was still hungry.

"Are you ready for dinner?"

He and Dot appeared at the top of the stairs like old pals. "I am. Actually, I'm starving. It feels like I just emptied my soul."

"Well, this is one of my mother's soul foods. Opa grows the basil, and she pounds it into pesto with a mortar and pestle. She got the recipe from her roommate one summer when she did a college exchange in Rome. They're still best friends—I call her Zia, meaning 'Aunt,' Paola."

Will snorted. "Your life could not have been more different from mine."

After the lasagna, she served him chocolate mousse with fresh strawberries in stemmed dessert glasses, another of Aunt Paola's recipes. They decided to save the dishes for after their walk.

"I don't have a leash for Dot yet, so I guess we'll have to leave her here." Ellie glanced down at her dog, who seemed to mirror her disappointment.

"I might have something down in Scarlett."

They all went downstairs and outside. Dot wandered around

the side yard while Will rummaged in his truck and returned with a bright yellow rope.

"What do you use that for?"

"I keep it in here for tying stuff down in the back. Think she'll go for it?"

"We can try."

Ellie called Dot over, and Will gently secured the rope around her neck. "This is a hillbilly dog for sure now, isn't it?"

Ellie snickered, but Dot appeared less than impressed. If animals could talk, she'd probably be saying, "Shoot me now, and get it over with."

"This is the only way you can go," Ellie told Dot. "And I don't want you staying in and peeing everywhere." Ellie knelt down to pet her new charge on the head. "You acted like you wanted to go with us. So let's just put on our big girl pants and make the most of it, okay? I'll get you a new leash tomorrow."

They walked together down to the boardwalk, Will holding Ellie's hand and Ellie holding Dot's "leash." They got more than a few looks, but since Will didn't seem to care less, Ellie decided not to either. *Another chance to channel my inner hillbilly,* she thought with a not-unhappy sigh.

Dusk was just settling in over the still waters of Lake Taneycomo. A light breeze kissed the faces of those who walked the boardwalk, blessing them with relief from what would have been a toasty summer night. There were no stars out yet; it was too early. But the sun had melted into mauve and then a dark purple color that washed the mountainside in majesty and spilled over the treetops into the lake like the train of a royal robe.

Gratitude filled Ellie's heart, and she sensed that Will felt it too. They were quieter than usual but walked closely and slowly together, just being. In some ways it felt like they had survived a shipwreck and made it to a peaceful island. Everything had changed between them, yet nothing had.

It was almost dark when they came back to Ellie's end of the boardwalk at Branson Landing. They stopped to gaze at the lake one last time. Will put his arm around her waist, and she leaned her head onto his shoulder. Neither spoke. They simply listened to the frogs and the rhythm of each other's breathing for a long time.

Dot lay down beside Ellie's feet contentedly. The first star appeared, then another, and soon the sky was smiling down at them—awash in radiant light.

Chapter Fourteen
....

10 March 1887

Papa is sending Mama, Heidi, and me away. He says it is only for two months. He says it is for Aunt Liesel's sake, because she has no children and is lonely. He says it will be the perfect opportunity for me to study for the teacher exam. He says the change of scenery will be good for us. He says this way he won't have to worry while he is gone out of town to work. He says all of these things, and I suppose they are true enough, but I know the real reason. There is not enough money or food for us to survive while he is gone. The last crop failed, and we are at the end of our food stores. So he is leaving with a group of men from the village to work on the railroad, and we are going to stay with Uncle Robert and Aunt Liesel in Branson.

Uncle Robert is Mama's brother. He owns a prosperous lumber mill in Branson. He and Aunt Liesel are very dear, and I do look forward to seeing them again. But the dark cloud of my family's financial predicament looms over me like a coming storm.

I heard Mama crying in her room last night when she thought I was asleep. She whispered softly, but I heard her pleading, "What shall we do, Friedrich? I never thought we'd have to break up our family."

My papa said, in his most soothing voice, "It's only for a little while, my love. I am most fortunate to have a chance with the railroad. And after that, we must trust the Lord to provide."

29 April 1887

Richard Heinrichs came today, as he has come almost every day in the past month, to take me riding in his carriage. There were two days he did not come—he was out of town—and I surprised myself by missing him. We do a great deal of talking while we ride.

At least I talk. He's rather quiet, but asks me a lot of questions. At first I didn't know how to answer, but I have become more comfortable with him on these trips. I even think of him now as a good and solid friend.

It is only when I imagine him as more than a friend— a beau, as people in town have begun to say—that I become unsettled inside. I still have no idea of what one should feel for a person like that. Perhaps while I'm in Branson I will be able to figure it out. I definitely need some time away from Richard to think about what happened today.

The ride began like normal. He gave me the reins as soon as we pulled away from my house. (I have become quite good with the horses.) When we came to his land, however, he asked me to walk with him awhile, so we stopped the buggy and walked up to the crest of a hill that looks out over the Missouri River. While squirrels and chipmunks scampered nearby, we rested in the shade of giant oaks, which stood like sentinels over the silver-green water so far below us. Wild poppies— my favorite flowers—bloomed at our feet.

I told him I was going away for a while and he seemed shocked, even saddened. I told him Papa was going to work on the rail for a while to make money and explained about Uncle Robert and Aunt Liesel in Branson. Richard offered to make my father a loan and I told him he must never say that— Papa is such a proud man.

Then Richard Heinrichs did something strange. He took one of my hands in his and held it tight. Then he looked into my eyes so long I was actually afraid that he might kiss me! (I have no idea what I would have done had he tried.) He said, "Elise, you must know how I feel about you. I want you to come back from Branson and be my wife—all of this you see will be yours—ours—together."

His eyes were kind and almost wistful as he spoke. I have never seen him look just as he did, so vulnerable and small in contrast to his usually confident bearing. I wish I could have known what to say to put his heart at ease. But panic overtook me. All I could say was, "Richard, you must take me home."

When we got back to the carriage, he drove. I sat beside him in silence like the first time we ever rode together. It was as if his proposal hung in the air between us. I got out as soon as we drove up in the yard, not waiting for him to assist me.

"Ellie?"

The ringing phone had broken her concentration—the deep concentration it took for her to translate Elise's story from German.

"Mom! Hi! How are you doing?" She set down the book.

"I'm fine. But I miss you—Opa and I both do. We were just talking about it. How are you? What are you up to?"

"Mom, you'll be so proud. I'm reading Great-great-grandma's diary."

"Oh! I am proud. So you like it, huh?"

"Have you read it?"

"It's been a long time." Katherine sounded tired.

"Do you remember it? It's so awesome. I can't believe how cool it is."

"Is she in Branson yet?"

"Huh?" Ellie realized what her mother meant. "Oh, I'm just coming to that part. She's getting ready to leave."

"Oh…then you're just now getting to the good part."

"What do you mean? What happens to her in Branson?"

"No way. I'm not going to tell you. You'll have to hammer out some more of that German to find out." Ellie sensed Katherine's smile through the phone.

"You are such a taskmaster."

"What about you? What's happening to you in Branson? Do you still hate it there?"

"Well…" Ellie wasn't sure where to go with her answer.

"Ellie? Tell me everything."

"I got a dog."

"A what?"

"A dog. A little stray followed me while I was running, and I did everything I could to find the owner but didn't get any leads. So now she's curled up here by me in the chair."

"Is that what I hear? It sounds like someone snoring."

"That's Dot. Will says she's a Boston terrier."

"Oh, Will says that, huh." Katherine grabbed on to that detail. "Well, that's wonderful. What else does Will say?"

"A lot, actually."

"Honey—you're making this very difficult for your mother."

Ellie laughed. "Mom, I don't know what to tell you. He's wonderful, and things are moving kind of fast, and I don't even know where it's all going, but I think I may be falling in love." There. She'd said it.

There was silence on the other end of the line. Then Katherine spoke, measuring her words. "Wow. I sure didn't see this coming, did you?"

"No. It was the furthest thing from my mind. And he's my director; it's just crazy."

"How is all of that working out?"

"Mom, this is one of the things you'd love about him. We were trying to figure out how to handle things. Neither of us wanted to to sneak around, but we felt weird about it too. Then he said, 'You know what? I'm going to talk to my boss. We need to face this head-on.' And he did. His boss was okay with it, so that's a load off for both of us."

"I see."

"But that's only one example of how he seems to be about everything. We had this huge talk a few nights ago. He wants to be totally honest and open in our relationship."

There was a pause from her mother's end of the line. Then, "That sounds good to me. I just don't want you going too fast and getting hurt."

"There's something else about him that's really different—from anyone I've ever dated, I mean."

"The church thing?"

"Yeah. I know I told you about that. But it's really more than church—I'm starting to see that it's everything he does. Everything he *is*."

"What do you mean?" Katherine sounded wary.

"It's the little things, I guess, but he's always praying, and talking about God—but it's not a fake thing or something that makes you uncomfortable. It's like God is his friend. I don't know how to explain it."

"Well, you and Beecher are pretty critical when it comes to that stuff. I can't imagine you with a religious fanatic."

Ellie snorted.

Katherine continued, "But if Will hasn't become the butt of your jokes yet with his spiritual talk, maybe he *is* the real thing."

"Maybe so."

"I'd love to meet him."

"When are you coming to Branson?" Ellie suddenly missed her mother.

"You know we'll be there on opening night, but Opa and I were thinking of coming sooner just to see you and do a few things for the winery. Would that be good? Is the guest room open this weekend?"

"It's totally open. That would be awesome." She could hear Opa saying something in the background.

"Opa says we'll take you and Will out to dinner Friday."

"Okay, wonderful. I'll see if he's available."

"Sounds good. See you in a couple of days."

"I love you, Mom. And tell Opa."

"I will. I love you too."

Chapter Fifteen

· · · · · · · · · · · · · · · · · · · ·

Beecher Heinrichs sat behind his desk, sipping his first cup of coffee of the morning. It was a taste of the good life, the life he'd designed for himself in this cosmopolitan city. He enjoyed looking out of his office window, as it constantly reminded of the reasons he fell in love with Munich from the first day he moved here.

The law firm where he worked occupied the top two floors of the Fünf Höfe, a swanky complex situated in the heart of Munich that offered spectacular views over downtown. Looking one direction he could see the looming green onion-shaped domes of the Frauenkirche— the tallest church in Munich and defining point of its skyline.

Just below the domes, Munich hummed with life. Beecher liked to observe the morning bustle of locals and tourists on Marienplatz, the city center of Munich where the picturesque Rathaus, Munich's Town Hall, sat. From another direction he could see the Residenz Hofgarten, the gardens of the historic Bavarian palace, which was now a museum.

Setting down his cup, Beecher rose from the chair behind his desk and stretched his long legs. He walked over to his office window and stood in the sun. Its rays filtered through the glass and warmed him, highlighting the gold in his bronze-colored hair. His eyes were blue and clear like his mother's and Opa's, and they hurt when they took in light. He squinted, therefore, and gazed out at the bell tower to Frauenkirche, which was pealing forth its regal chimes. They sounded lonely this morning, farther away and more hollow than usual. Beecher thought about the architect of the church and his supposed deal with the devil. What a story. He was glad nothing in Munich would ever be taller than those bulbous domes.

Beecher shifted his weight. From a certain angle he could see, in the corner of the museum gardens, an oak tree soaring high into the air, with a patch of blue sky behind it. Somehow this tree, this patch of sky brought him comfort. An unfamiliar feeling was settling over him this morning. Homesickness.

The sort of mind Beecher had, not by conscious effort but by instinct combined with force of habit, searched about for a reason for this condition. Like a spider throwing threads of silk, he cast thoughts outward, seeking a source where one would catch hold, and from that anchor he could begin to construct a web. It was in this manner Beecher usually began to analyze and then make reasonable sense of his feelings.

He thought first of his family. He was deeply connected to his mother and sister and Opa, to be sure. It was logical that he missed them and that could account for the homesickness he was experiencing. Yes, perhaps that was it. Opa had not been feeling well, after all. And Ellie was dating someone new—someone who seemed to have potential. Beecher wanted to meet him and form his own opinion.

But as Beecher looked out the window, he could see there were holes in his argument, the biggest one being that whenever he missed his family before, he could make plans to go home and see them, or have them come to where he was, and the feeling would be assuaged. Even the plan-making was a remedy that worked quickly to dispel the symptoms. He'd gotten his plane tickets and was going home for Ellie's opening night. So why could he not return his attention to Munich at least till then?

Maybe it was Vivienne. As he requested, she had really let things go this time. There had been no contact between them since the breakup. Through one of their mutual friends he had heard she was dating someone else—and she seemed really happy. While this was uncomfortable for Beecher's pride, in his heart of hearts he was okay with it. Even glad. He knew there was no future together for them. No, if anything the breakup with Vivienne made him happier to be in Munich, across the ocean from where she was.

So that left what? *Audrey.* The name popped into his head like a surprise visitor, someone you least expect in the least-expected moment. He didn't know what to do with it. *Audrey? Really?*

He re-read her latest e-mail.

To Beech or not to Beech?

That is the question, and my answer, obviously, is to Beech when I should be studying, or doing some other constructive activity with my time. But I find myself thinking of you, and wanting to write as you encouraged me, so here I sit with my laptop in the NYU law library looking for all the world like a responsible law student while really I am nothing of the sort. Unless our conversations might be counted as research. Which is, admittedly, a stretch (though at least you are an attorney).

How's it going?

Thank you for the invitation to come for Oktoberfest. I have not talked to Ellie in a week, but I hope she'll be free and we can both come, and you can treat us to the real German experience. (Have you talked to her?)

I already promised Katherine I would work for Heinrichs Haus, like every year, during Weinfest. She is going to order dirndls for me and Ellie that we can wear over there as well. We can all go in our tracht! I'm excited, especially since you sent me the photo of you and your friends last year. I cannot believe even you dress up. I remember you stopped doing that for Hermann's big festival in what—about the second grade? The last time you wore lederhosen Katherine bribed you with promises of a plastic sword. Do you remember that? I do, because when you got it you chased Ellie and me with it, threatening to cut off our heads. You were quite the little barbarian back then.

Mom and Atticus came to visit me last weekend. Dad hates the city; we had to drag him around to anything non-historic, especially in the evenings. And he refuses to take the subway. Says it's too dangerous. He got into conversations with every taxi driver we met, mostly immigrants, about our country. One Laotian man told us he arrived in NYC with five dollars in his pocket and went on to say, "America is a great country—you can make a great life here if you are willing to work." I could not help but wonder if his life is truly great. How he survives driving taxis all day long…what kind of a job that must be. Can you imagine? What was his life like before? Was this what he dreamed of?

We went to that restaurant I told you about (the one with the Southern food). Atticus loved it. Mom and I were beside ourselves because Alec Baldwin was eating there too. And later we passed Christopher Plummer on the street in the theater district. He's so old now—white-haired and not anything like when he was Captain Von Trapp, Mom said—but it was unmistakably him.

We went to see Beauty and the Beast on Broadway—us and a bunch of little girls dressed like princesses. Atticus was unmoved, but Mom and I—well, we might as well have been little girls ourselves. The costumes were amazing! There was the candlestick character, Lumiére, who could light up his own hands—and a woman dressed up as a dresser, complete with pull-out drawers! Regardless of whether it's a kids' show, I do love that story, don't you, Beecher? Such a beautiful message.

Well, I just thought I'd write a note to say guten Tag, and here I have bored you with the minutiae of my life in New York. Write back and bore me with the minutiae from München, okay?

A.

A. Beecher grinned to himself as he studied her signature. She'd been doing that as long as he could remember, probably since she learned to write. He'd known her that long, knew her better than most people did, and she knew him. He loved her almost like a sister. As Ellie's best friend, she was a permanent figure in his life. But there was nothing more than friendship between them, was there?

Audrey, five-foot-two in high-heeled shoes, with her dark curly hair and coal-black eyes. Her skin was so white she looked like an old-fashioned china doll. Beecher had teased her mercilessly one time about a straw hat she wore to shade her face on a fishing trip. She took it off and got a sunburn. Turned red as a lobster. He had teased her about that too. Now he felt bad about both things. *You are definitely going crazy,* he told himself as he hit REPLY.

Dear Audrey,

I am glad you decided to Beech, even though you probably should be studying. Don't ask me why, but as I read your e-mail I got a vision of the time we all went fishing at the pond and you wore that ridiculous hat. I teased you, and you took it off and got sunburned, and so I teased you more. Did I ever apologize for my unchivalrous behavior? I am truly sorry. I was a terrible arse in those days.

Beauty and the Beast sounds lovely, at least for tender-hearted, idealistic people like you. It does have a good message, but like your dad, I suppose, I am unmoved by talking candlesticks. I'm afraid my tastes are more attuned to the realistic, or as Ellie would say, the dark and dreary side of the theater: Chekov, Eugene O'Neill, Arthur Miller, Tennessee Williams. I even like David Mamet, though his diction is admittedly far beyond foul. (You would never approve.)

I am feeling homesick and I can't imagine why, because I did something very cool over the weekend, and my life in Munich affords me all kinds of these opportunities. At any rate I went with a group of friends, Americans and Germans, by train to Amsterdam to see U2 in concert. They were amazing. The band Muse opened for them—Ellie knew who they were because of that blasted Twilight—*and they were moderately good, but when U2 came on stage Muse was instantly forgotten. My friends and I sang along to all of the songs. We were the only ones in the stadium, it seems. Europeans are so funny about concerts. They sit like sticks in the mud rather than cutting loose and having fun. But on this occasion we showed the Euro-dorks who went with us how a rock concert is done. Do you still like U2?*

Speaking of concerts and cool opportunities, just last weekend I was in Paris and I went to see the Avett Brothers. Are you familiar with them? This was their first European tour. U2 they are not, but I like them, and I believe you would too. They're from North Carolina, quite good musicians, intellectual and spiritual and honest like you.

Will you be in Branson for Ellie's opening night? I think she said you couldn't come, but I can't remember why. I have scheduled a trip home around it. Will be doing some work for

Heinrichs Haus too. My flight goes through New York, so if you are going to be around, perhaps we could see each other briefly? Let me know.

Affectionately,

Beecher

"Vat's that silly look on your face?"

Gretchen, his assistant, was always coming to the door at inappropriate times with things like important files.

"Nothing that concerns you. Whatcha got?"

She plopped down a manila folder that landed like a brick on his desk. "It's a new document from dat pharmaceutical company. They vant you to vord it correctly for dem so der butts are covered."

"Well, that's what I do best."

"Vant a cup of coffee?"

"No thanks, Gretchen."

She smiled curiously at him and left the room.

Beecher hit SEND and picked up the folder. *Silly look? What silly look?* Gretchen clearly didn't know what she was talking about.

Chapter Sixteen

....

Ellie's excitement about the weekend bubbled over into all kinds of preparations around her condo. She made a trip to Home Depot, where she picked up some terra-cotta flowerpots, a watering can, a few tools and potting soil, and then stopped at a local nursery where she chose a variety of healthy-looking plants. Dot kept her company in the side yard, chewing open a sack of potting soil and carrying off her gloves, while she combined green and purple sweet potato plants, ivy, geraniums, gerbera daisies, and decorative grasses in several arrangements for her front porch and balcony. When Ellie was satisfied that Katherine would be impressed, she moved on to groceries.

Will had told her about a fun market where she stocked up on granola, organic milk, artisan cheeses, German chocolate, and French bread. Going back to the fruit stand she frequented regularly, she got everything she knew Opa would love—a half-bushel of white peaches, two watermelons, a cantaloupe, raspberries and blueberries, and ripe tomatoes. With those she planned to make marinara sauce to go with pasta for their Friday night meal.

When Friday came, Ellie bought fresh flowers for the guest room, bar, and master bedroom. She got a bundle of sunflowers for the guest room, roses for the bar, and because she knew Katherine would sleep with her, peonies for the master bed and bath. They were Katherine's favorite. She had Dot groomed, which Dot hated, and was dressed in a ruby-red V-neck dress, tiered with embroidered detail, and a pair of burlap-colored Tom's shoes, when the doorbell rang. Gathering her hair up into a French twist, Ellie clipped it loosely as she descended the stairs.

"Wow." Will stepped inside the door in khaki shorts and a linen shirt the exact color of his eyes.

"Wow yourself." Ellie smiled at him, approving. He pulled her into his arms, kissing her on the lips, then nuzzling her cheek. His face was as smooth as satin, and he smelled like fresh rain.

"You shaved."

"Katherine doesn't sound like the five-o'clock shadow type."

Ellie laughed, shaking her head. "Nope."

"You've got your hair up." He wound his finger through a wisp of her hair that had escaped the clip. "That could be very danger-ous." He kissed her neck, sending tiny electric impulses up and down her spine.

Ellie arched her back, offering him her throat, and held him firmly around the shoulders. His taut muscles pulsed under her hands, and his lips felt like velvet on her throat, awakening every nerve ending in her body.

"Remind me to wear it up more often," she whispered into his ear.

It was Will who finally pulled away. "You know, if you weren't so darned good-looking, I could focus."

"Focus on what?" Ellie patted her hair, looking around for her clip, which had fallen out.

"Well, helping you get ready for your guests. We want this meet-ing to be successful."

"You sound like a director."

He handed her the clip. "What can I do? Chop onions?" He smoothed a wayward brown tress back from her face. "Give me some-thing to do with my hands besides mess up your hair."

Dot barked at their feet, dancing around impatiently as though she'd waited long enough for Will's attention.

Ellie wound her hair back into the clip. "Could you take Dot for a potty break? And then we'll get started on the marinara. Katherine called earlier and I'd say they're about thirty minutes out."

She climbed back up the stairs to the kitchen while Will and Dot took a trip to the side yard. She put on an apron, then preheated the oven and started on the bread. Taking out a bread knife, she cut the loaf of French bread lengthwise and placed it on a cookie sheet. Then she buttered it generously, sprinkled garlic powder and Parmesan cheese over it, and placed it in the oven.

"Something smells good." Will and Dot reappeared at the top of the stairs.

"That's what Beecher calls 'smashed bread.'" Ellie giggled, holding up a hot pink and green apron and shaking it at Will. "Here, come put this on."

Walking over to her, Will turned his back as she slipped it over his head and tied it behind his waist.

"Perfect." She patted the knot.

"I wouldn't wear this for just any girl, you know."

"I am very honored." Ellie snickered. "But it does look nice on you, you know. Matches your eyes."

Will set to work washing the tomatoes Ellie bought at the fruit stand, and then cut them in halves, placing them in a deep baking dish he'd already lined with foil, as she instructed him. While Ellie put the finishing touches on her Italian cream cake, dousing it with cream cheese and pecan icing, Will drizzled extra virgin olive oil over the tomatoes. Next, he sprinkled them with basil, oregano, sea salt, pepper, and fresh garlic.

"Now put this in the oven?"

"Yep—the bottom oven. I've already got it preheated."

Ellie was boiling the water for pasta when the doorbell rang again. "I bet that's them!" She dashed toward the stairs while Will pulled the apron over his head, stashing it in a drawer. Dot began to bark, joining in the excitement.

"Mom! Opa!" Ellie gathered them both into her arms, practically pulling them through the door.

Will stood back and watched as she hugged her mother and kissed Opa on both cheeks.

Then she turned directly to him. "Mom, Opa, this is Will Howard."

Katherine stuck out her hand. The incline of her head was almost regal as she said politely, "It's so nice to meet you, Will."

"You too, ma'am." Will shook her hand first, and then Opa's.

Opa's eyes crinkled around the edges as he studied Will. "So you are Ellie's famous director."

"Infamous, I'm afraid."

The timbre of Opa's laugh was warm and deep. He clapped Will on the shoulder.

"But you are the truly famous Opa." Will looked from Opa to Katherine. "Ellie has told me so much about you both. I'm glad you could come to Branson this weekend."

Dot barked, jumping up on Katherine's leg, and Ellie introduced her as well.

"Well, aren't you just precious," Katherine cooed as she patted the dog's head with a manicured hand.

Dot looked at her with satisfaction, as though she concurred.

Ellie and Katherine ascended the stairs first, Katherine nodding her approval of Ellie's placement of the glass bowl for her keys.

"Your flowers outside are beautiful, Sunshine," Opa commented, as he and Will brought up the rear. "Everything looks so much cozier with you here than when I visited with the Realtor."

"Thank you, Opa. I've got more you'll have to see on the balcony."

When they got to the top of the stairs, Will made his way over to the kitchen. "Why don't I put in the pasta while you give them the fifty-cent tour?"

* * * * *

After Ellie had shown her mother and grandfather around the condo, she seated them at the infinity table. She had set it beforehand with the elegant white dishes Katherine selected and Opa had bought for the place. Will served their salads while Ellie took the bread out of the oven, turned it over, and pressed it down. Then she returned it to the oven for just another few minutes.

Taking the baking dish out of the oven, Ellie used a fork to pop the skins off of the tomato halves. Then she used a potato masher to crush the roasted tomatoes and mix them with the herbs and spices, releasing an irresistible aroma. Throwing a piece of fettuccine against the tile backdrop to her stove, the way Zia Paola had shown her, Ellie determined the pasta was al dente. She dished heaping piles of it onto the white plates and crowned them with marinara. These she set in front of Katherine and Opa while Will cut the "smashed bread" in slices and deposited a plateful on the table.

"This looks wonderful, honey."

"Aren't you two going to join us?" Opa looked concerned.

Will answered his question by holding out a seat for Ellie. She sat down, and he took the seat next to her.

Ellie reached out her hand to hold his. "Would you mind blessing the food?"

"Sure."

Katherine and Opa joined hands too as Will began.

"Thank You, Lord, for this day and for the safe trip You gave Katherine and Philip. We are grateful for the joy of their company. Please bless our conversation and this time we have together; let it be something that brings honor to You. We thank You for the meal Ellie has prepared, and ask that You would nourish our bodies with it, just as You nourish our spirits with Your presence here. In Jesus' name, amen."

Ellie thought she saw Katherine wipe a tear. This was such a rare occurrence that it made her want to cry too.

The dinner—and the meeting, to coin Will's phrase—were both wildly successful. Katherine was a little bit more quiet than usual, and contemplative, but Opa put everyone at ease. He and Will took turns asking get-to-know-you questions. By the time dessert was served, they were laughing together like old friends.

"Why don't I clean up the kitchen and you guys just relax?" Will started to gather the dishes after everyone had finished the Italian cream cake.

"No—I'll help." Ellie rose too, then offered, "Mom and Opa, the balcony is breezy in the evenings. Go on out there and sit, and I'll bring you some coffee."

When she had served them their decaf, she rejoined Will and began to load the dishwasher. He handed her a dish he had rinsed, and she squeezed his hand. "Thank you, for everything you've done tonight."

"I haven't done much. You're the amazing cook."

"You helped me with everything. But most of all, thank you for being so kind to my family."

"They're a part of you, so that's easy." He wiped his brow with a sudsy hand. "Anyway, it's been fun."

"Do you think we should go on a walk now, on the boardwalk? Dot needs it, and it might be nice."

Will squinted toward the balcony as though he was thinking about her question. "To be honest, I think your Opa is tired."

"Really?"

"Yeah. I do."

Ellie hadn't thought so by the way he looked, but she knew Opa would never want to say so. "Okay, we can visit here, I guess."

Will straightened his back from where he was bent over the sink. "Would you like to take Dot on a walk with your mom? I could stay here and hang out with Opa."

"That would be great."

* * * * *

As Ellie and Katherine strode down the boardwalk, Dot at their heels on her "real" leash, Ellie noticed people staring at Katherine. Couples looked up from their meals on the verandas of the stylish restaurants. A shoe shiner stopped shining a shoe in midair. Vendors paused in the hawking of their various wares, and one man, sitting on a bench talking on his cell phone, actually dropped his jaw.

She was a striking figure, with the height and build of an aging supermodel. She wore a peacock-feather-printed skirt of polyester chiffon—long and flowing—with a beaded waist, paired with a simple combed cotton scoopneck T-shirt. Her short blond hair was gently tousled by the light wind blowing off the water, and she wore big blue and gold beaded dangle earrings that perfectly matched her skirt. Her feet were adorned with designer Italian calfskin sandals, T-straps, in the ideal shade of bronze. Even her toes were done in a faultless French manicure. She walked deliberately, with her head held high.

"Mom, you are so not Branson."

Katherine laughed faintly. "What is that supposed to mean?"

"It means everyone is staring at you. You look like you just stepped off a New York runway."

"That's very kind of you to say. But no one is looking at me, Ellie. Not when I'm walking with my daughter."

Ellie shook her head. "You're crazy."

"Even if I were young, I am small potatoes compared to you."

"Mom, that is so not true. It never has been."

They stopped to look out at the lake, and Katherine leaned over, resting her elbows on the railing. "Perhaps we should ask Will Howard if it's true."

Ellie was unable to look her mother in the eye.

"I love the way he looks at you, Ellie."

"What do you mean?" Ellie thought she knew, but she wanted to hear someone say it—wanted to see what her mother saw.

"He looks at you with wonder—and respect."

"That's an interesting observation."

"It is." Katherine gazed over the greenish water toward the mountainside. "I'm still trying to get my head around it."

"What do you mean?"

"Well, I don't want to jump to conclusions. But the things you've told me and the things I've seen tonight add up to a pretty compelling package."

"I think so too."

"Can you believe this is happening? I mean, when you did your best to avoid coming to Branson?"

"The irony of it dawns on me—fresh and new—every day." Ellie chuckled.

"It's like you were running as fast as you could in the other direction, but some force—some fate—pulled you here, toward him."

"I think that force was God."

Katherine raised an eyebrow. "You may be right."

"So you like him?"

Katherine's smile was dazzling. "Ellie, I like him a lot."

Chapter Seventeen

....

Will sat on his porch, watching the sunrise over the cove that was his little piece of Table Rock Lake. It began like a whisper, with only the vaguest notion of light pervading the darkness. He couldn't see the sun yet, but he knew it was there, making its presence *felt* before it would burst on the scene and be *known*...in all of its splendor.

He hummed an unknown tune. He had slept well but awakened suddenly right before dawn, and with urgency. What was coming, he did not know.

This had happened to him before. Not often, though—it was a cherished occurrence, like dreaming of someone loved and lost. The kind of dream so real he didn't want to wake up. But this was better. Will had been summoned. This was a divine meeting.

He went inside to grab his guitar and returned to the porch. Putting chords to the tune he was humming, he began to sing:

> *"I am here*
> *I am Yours*
> *Do with me what You will*
> *For You are God,*
> *You are good,*
> *And all Your ways are love."*

Will could see a crease of light peeking over the mountain. He fixed his eyes on it as he played, and in what seemed like only a few seconds, the crease became a half-circle, rose to three-quarters, and then the giant flaming orb filled the sky with its opulent beauty. Will stared at it till his eyes burned with tears. He had to look away; it was too bright and brilliant for him.

Be still.

The thought came to him like a drop of dew falling on a leaf. It was gentle and light, yet profound. Nourishing. He stopped his fingers on the strings.

Be still, and know that I am God.

A steady stream of images began to fill his head then, and he held each one up, as though to study it beside the command of Psalm 46.

Ellie. *Be still, and know that I am God.*

The past. *Be still, and know that I am God.*

The play. *Be still, and know that I am God.*

The future. *Be still, and know that I am God.*

What does it really mean to be still? Will had the feeling that seeking the answer to that question was his assignment for the day.

* * * * *

"Sam?"

"Sam I am."

"You sounded exactly like Jesse Jackson when you said that." Will laughed into his cell phone.

"Will Howard. I didn't know spiritual people like you watched *Saturday Night Live.*"

"Only when there's a reverend on it."

Sam hooted. "That's a good one. That's right—that's when I watch it too. What's up?"

"What are you doing for lunch?"

"Today? I'm not doing a thing. I've got appointments till twelve o'clock, but I could meet you at twelve thirty."

"Great."

"The usual place?"

"I'll be there."

* * * * *

The usual place was Uncle Joe's, a barbecue joint. It had been a Branson staple for years, especially among locals. Since Sam had been the public school superintendent in Branson for twenty years and had been eating at Uncle Joe's for almost that long, he qualified as a regular. He and Will ate there every time they went to lunch.

Uncle Joe's was at the end of a cabinesque strip mall on the main drag in Branson. It was right next to a T-shirt shop and shared a parking lot with an ice-cream parlor. It was a bit tricky to get to without fighting traffic, but Will knew a back way, and he arrived before Sam. He parked Scarlett in semishade and went in to get a table.

The scent of Uncle Joe's was pure barbecue heaven. Hickory smoke, salt, spices, and sugar suffused the atmosphere around it, beginning with the parking lot and growing stronger as he made his way inside. Will was lucky enough to get a table without waiting. A girl with enormous hair-sprayed bangs and electric-blue mascara seated him in a booth and brought ice water for two in mason jars.

Will's table was covered with red plastic and set against a wall that looked like distressed barn wood. On the wall hung a red telephone, the old rotary kind, and it was into that phone one placed his or her order. Since Will knew Sam's order by heart, he called in both of their orders. Then he sat and waited, rearranging a tray that held ketchup, hot and mild barbecue sauces, salt, pepper, and packets of assorted sweeteners, and a roll of sturdy paper towels.

"Hey, man!"

Will rose to hug Sam, who sat down in the booth, smoothing his tie, which was navy with what looked like a child's drawing of stick people.

"Nice tie."

"Thanks." Sam smiled, revealing white teeth that were large and square like a row of Chiclets. "Sorry I'm late."

"How's the school business?"

"It's usually slower in the summer, but today I've had to work hard for my money." Sam shook his head and whistled, blowing out air. "Whew."

"What happened?"

"Oh, just some crazies. It always gets me how much energy gets wasted by people who want to stir up trouble. If they'd put all that into something positive, we could get a lot done."

Will took a sip of his water.

"It's a long story, Will, but the bottom line is that this lady got her feelings hurt because her son didn't get to play on the ball team last year. The kid was a good player, but he didn't make his grades, and that's our policy. Can't change it for the star athlete, you know? Even if it makes us lose games. We got more important things than that to worry about."

"Like character."

"That's right, like character. You get it, but she doesn't." Sam took a sip of water from the jar. "Made a big stink last year, but I thought it was over. Now she's saying she's going to run for the school board, and that's fine with me, but she didn't make the deadline to file so she was disqualified to run this term. State law. So she comes up to my office as I was leaving and proceeds to make a scene in the parking lot. Says it's a conspiracy against her and her family. Really flipped a switch."

"What did you do?"

"I tried to reason with her, which of course didn't work. She started screaming. I guess I could have called the police but decided to get in my truck and drive away instead. Decided it was the merciful thing." Sam exhaled. "It was kind of funny too. Left her standing there just hollering. The office was locked; Thelma's on vacation, and Gerry and Janie are gone for the rest of the day, so I headed out. Hopefully she'll be gone by the time I get back."

"What a story."

"You wouldn't believe what I've seen in the school business." Sam paused while the server set down their food, then walked away to refill their waters. "But it's a good business."

Sam said a quick prayer of thanksgiving for the meal, and they dug in. Each of the men got a half rack of pork ribs with french fries, and Sam got coleslaw.

"So how are you?" Sam asked.

Will swallowed a bite and washed it down with some water, wiping his mouth on a paper towel. "I'm good. Having an amazing summer."

"Work going well?"

"It is. You know, as crazy as it seems, I really have a passion for the Shepherd story and getting it told in an excellent, meaningful way."

"Doesn't seem crazy to me. Seems cool."

"I've got a great cast, and just hired a codirector who is really helping out. So I think we're going to have a great season."

Sam nodded, finishing off a rib. "Now maybe with that help you can simplify your life a little more, live out that vision you came here with."

"Yeah. I believe that's coming. That's the goal, anyway."

"You still seeing that pretty little thing you brought with you to church?"

Will's eyes lit up. "Ellie. That's one of the big things I want to talk to you about."

"Well, spill the beans."

As they ate, Will told Sam how strongly he'd come to feel for Ellie in such a short time. He shared about talking to his boss, and he and Ellie praying together, and how he'd been honest with her about his past. "You know, you're the only other person around here who knows that story."

"That's pretty heavy-duty stuff."

"I know. I never would have put it on her if I didn't feel the Lord was in it."

"Sounds to me you've got a good thing going. So what's bothering you? You know I don't have all of the answers, but I'll sure listen and pray for you."

Will's voice dropped to a half whisper. "This morning I woke up early and sat out on my porch. I felt like the Lord wanted to meet with me. I was singing and playing my guitar, and I felt Him speak to my heart and say, 'Be still.'

"I started trying to figure out what He meant. I mean, I know what that means, sort of, but since it was so direct for me in that moment I started thinking about my life and wondering what areas I need to be more still in, and Ellie kept coming to mind."

"What's your physical relationship like?" Sam leaned forward. His eyes were kind but penetrating.

"It's pretty—hot." Will's throat suddenly burned from the spicy barbecue. "I mean, we haven't done anything wrong, but—"

"But it's smokin'."

"Yeah." Will took a drink of water.

"And where there's smoke…"

"There's probably a fire?"

"Sorry, dude." Sam reached over the table to pat Will's shoulder, and they both laughed.

"I know the Bible says it's better to marry than burn, but we can't get married yet, can we? We haven't dated long enough. She'd probably turn me down flat."

"What do you think you need to do?"

Will took a deep breath and let it out slowly. "Be still." The words from the early morning dawned on him again. "I never thought of it that literally."

"I'll tell you something about me and Clara. I know you think we're just two old folks now." Sam chuckled.

"I do not."

"When we met as juniors in college, it was like two pieces of flint rock coming together. Sparks flew. She was gorgeous—just like she is now—and I was lifting weights every day for football."

Will could hardly imagine Sam more fit than he was today. His shoulders hardly fit in the booth.

"I became a Christian my first year in college, you know, and when I met Clara two years later I had just made a big commitment to the Lord that I wasn't going to kiss another girl till my wedding day."

Will's eyes widened.

Sam laughed at him. "I know, man. I met Clara, and it was like, 'Lord, You are messing with me here, aren't You?'"

"Bummer."

"It seemed like it, but believe it or not, we stayed the course. Clara was a good girl, never messed up bad before. But I had failed in that area so many times, even after I became a Christian, I just knew it was the only way. That's why I made that drastic commitment. Thank goodness Clara was willing to wait."

"So you didn't even kiss her—at all—till your wedding day?"

"Nope."

"How long did you date?"

"Six months. And that includes our three-month engagement."

Will was in shock. He'd never heard anything so radical. "That must have been so hard."

"It was." Sam nodded. "But God gave us the strength to resist temptation. I set my mind to getting to know Clara's heart before I knew her body. It was an awesome experience."

"I don't think I could do that. I mean, I guess if God called me to it, anything is possible—"

"That's true." Sam dipped a french fry in ketchup. "But I'm not advising you to follow me. That was my particular calling. I'm just telling you this story to encourage you that you can walk in purity. Believe me—if I could do it, anybody could." Sam's voice was unassuming. "God gives us the grace for anything He calls us to. You've just got to hear from Him on what purity means for you."

"How did you decide where the line was? I mean, no kissing?"

"I got honest with myself about where everything started going south. For me, holding hands was okay. But kissing—nope. It was like rolling a snowball down a hill. Once I started kissing a girl, that thing was gone, out of control fast."

Will looked into Sam's eyes. The metaphor was right on for him too, but Will couldn't imagine not kissing Ellie. He was not that strong. "You are an amazing man, you know that?"

Sam snorted. "Nah. I'm just a guy clinging to grace."

Will took the check when the server came to offer it.

"You let me get that." Sam reached across the table.

"Nope. It's mine today. I am in your debt, though I don't know what to do about what you've told me." Will felt a little sick to his stomach.

Sam smoothed his tie. "Listen, Will, you've got to hear me on this."

Will set down the tray with his money for the server and gave his friend his complete attention.

"Sex is from God. We're created for pleasure. It's an awesome gift. You don't have anything to be ashamed of, falling in love and feeling desire for Ellie. So don't you start feeling condemned. Your past is over, and you're a new creation."

The knot in Will's stomach loosened somewhat. "I want to get it right. I want to please the Lord, and I honestly don't know if I can without stepping out of my relationship with Ellie." Even the thought was physically painful. "I don't want to do that. But I'm not strong in that area. Not at all."

"What you've got to remember is that Jesus is strong in our weakness. And you'll have to search this out, but I don't believe God wants to take your relationship with Ellie away. There's too much good going on there."

Sam's words brought Will relief.

"Will, all of His ways with us are kindness. Not condemnation. The Bible says *no good thing will He withhold*."

They rose from the table and walked toward the door together. When they were outside, Will squeezed his friend's arm. "Thank you, Sam, for all you've shared. I think I need to spend more time alone with God now to sort some of this out."

Chapter Eighteen

....

4 May 1887

It is my first night at Uncle Robert's and Aunt Liesel's home in Branson. Heidi and I still share a room, like at home, but what a room it is. It is beautifully appointed. We have an ornate iron bedstead with soft sheets and satin covers, instead of a patchwork quilt. The pillows are of finest down— not straw like at home. They feel like clouds billowing underneath your head.

Our lamps are kerosene, not candles, and we each have our own, on lovely walnut nightstands that frame the sides of the bed. We each have our own drawers in the nightstands where I will keep this diary, my Bible, and my pen and ink. It's a brilliant situation for writing.

Papa drove us here with the team. The trip was long and hard. He and Mama are in the parlor now, visiting Uncle Robert and Aunt Liesel, and he will spend the night with us tonight. It is too dangerous to drive in the evenings because of the Baldknobbers, a terrifying gang of outlaws that plagues the area. We hadn't heard of them in Hermann, but in Branson they are feared as a very real threat. Papa will leave us in the morning, as early mornings are the safest time to be on the road, and it will be weeks before we see him again. I pray for his safety.

At one point in the trip to Branson I rode up front with Papa and we talked about Richard Heinrichs. He told me he thought Richard was a good man, the type of man who would be successful. He said if I married him I would want for nothing, that my life would be so much easier than what it has been for my parents as new people in a new land. He said he trusted Richard Heinrichs. "What are your feelings, Elise?" he asked me.

I wanted to rest my head on his chest and hide my face in his beard like I did when I was a little girl. I wanted to say that I was too young to marry, too young to know what my life would become. Instead I kept my head erect and said none of that. I told my papa that Richard was a good friend, and I enjoyed his company. Beyond that, I had no feelings for him I could describe—yet.

"All in good time" were Papa's words. "All in good time."

O Lord, I know You hear the prayers of country school girls just as You listened to Ruth, Abigail, Esther, and Mary so long ago. Hear me now as I plead with You for wisdom and direction. As much as lies within my realm of control, I want to do the right thing, to make right choices about the future for my family, for myself, and for Your perfect will to be accomplished. Amen.

21 May 1887

I met someone today. A man with the kindest eyes and gentlest voice I have ever heard. It seems unreal—he does. Yet he was there in flesh and blood.

I was on an errand for Uncle Robert, carrying a letter to the post office. It was a short, straight walk across town. I gave my letter to the postmaster, turned from the window, and he *appeared. I don't remember what he was wearing. I just know that if a person's life can be changed in one moment, mine was changed forever the moment he looked into my eyes.*

God, help me.

22 May 1887

I could not finish writing the whole story last night because Heidi was pestering me to tell her what was wrong with me. I didn't eat a bite of dinner and turned in early for the night. But that was just because I wanted to be alone with my thoughts and to record the events of the day here. Well, Heidi would have none of that. She came straight to bed too, under the guise of nursing me, and demanded that I relate to her every detail.

By the time we had finished talking, I had to frantically write to get even one paragraph. Then Mama was here to tell us good night, and I certainly didn't want to raise her suspicions. So off went the light. Tonight I have more to record, as I saw him again today, and I want to remember every single moment we spend together. I have the feeling this may be the most important summer of my life.

His name is William Daniel Howitt. He says where he is from everyone calls him Daniel, but down here he goes by William, because it is easier with his identification papers. Anyway, that is of no consequence. After our encounter at the post, I walked back toward home, perhaps a bit slower than usual. I can't explain this, but there was an inner knowing— just beyond a hope—that he might follow me. And sure enough he did! Within a few moments his business at the post office was complete, and he jogged up behind me. "Excuse me, miss," he said breathlessly. "What is your name?"

I will never forget the sound of his voice as he asked me that simple question. It was the sound of meekness—the meekness I've heard the reverend talk about in reference to Jesus—power and strength under control. His whole appearance is like that too. He has large, intense green eyes with long eyelashes, framed with serious brows. His skin is ruddy with a few freckles and his hair the color of wheat. His shoulders are broad and his chest like a rain barrel. His legs are long enough that he had to take small steps to stay beside me. His big lips seem always to want to curve up in a smile.

We walked together to the end of the road. He asked to walk me to the house, and I don't know why I said no. I felt like a different person than myself refusing him that. But there's a caution in my heart, a desire to know him myself first before sharing such knowledge with my family. I can't explain it. It's not proper. I only know it was my choice to make that day, and I made it.

I stood by that choice today when I met him at the river. He asked me yesterday when we parted if we might be able to talk a little more, and I said I could get away after breakfast, because Mama and Aunt Liesel were going to call on some people in Aunt Liesel's church. Heidi and I had the option of going, but I didn't want to. So I hiked down to the river, through the pasture behind Uncle Robert's house, and a ways through the woods. William was waiting for me in a shady spot on the bank. He had brought coffee and two little bought cakes to share.

We were only together for two hours, but they were the best hours I've ever spent. We talked without ceasing, as though drinking in one another's thoughts. At last I have found another soul who understands me, who has some of the same feelings and fears about life, who dreams the same dreams. Other than my sister I have never known another person like that.

Perhaps William is God's answer to my prayers for clarity about my involvement with Richard Heinrichs. Richard is a good man—of that there is no doubt. And he will be a success in his life. But my passions are not stirred toward him as they have been, in only two days, toward this man. It is as though William Howitt was handmade for me. We are cut from the same cloth.

The alarm clock beside the bed read 2:00 a.m. Katherine was fast asleep, and Dot was snuggled under the covers in the middle of them, snoring, but Ellie was wide awake. The similarity of the name *William Howitt* to her own Will Howard's astounded her. Surely, surely there was no relation. But was it possible? And the similarities did not stop with the name. William Howitt's description fit many of Will's features as well: intense green eyes, sandy red hair, strong physique. But, perhaps most of all, it was her grandmother's feelings for William Howitt that resonated with Ellie. What had happened between them? Even though she knew Elise ended up with Richard Heinrichs—perhaps *because* she knew that—Ellie had to keep reading.

31 May 1887

Heidi thinks I am crazy. She says things are moving too fast; that I am not my usual self; that William Howitt has bewitched me into doing things I would never have done before, things that are of the devil. And it is true that I would never have gone to meet a man in secret, or spent this much time with someone without my father's blessing. But I do not, cannot believe any of it is of the devil. On the contrary, I believe William is God's gift to me—His answer to my prayers—

and as soon as I figure out a way to tell my mother, I will. Meanwhile, Heidi is going with me to meet him by the river tonight. It is a full moon.

1 June 1887

William surprised us by meeting us by the gate that leads from the barnyard to the pasture. He said it was too danger-ous for us to be out at night very far from the house, even on our own uncle's property. "There could be Baldknobbers anywhere," he said, "and you don't want to be anywhere near their lot."

This protectiveness impressed Heidi right away, I think, and set her mind more at ease about the sort of man William is. He explained about how his family doctor had sent him to Missouri for fresh air, and how at the summer's end he'd go back up north to finish his schooling to become a preacher. She was even happier when he told her, "I don't like this sneaking around. We don't have anything to hide. Can't you talk your sister into letting me meet the rest of the family?"

Chapter Nineteen

....

"I wish they could have stayed longer." Will stood in the driveway of the condo with Ellie, waving at Katherine and Opa as they drove away.

"I know. And I'm sorry about church. They were both willing to go, but Opa started feeling terrible. I hope he's okay."

"Me too."

Ellie lingered a moment, staring after the car even when it was out of sight. Then they walked together around to the front and opened the door for Dot, who scampered down the stairs and out. Ellie clipped Dot's hot-pink leash to her zebra-print collar. Then they headed through the side yard and around the condo to the left toward the walking park.

"How did things go with the music?"

"Fine. I talked to McKenna beforehand, and we led the praise and worship together and then I left. She was going to handle the end of the service."

"It was really nice of you to come say good-bye."

"Well, we had a great time Friday, but I didn't see you guys yesterday, and since they weren't going to be able to keep our plans today, I wanted to."

"Thanks."

"What about your day yesterday? How did that go?"

Ellie stopped to let Dot do her business. "It was good. A lot of hard work, though. Maybe that's why Opa is so worn out."

They continued up the walking path.

"What sorts of things did you do?"

"We basically set up a lot of the tasting room. The bistro furniture was there—it all had been delivered—but Katherine and I arranged and rearranged it till we like the way it looks. Then we worked on some signage and stocked the tasting bar. It's ready to open."

"Wow. When is that supposed to happen?"

"We may do a quiet opening in the next week or so, for a test run. Then there will be a grand opening we'll advertise." Ellie covered a yawn with her hand.

"You seem really excited about it."

She laughed, dropping her hand, and another yawn escaped. "It's not that. I stayed up late last night reading."

"Must have been a good book."

"It is. I've told you about it, haven't I? I'm translating my great-great-grandmother's diary."

"You did mention something about that. Your mother gave it to you to help you connect with us hillbillies."

"Well, yeah. To connect with my own family's hillbilly history."

Will looked perplexed. "I thought your family was German."

"They are—we are."

"German hillbillies?"

"In a sense, I guess. They were immigrants and pioneers."

"I see."

"Anyway, I got all caught up in it last night because I'm at this part where my grandmother visits Branson."

"Cool."

"I know, but that's not what kept me awake. She met this guy and seems to be falling in love with him—"

"Your grandpa?"

"No." Ellie grabbed his arm. "That's the clincher. A man named William Howitt."

Will gaped at her. "No way."

"I know. I couldn't believe it either. At first I thought I was trans-lating it wrong. But it's not wrong. That was his name."

"That is unbelievable!"

"Do you have any relatives by that name?"

Will's brows furrowed. "You know, Ellie, I don't think so, but I guess it's possible. I've told you a bit about my family; there aren't many of us, and I've never gotten into genealogy."

"It might be fun to do some research. What if our ancestors are connected in some way?"

They sat down on a bench together, and Will put his arm around Ellie's shoulders, hugging her to him. "If we're related, I don't think I want to know that."

She smiled, leaning her head against his chest. "I don't think we're related. My grandmother married Richard Heinrichs, remember?"

"Well, if she dumped my relative for him, that might be even more depressing."

She punched his knee. "He couldn't have been as wonderful as you."

Dot lay down by Will's feet as if to express her agreement.

"On that note, do you want to go out with me today?"

"What do you have in mind?" Facing him, Ellie raised an eyebrow.

"I think it's time you experienced a major Branson tradition."

"You're not proposing a country music show, are you?"

"That's a thought—maybe later." Will smiled crookedly. "But no, that's not what I had planned for today."

"Okay. I give up."

"Let's go to Silver Dollar City!"

* * * * *

Once they were back at the condo, Will grabbed a bag from his truck. He changed into khaki shorts and a brown polo in the guest room while Ellie went to her room to change. When she came out she was wearing a dainty black V-neck T-shirt with sand-colored cropped cargo pants. Her hair was loose and straight, and she wore black Sesto Meucci leather toe-ring slides. No jewelry.

"How do you do that?" Will, who was sitting on the couch petting Dot, rose.

"Do what?"

"Make everything you wear look so good?"

Ellie's cheeks turned red.

"Dot here was just telling me that she hates Silver Dollar City."

"Really? Why is that?" Ellie crossed to the kitchen where she filled the dog's bowl with plenty of fresh water. Then she put it in the guest bathroom.

"No dogs allowed."

"Oh. Of course." Ellie made a sad face to match her dog's. Then she grabbed Dot and set her down on the soft rug of the guest bathroom, patting her head before shutting the door.

Going to her desk, she grabbed her debit card and a bit of cash from her purse. These she stashed in the zippered pocket of her pants. "I'm ready if you are!"

* * * * *

Will, clever about shortcuts as usual, took the red route and avoided most traffic till they ran into a line of cars waiting to enter Silver Dollar City. Crawling along then, Ellie saw a sign advertising *The Branson Belle*, a showboat with dining and entertainment cruises on Table Rock Lake.

"That looks like Dot!" She pointed to the sign, which, interestingly, featured a man and three dogs, one of which was unmistakably a Boston terrier.

"It sure does," Will agreed. "Maybe not quite as cute though."

"She'd be proud to hear you say that."

"Dot has really been a blessing to you, hasn't she?"

"She has. It was so out-of-the-blue. I feel badly that someone may have lost her, but I definitely gained a precious friend."

"I don't think you should feel bad. You tried everything you could to locate the owner. And after the shape she was in, I believe it was a God thing she ended up with you."

Finally they came to the parking area of Silver Dollar City, and Will parked Scarlett in section F, one of the many massive parking lots. Hiking about a quarter mile, they queued up with other visitors for a trolley that would take them to the park's entrance.

It had been a long time since Ellie had been to Silver Dollar City. She had gone, as a little girl, with her mother and father and Beecher, but she didn't remember much about their time there, which she thought might be a good thing. The last time she'd been there was as a freshman in high school, with Audrey and her family, during "Young Christians Weekend." That trip had been a blast. Audrey and she had poked fun at a lot of the shops with their pioneer motifs, while riding every ride and having a ball. They even got their picture made in the old-fashioned photo shop. Mr. DuPree, or Atticus, Audrey's nickname for her father, had bought each of them a copy, and one for himself, which, to their horror, he kept to this day on his law office desk.

"The flowers are amazing." She and Will stopped to admire the extravagant beds that surrounded a water wheel and pool. A lady they didn't know asked Will to take a picture of her and her two kids with her camera, which he did.

When it came time to pay for their tickets, Ellie tried to pay for her own. "Those are expensive, Will."

But he would have none of it. He purchased their two tickets, at close to fifty dollars each, and said, "How about I let you get lunch?"

The first diversion they came to, once inside the park, was Marble Cave.

"Do you want to do the cave?"

Ellie was game. "Sure, why not?"

They stood in line, but not for too long, then listened to a park ranger type give a short speech about how many steps they'd take, and how steep it was, and basic cave safety. Ellie felt a sense of adventure as she and Will descended, watching upward as the shaft of daylight grew narrower and narrower till it was out of sight.

The air in the cave was cool and damp.

"Maybe we ought to have saved this for later, when we get hot."

"There are always the water rides." Will grinned wickedly. "In fact, I believe there's a new one where I get to shoot you with a water gun."

He held her hand as they climbed down the hundreds of stairs, drawing closer to the belly of the earth. Ellie could hear a faint dripping noise. The only light was provided by the guide's flashlight and other artificial lights placed at intervals as checkpoints along the path. When they stood with the group to hear a lecture about stalactites and stalagmites, Ellie shivered. Will pulled her close, and she breathed in the welcome scent of cedar. The warmth of his skin was luxuriant, like a blanket over her goose bumps.

The cave was beautiful in its own way, with a waterfall and formations of rock nothing short of fantastical. Much of the time they had to walk single file to get through the narrow passageways. Ellie thought several times of the *Lord of the Rings* movies. "My precious," she said to Will in her best Gollum voice, and he laughed.

Happy to have done it, they were both happy as well to board the train that took them straight up and out of the cave. Passing through the obligatory shop at the end, they decided not to purchase the photo that had been taken of them by a Silver Dollar City photographer down in the cave. It was showcased, along with everyone else's, in a twenty-dollar frame.

"We look like ghosts." Ellie placed it back on the shelf.

"You know, we do that at The Shepherd of the Hills too."

"What?"

"Take pictures of people for them to buy."

Ellie frowned. "Do you think that's okay? I mean, what do you think about that practice?"

He shrugged. "We don't do it without consent, but…it's a little cheesy."

"That's how I feel too. Money, money, money." She waved her hand to the rhythm of the repeated word.

"Of course, the boss would say we're in the business to make money."

Ellie rolled her eyes. "I'm glad I'm not a businesswoman."

"But your mom is."

"Yeah. But I've never seen her do anything cheesy."

"What about wine and cheese?"

Ellie punched him in the ribs.

* * * * *

They decided to ride the swings next. Then they strolled through the rest of the kiddie section, stopping for cotton candy and a rainbow-colored slush that they shared, using two straws. Their plan next was to ride the famous Fire in the Hole roller coaster. When they got to the entrance, however, an attendant was fixing a chain across it. He was dressed like an old-time coal miner, complete with black powder scuffed across his face.

"Sorry, folks, we've been notified there's lightning within a five-mile radius of here. All outside rides are closing till the storm is past."

Will and Ellie glanced up at the overcast sky. A huge dark cloud loomed in the east like a spreading bruise.

"How long will that be?"

"I don't know, miss. Sometimes it's fifteen minutes, and sometimes it's an hour or longer. You just can't tell about a Branson summer. The weather is unpredictable."

The man put a lock on the chain and pulled it tight. "Hopefully we'll be back up and running soon." He nodded to them and walked away.

"Hmm." Ellie tossed the empty paper cone from their cotton candy into a nearby trash can. "Bummer."

"Why don't we go do the stuff that's indoors?"

Will, who knew his way around better than Ellie, led them to a ride called The Abandoned Mine. They queued up near the Silver Dollar City train station, which was also closed down. It was quite a distance from the ride's entrance.

"I guess a lot of people have the same idea."

Ellie took the opportunity to people-watch while they stood in line. There were a lot of families with young children and a few groups, like church youth groups, who walked by. As her eyes scanned the crowds, she saw a familiar black ponytail and the outline of muscular shoulders under a tight T-shirt. "Don't look now, but I think that's Seth Young across the way—near that food stand. Is that...that Cristal girl with him?"

Will turned to look. Seth was seated on top of a picnic table with his feet on the bench where Cristal sat facing him. They were eating giant sausages on sticks. "Well, speak of the devil. I believe it is."

Ellie turned her face away quickly.

"Hey girl." Will gently cupped her chin, nudging her to look up at him. "Want to tell me what that guy did to you?"

She laughed lightly. "Yeah. I want to tell you so you can go beat him up."

"I will if I need to." He made a fist and shook it in Seth's direction, playing.

Ellie reached out and took his hand in hers. She uncurled his fist, tracing the calluses on his fingers that had formed from years of playing guitar. "It's not that bad. Just stupid, immature stuff. Sometimes I wish you were the only person I'd ever dated—the only person I'd ever given even a part of myself to."

"I understand that."

They inched forward together in the line for the ride.

Ellie spoke softly, still caressing Will's hand as though mapping the train of her thoughts. "We were in a play together in college. That's how we met."

"Hmm."

"It was a bombshell romance—and I thought it was real." Ellie glanced in the direction of Seth and Cristal. "Looking back, I feel like an idiot that I couldn't see through him. He moved so fast, made all of these promises, told me he loved me on our very first date. Even though it went against everything I'd been taught, I believed him. We moved in together. I thought I was living a modern fairy tale, until it became a nightmare."

"What happened?"

"He cheated on me."

"Oh."

"Yeah. It was rich. He was in a band and had this gig in a bar called Juanita's. I went to watch him all of the time, but this night I couldn't—I can't remember why. Anyway, he got in real late, and the next day he was acting weird. Turns out he met up with an old girlfriend at Juanita's."

"Ouch."

"He tried to justify it. Like he had no choice—he was in a bar playing music, the ambience was just right, and his old girlfriend walked in." Ellie laughed. "It's sort of hilarious now. But it was so painful then."

"Did you break up with him immediately?"

"No. I still loved him—or thought I did—so I degraded myself awhile and stuck around. Things only got worse. He eventually dumped me."

"*He* dumped *you*?" Will looked like cold water had been thrown in his face.

"Yep. 'Fraid so."

"That's insane."

The line took another spurt forward, and Will and Ellie moved with it, stepping onto a wooden bridge shaded by willows. It would take them across a man-made pond and into The Abandoned Mine ride.

"I almost transferred schools. I didn't want to be around him in the drama department or have to deal with any of that."

"But you stayed at Saint Louis?"

"I went home crying to my mom, and she was wonderful—very sympathetic. But then when I told her about my plan to change schools, she pulled a good one on me." Ellie raised her eyebrows just as Katherine had. "She said, 'Ellie, you've always made your own decisions, and if you want to change schools, you can do that. But if that's what you choose to do, you need to know it is not with my blessing.'"

"Wow."

"I was shocked. I asked her why not, and she said, 'Because I believe you have to face your fears to overcome them, or they will always haunt you.' That's it. And so essentially I went back and faced Seth Young and dealt with all of that junk and got over it—in time. And I'm really glad I did, because here he is to haunt me."

"You're matter-of-fact about the whole thing." Will took a strand of her hair that had fallen in her face and tucked it behind her ear. His eyes shone with wonder and...something else. Discovery. Admiration.

"It took quite a bit for me to become so. But you live and learn." Ellie shrugged.

"I think the next time I see Seth I'm going to shake his hand."

Ellie was repulsed. "Why would you want to do that?"

"Because his loss is my incredible gain."

* * * * *

They boarded the little rickety boats that would take them through the supposedly flooded—and thus abandoned—mine. Resetting the digital counters in front of their seats, they each took a toy pistol in their hands and competed vigorously for points all along the ride: 100 for hitting the stuffed yellow canary in its cage and making it sing; 200 for ringing a bell on a distant spittoon; 300 for "igniting" a stack of fake dynamite and setting off a loud boom. If you freed trapped miner-mannequins by shooting the lock on their iron bar jail, you got 500 points, and so on. Will was proud at the end to display his 10,000 points in comparison to Ellie's 7,000.

"You beat me, fair and square." She took the hand he offered as she climbed out of the boat. "Congratulations." They followed the line of people exiting out of the ride into a still-sunless day. "Want to celebrate your victory with some lunch?"

"I guess that could be another indoor activity, couldn't it?"

Someone had recommended the barbecue to Will, so they walked to a large red, white, and blue warehouse labeled THE HOUSE OF BARBECUE and found a seat inside at one of the long picnic-style tables covered with blue-checked plastic. It was crowded. A large stage was lit up on one end of the building, and stands touting regional barbecue fare from Texas, Memphis, and North Carolina lined both sides.

"What can I get for you?" Will asked Ellie over the din of voices. No one was performing on the stage at that moment, but The House of Barbecue was still noisy.

"I don't know. What is there?" Straining her eyes toward the food stands, Ellie could see heaps of corn on the cob and what looked like chicken legs, ribs, and rolls under the North Carolina sign. "Just get me whatever you're having."

"Okay."

Will started to walk away, but Ellie stopped him. "Take this money. I said I'm getting lunch." She shoved a twenty into his hand.

"Yes, ma'am." He nodded obediently.

Ellie smiled, watching the way he walked toward the line for food, with his shoulders back and a spring in his step. She didn't have any fears about Will. And that was an amazing feeling.

Chapter Twenty

....

After two more hours at Silver Dollar City and careful study of the theme park's map, Ellie and Will had done everything else there was to do indoors. They played in the big house of balls, shooting air cannons at each other in a place so colorful and imaginative it could have belonged in Willy Wonka's Chocolate Factory. They watched a couple of shows, getting their fill—perhaps for a lifetime—of blue-grass music and having a "hand-clappin', foot-stompin' good time." They attended a glass-blowing session. Watched old-fashioned iron making. Finally, they ended up in the candy shop, where they sat on wooden benches with other tourists and learned how to make salt-water taffy, pecan pralines, and peanut brittle. As they exited with a bag of giant chocolate-covered strawberries, which cost a few dollars each, the sky was still gray.

"Will, I think we're going to have to call it a day before I gain ten pounds. I'm sorry you paid so much for us to get in here and the rides have been closed."

"No problem, little lady." Will mimicked the friendly ironsmith's jargon. "I'm still glad we got to spend the day together."

On their way out, Ellie noticed a customer service sign hanging over a small white house. The porch was adorned with hanging flowerpots full of pink and purple blooms and white ladder-back rocking chairs for people to sit. "I think I'm going to go in there a minute."

Will sat down in one of the rockers while Ellie went inside.

A kind-looking woman, the kind you wished was your grandma, sat behind the counter.

"Ma'am," Ellie said in a friendly tone, "we've been here all day, and just an hour or so after we got here, all of the rides closed down because of lightning. Is there any way we can get a refund, or possibly a discount for the future?" Ellie knew there wasn't much of a chance, but she had to try anyway.

The woman peered at her from behind wire spectacles with keen blue eyes.

Ellie braced herself for the condescension she found rampant in big businesses, even those that labeled themselves "family centered."

The woman smiled warmly. "We can't control the weather, now can we?" She wrote *good through the season* on two new tickets and slid them across the counter to Ellie.

Ellie burst into a smile. "Thank you so much!"

Will declared, as they waited for the parking trolley to take them back down the hill to the truck, that she was amazing.

* * * * *

"I've got an idea."

"Okay, let's hear it." Ellie scooted closer to Will in the cab of Scarlett, thinking that her inner hillbilly—or perhaps redneck—was taking over. She didn't even care.

"I'm going to take you to my place."

"The woodland sanctuary of the elusive Will Howard?"

"That's the one. Except I'm not elusive."

"Celebrity reporters say you are, or at least they used to."

"I do like my privacy. But—obviously—not when it comes to you." Will took a deep breath and let it out slowly. "It's time."

"Awesome. I'd love to see where you live."

"There's only one problem."

"What's that?" Ellie couldn't imagine.

"Dot's not going to be happy with this arrangement."

They laughed at that together. Exiting the parking lot, Will turned down Indian Point Road in the opposite direction from which they had entered. After winding through the Branson hills for a few miles, he turned to the left on an unmarked drive.

It was a paved road, but narrow. Just off the big road, they began to meander through dense trees that opened at a small creek. A quaint bridge from a different century crossed the creek. Out of Scarlett's windows Ellie could see on either side the trickling clear water, polished stones around the edges, and an overhang of forest that shaded much of the creek from the sun. It resembled a scene from a storybook.

"Will, this is beautiful!"

He beamed.

On the other side of the bridge were more woods. They were driving downward, and Ellie had the sense she was delving into a secret. Oak, hickory, cedar, and pine trees congregated to form a canopy above them. The forest floor on either side of the paved lane was mossy and blanketed in leaves. Beautiful rocks—some very large— were scattered throughout, and more than once Ellie saw a rabbit dash by, no doubt on an important and mysterious mission.

At the foot of the hill was a stone gate, understated in its height. Will pressed a button on a remote control clipped to Scarlett's sun visor and the gate opened inwardly. Will drove through.

What Ellie saw next made her insides dance. She leaned forward in the truck, gaping. "Oh my goodness! Will!"

His voice was shy. "Do you like it?"

"Like it? Are you serious? I love it!"

Will pulled the truck up to the side of the cabin.

Not waiting for him to open her door, Ellie jumped out. "I don't know what to look at first!" Ellie twirled around, arms extended. "It's all so beautiful!"

Will's cabin was set on a tableau of land that backed up to lovely woods. His back porch, running the length of the cabin, overlooked a rock formation that featured stacks of limestone in uneven patterns about two stories high. A natural spring high above created a waterfall that gathered in a pool mere yards from the porch. Will had nurtured the dogwoods, redbud trees, wild ferns, and moss that grew around the pool into a woodland dreamscape.

Ellie plopped on one of the wicker rocking chairs and leaned back. From the copper fire pit, to the mission-style ceiling fans and the wine-red cushions on all of the furniture, the porch was perfectly appointed. "I see why you love it here so much, Will. You've created an astonishing place."

Will was obviously pleased. Taking her hand, he pulled her to her feet. "Well, don't stop there. I want you to see everything."

He led her through the French doors of the back porch and into the living room. A natural stone fireplace filled one wall, and there was an old chest in the center of the room for a coffee table, flanked by two chairs and a small couch. The gold walls were rough, like stucco, and the floors were aged, wide-board red oak. A Persian rug anchored all of the furniture, providing boundaries for the room.

Behind the living room was an antique carved dining table with ten chairs and a matching buffet, which Ellie thought she recognized as German. A long, rough-hewn wooden bowl was set on the table, full of Anjou pears. An iron chandelier with cut crystals glowed softly overhead.

The dining area flowed openly into a functional kitchen with zinc countertops and painted green cabinets. The all-glass doors opened with brushed nickel pulls, and the large gas cooktop was stainless steel, as were the refrigerator, double oven, and dishwasher. The breakfast nook at the end of the kitchen held a small round table made of iron and a bay window with cheerful toile curtains.

Feeling nosy, Ellie walked to the doorway just off the kitchen and pushed through the white saloon doors. She was pleased to see a neat laundry room with a deep sink and terra-cotta tile floor. A door led into the room from outside, and on the wall beside it was a three-tiered wooden rack for shoes. She recognized Will's tennis shoes, boots, and a pair of Birkenstocks.

"What do you think?" Will's voice echoed his amused expression.

"It's great—especially for a man."

He laughed. "Thanks so much."

As they moved through the house, Ellie noticed something different about Will—about the way he related to her. *Distant* didn't seem the right word, for his eyes were just as kind and his mood was warm as usual. But he wasn't quite as affectionate, as if he was holding back somehow. Yet he acted so happy to show her his home. Ellie couldn't quite put her finger on the problem. But when he showed her his bedroom, he stayed outside the door and let her go in and walk around.

"Will, are you okay? Is something going on?"

"Let's go out front, Ellie. I want you to see the water, and I need to talk to you about something."

They walked through the foyer and out the front door of the cabin. Ellie gasped at the view of Table Rock Lake. "Honey, I am *so* happy for you…to know you have this incredible place to come home to—to call your own. It's like a haven."

"I knew you would get it."

He led her down the flagstone path he had laid from his porch to the water. When they reached the dock, she scampered ahead of him and flung off her shoes, sitting down on the edge and sticking her toes in the water. Will followed, leaning back on his palms beside her.

"What do you need to talk to me about?"

"You are so direct, you know that?" When Will smiled, Ellie noticed there were no more clouds in the sky.

"It's inherited."

"It's disarming sometimes."

"I want to know what you're thinking about." Ellie turned her face totally toward him.

Will's green eyes smoldered, and his voice was husky. "I'm thinking about you, Ellie. I'm thinking about how right it feels to have you here. I'm thinking about how much I want to be with you and give to you—"

She touched his face with the tips of her fingers, moving closer to him and kissing him gently on the lips. Then he slid his arm around her, cradling her to him, and kissed her more firmly, entering her mouth with his tongue. In that moment Ellie felt something open within her. She wanted to receive him—to taste and embrace all that he was. She urged him to scoot backward just a bit, climbing onto his lap and facing him. Throwing his arms around her, he hugged her and buried his face in her chest. She wound waves of his hair around her fingers and caressed the nape of his neck. Then Will lay back on the wooden planks of the dock, bringing her with him. He smoothed her hair as it fell forward, and stroked her face with the back of his hand.

For a fraction of a second the universe seemed to stand still, and Ellie and Will looked into each other's eyes. Plunging deeper than she ever had before, Ellie thought that she had never seen such...dare she think it? *Love.* Will was correct that it felt right for her to be there. In that instant, everything felt more right to Ellie than it ever had in her life. She reached for the button—only the bottom one was buttoned—of his polo shirt.

"Stop."

The word was a whisper. Ellie glanced from the button she was holding back to Will's eyes. They were closed. His hand—the hand that seconds ago had been on her face—was now holding hers, the one on the button, tightly, as if to keep it still. Her hand felt like a captive bird. She wriggled her fingers, and Will set it free. Ellie moved wordlessly from where she was and lay down on her back beside Will. They were not touching.

Ellie's face—her whole body—was on fire. She swallowed hard to suppress a scream, feeling it rise with the bile in her throat. *What just happened?* She felt confused, rejected, in need of an explanation. But, most of all, she felt ashamed. It was as though her directness—her assertiveness—had somehow offended Will's sensibilities. Her heart sank like lead, pinning her to the dock. She wanted to slap him. She wanted to get up and leave. But she also wanted to cry. She closed her eyes to force back the tears, and then opened them again, fixing her gaze on a clear patch of sky.

After what seemed like hours, Will finally spoke. "I'm sorry."

His voice sounded pained, but Ellie didn't care. He was confusing the heck out of her. "Sorry for what?"

"I almost blew it."

Ellie sat up, glaring down at him. "Will, what are you talking about?" She hugged her knees to her chest and stared out over the water.

Will sat up beside her and tried to take her hand.

She shrugged him off. "You've been acting a little weird...sort of, I don't know, distant. But then I thought everything was fine, and you say how right we are together. You pull me to you and then you push me away. Then you say you're sorry and how you almost blew it. I don't have a clue what your problem is. I feel like you're talking to me from the other side of the Grand Canyon. Maybe you are."

Will looked her in the eyes. "Ellie, please forgive me."

"For what? Resisting my advances? I know I'm too direct." She blew out an exasperated sigh.

Will did something that shocked her then. He laid his head back and laughed—loudly.

"You're laughing at me."

He laughed louder, holding his stomach.

"You're such a jerk. I'm leaving." Ellie started to rise, and Will reached out to stop her. She shook his hand off her arm like it was an insipid bug but sat back down. She focused on a groove in the wood.

"Ellie, you never cease to amaze me."

She raised a wary eyebrow.

"Don't you know, girl, how much I want you? More than I've wanted anything else in my entire life."

The vise around Ellie's heart started to loosen. An unexpected tear rolled down her face.

Will wiped it away with the pad of his thumb. "Oh, no, please don't cry. I can't stand it that I've made you cry."

Another tear dropped from her eyes, and another. And another.

"God, forgive me. Ellie, I'm so sorry. I am a jerk."

She viewed him through her tears—it was like seeing through old glass. "Explain yourself."

"Okay." Will swallowed hard. "After the last time we were together, I felt convicted. You're so beautiful—so amazing—I am so attracted to you."

"That's a lot of sos."

"I know...right. So anyway—" Will let out a long sigh that was more like a groan. He turned his body to totally face Ellie and motioned for her to face him. "I. Want. You. When you asked me what I was thinking about, there was so much more I needed to tell you. But all I could think was how great it feels to have you here with me, and how much I want to be with you and give to you. And how much I want to make love to you."

"I want you too, like I have wanted no other." Ellie looked away. "So why did you stop?"

"Because I want to do it right."

"What do you mean?"

"I mean, I believe we should wait."

"Like until we're married?"

"Yes."

Ellie blinked her eyes. "Oh."

Will moved closer and took her hand. He told her about his talk with Sam and more about his growing relationship with Jesus and how he was getting free from the past. He also told her he believed God had brought them together, that she was a treasure and a gift.

And then he ran up to the cabin and came back with his Bible. He read to her from Ephesians about how Christ loves the church. "And here's the deal, Ellie. Here's what got me. Listen. Jesus loves us like a husband loves his bride. And He gave His life so He can *present her to God holy and blameless, without spot or wrinkle.*[3] After searching it out, I believe that's the way He wants me to be toward you. Not to take from you, but to protect you and give up my desires for your good. To keep our relationship sacred and learn to love you—heart and soul—before the physical stuff. I made a promise to God I would do that, just yesterday. And I almost blew it already!"

Ellie sat still, letting Will's words sink into her soul. "This is definitely a new one."

"Not having sex till marriage?"

"No, not exactly. I did grow up in church." She cut her eyes at him. "What's new is having the guy be the one to enforce it."

Will grimaced. "That's unfortunately new to me too. And believe me, it's not what I want—at least not what my body wants. But in my spirit it's what I believe God wants. Can you help me with it?"

"I don't know. It's not what my body wants either."

"I understand that. And it would kill me, but if you don't want to date me anymore—"

---

3. Ephesians 5:27

"What exactly are the rules?"

Will brightened. "You'll think I'm crazy."

"I already do."

"I'm thinking no kissing." He seemed to shrink as he said the words.

"No kissing? Are you a monk?"

That produced a grin.

"Girl, here's the deal. You are so smokin' hot it's taking every ounce of strength I've got not to kiss you right here and now on this dock." Will ran his hand through his hair. "Maybe I'm a freak. But, like Sam says, it's like a snowball rolling down a hill. Once we start kissing, I start to go all out of control. I'm afraid I won't be able to stop myself."

Ellie thought for a fleeting moment that maybe he *was* a freak. This was certainly a radical concept. But the heart of it was what— honor? Commitment to God? She had to admit that, underneath it all, these things were what attracted her most to Will…that set him apart from anyone else.

"Okay. I'll try it."

Will's grin spread across his face. His shoulders straightened.

"But I have a little rule of my own."

"What's that?"

"The words *I love you* have become pretty cheap in my experience, both with my dad and other guys. But love is supposed to be forever. So I don't want to hear those words from you—not *ever*— unless you're ready to put a ring on my finger."

"I can do that." Will held out his hand for a shake. "You've got a deal."

Chapter Twenty-One

. . . .

Audrey DuPree paced the tiny apartment that was costing her parents dearly every month to rent for her because it was within walking distance of the law school at NYU. Her red patent heels, which she wore to make herself look taller, tapped out an allegro staccato on the ceramic tile floor. She was still dressed in the red crepe suit she'd worn to work today at Ray's less-than-subtle suggestion. He'd sent her to the jail again, this time to interview a petty criminal they desperately needed information from. A male. She'd gotten the information.

She stopped pacing long enough to take off the shoes and toss them down the hall in the direction of her bedroom. A bit more comfortable after that, she resumed her trek back and forth from the living room to the kitchen. Each time she passed the kitchen counter she grabbed a few M&M's from the dish she'd placed there. When the dish was empty, she finally stopped pacing and plopped on the couch with a sigh.

Slouched there, with her feet up on the ultra-modern black metal and glass table in front of her, Audrey mentally prioritized her concerns. For her, this was a form of prayer—laying things out between her and God. Number one, and always hanging over her head like a black cloud, was the problem of law school, her desire to quit, and the subsequent effect that would have on her family. She knew all of the Sunday school clichés about God making a way for His children, and nothing being too hard for the Lord. *Yada, yada, yada.*

But at the present moment it seemed to Audrey that she'd come up against an insurmountable problem. Beyond her own sense of pride, and the horror of being labeled a "quitter," was the fear of disappointing her father. She may have been twenty-three years old, but when it came to her dad, she still felt as young as Scout. And Atticus was Atticus. He never changed. Besides, what else was she going to do? Law was the only thing she knew.

Second on her list of problems was the conundrum of Ellie's father, who was also Beecher's father, of course. Her search via Ray's easy access to public records had turned up no less than twelve Andrew McMurrays living in New York City. Upon further examination, three of them were within the age range of Drew—Ellie and Beecher's estranged dad. One was a bartender, one a radio DJ, and the other a history teacher at Stuyvesant. What to do with that information felt like a non-choice for Audrey. But, in her opinion, it was opening a can of worms.

Third on her list was the related problem of Beecher. Beecher, her best friend's brother. Beecher, the legal genius. Beecher, on whom she'd always had a crush but suppressed it following grade-school playground humiliation. Beecher, who was now single and coming to see her in New York.

As far as problems went, the third was by far the least unpleasant. She decided to dwell on it for a while. Regardless of the fact that Beecher would never look at her romantically, he was a loyal friend. They had scads of great memories together. In fact, Audrey being an only child, Ellie was the closest thing she knew to a sister, and by default Beecher had become her brother. They knew each other like a book—a very old book you've read a hundred times. If she could get past his sex appeal, which she'd trained herself to do, and see him only as a friend, Audrey enjoyed Beecher's company immensely. He was a comfort to her—as he had been lately in his e-mails. Like a favorite jacket that fit just right.

The analogy only broke down if she considered him as anything other than a friend. Then the thought of Beecher as a jacket that fit her became a joke. *Like putting Armani on a bag lady,* Audrey thought. She simply couldn't—shouldn't—view his visit in any other light than friendship. But still, it seemed a bit odd. Ellie was always the glue that stuck Beecher to Audrey. She never thought of him in any other terms. It was a surprise to Audrey that he mentioned coming to New York without Ellie—just to see her. *Of course it isn't just to see me,* Audrey reminded herself. His trip was bringing him through there. But still, they would be alone.

God, help. Audrey rubbed her temples. Beethoven's "Für Elise" signaled the ringing of her phone.

"Hello?"

"Miz Audrey?"

"Yes. This is Audrey."

"This is Chuck Filson down at the Manna Soup Kitchen."

Audrey's mind clicked through the files of faces she'd met over the summer. She finally placed the name with the image of a wiry, dark-haired man whose face reminded her precisely of a hamster.

"Oh, hi. How are you, Mr. Filson?"

"Call me Chuck." There was a pause, apparently for effect. "Miz Audrey, the reason I'm calling is that you gave me your number. You said you might be interested in working the soup kitchen sometime, and we've got an emergency situation. One of the ladies who volunteers called in sick, and our backup person called in sick. Would you happen to be available this evening?"

"Are you located in Greenwich Square?"

"Yes, ma'am, we are."

"I can be there in thirty minutes."

"That's perfect. We'll see you then."

Audrey changed out of her red suit, grateful for the distraction.

She put on a pair of army fatigues, a gray T-shirt, and a pair of clunky black lace-up boots. Locking everything up tightly, she walked the few blocks from her apartment to the soup kitchen, where a line was gathered outside.

"Miz Audrey!" Chuck Filson was at the door, waving her in. He pumped her hand up and down. "We're so pleased you could come."

He introduced her to several others who'd be assisting with the meal, which was served like a cafeteria line. Audrey's job was to man a vat of soup the size of a small swimming pool. It was steaming hot and the scent wafting above it smelled incredibly good. Audrey licked her lips. On either side of her were a man and woman handing out bread and silverware, respectively. The other two people in the line were in charge of drinks. An identical setup mirrored theirs on the opposite side of the room.

From the time the door was opened until the soup ran out two hours later, Audrey was busy filling bowls. Manna Ministries worked on the premise that people could pay whatever they could afford in order to eat, even if what they could afford was nothing. Audrey was astonished to see the money that collected in a simple jar near the door. The clientele ranged from NYU students to working-class families to homeless people.

"Can I come back again?"

Chuck Filson had just finished thanking her and shaking her hand. He smiled, and his small black eyes sparkled. "We'd be happy to have you any time."

"Please keep my number, and feel free to call if you're short of help again."

"Will do, Miz Audrey. Will do."

* * * * *

Back at her apartment, Audrey typed out an e-mail to Ellie:

Ellis Island,

I think I may have found my calling at last. It is far less glamorous than the famous actress you are sure to become. And it is less intellectual than the promising law student I am supposed to be. I will never make any money. But I think I could be happy if I could do some kind of community outreach— maybe start my own homeless center or halfway house. There is such need here in New York, and I never would have seen it, had I not come to law school.

How are you?

A.

Chapter Twenty-Two

....

It was the end of the first week of play practice since Ellie and Will made their "purity pact." Opening night was drawing close, so practice had been very intense, which was more than Ellie could say for the rest of their time spent together. For dates they had intentionally gone to public places, like the ice-cream shop and the park, instead of being anywhere alone. And instead of cooking at home, they'd done a lot of eating out. For someone as private as Ellie, it was exhausting. But worth it, she supposed. They'd stood by their commitment to no kissing.

This night, as on every other night of the week, Will had walked her to the door but not come in. He waited while she got Dot, and they went for a short walk. Then, back at her doorstep, he hugged her tightly and said good night. Watching him go, Ellie felt pain rip across her chest. She put on her comfiest pajamas and piled into the bed with Dot, hoping that reading her grandmother's diary might help take her mind off her unrequited desire to be with Will.

8 June 1887

If I die tomorrow, I've just had the best two days of my life. I know that sounds dramatic, but it is no exaggeration. I never knew life could be so wonderful, or that I could be so happy.

Uncle Robert had business in Springfield, and he took Aunt Liesel and Mother along. They left early yesterday morning and made plans to spend the night, returning today midafternoon. Heidi and I were to stay here and look after the place.

We saw them off before tending to the breakfast dishes and other morning chores. Mother looked grand in her nice dress and bonnet sitting beside Aunt Liesel. I was excited for Mother, especially, to get out and have a good time. She misses Papa and home excruciatingly; Heidi and I can read it on her face. Though it is comfortable here and our relatives are kind, I think it is hard for Mother to be in Aunt Liesel's shadow. She is used to being the mistress of her own house. I feel a bit guilty in writing this, and feeling as I do, but it can't be helped. It is ironic that while she seems displaced, I am finding out where I truly belong.

William came at ten o'clock. He brought candy for us both and a book for Heidi, Pride and Prejudice, which, I believe, unintentionally buttered her up. It was she who suggested we spend the day together—that she would enjoy the time alone with her new book. We tried to persuade her to come with us to the river, but she insisted against it. And although she would have been welcome—is always welcome wherever I am— I've never loved her more as a sister than I did in the moments I spent alone with William that day.

We walked, as usual, to our favorite spot by the river. William's horse was tied there, and instead of sitting down on the bank, this time he asked me if I wanted to go on a ride. It was a bit awkward with my dress, but he helped me, and I climbed on—not sidesaddle. He then mounted the horse in front of me, and fixed my arms around his waist.

At first I could not pay attention to my surroundings. I was dizzied by the scent of his shirt, which reminded me of the river, and wood smoke, and pine. It was soft against my cheek, worn. I lay my head against it and breathed it in, wanting to memorize the smell and the texture to keep with me forever, as if trying to capture a dream.

William squeezed my hands. They were clasped together, and fit—the both of them—under one of his. For a moment he rested his hand there, holding the reins with the other. I could feel the rough calluses against my soft fingers. His big hand was like a shelter, a cave, where mine could hide.

We didn't talk much as we rode. There was no need for words. It was enough to have each other and just to be. He led us along a path that was narrow but seemed timeless as it was carved into the hills. It went along the water for a piece, and I closed my eyes and listened to the flow. William agreed—there is nothing like the sound of running water. It's peaceful, and at the same time active, busy, alive. He showed me where he camped and caught trout before the river became too swollen and he had to move.

At one point the trail departed from the river and ascended up and up into the hills. We saw deer, rabbits, and squirrels, and all kinds of birds. The trees formed a canopy above our heads, but the day was so bright and sunny that beams of light shone through in shards, glancing off rocks, illuminating specific branches or highlighting patches of lichen: moss green, brown, pale gray-blue.

Finally we reached the place where he has set up camp now and hopes to remain till the end of the summer. He calls it "inspiration point" and made me close my eyes while he tethered the horse and then lifted me down, holding my hand and walking me over to the edge of the ridge at the edge of his camp.

"Now you can open," he said, and I learned why he calls it inspiration. It is the loveliest place I have ever seen. Rolling *hills stretch out before one's eyes to what seems like infinity. It's like I imagine the ocean, except the waves are green trees. They reach on and on forever, rising up to meet the blue sky. And snaking down between them all, like a silver ribbon, is the shining White River.*

"I wish I could stay here forever." His words were resolute, a bit sad.

"Can you?"

"No. This place is already taken. The homesteaders who own it have been most generous to let me camp for the summer. They've welcomed my help clearing some of the acreage— that's been my keep." William kicked at the corner of a rock stuck in the ground. "We've become friends, and they are a lovely couple, but they have their own son who will inherit the land."

"You have a life anyway in Chicago."

"Yes, and I'm expected back there for the fall term."

We sat down together on Inspiration Point and talked the day away. William asked me all sorts of questions, from the biggest things to the smallest. "What is your favorite color? What's your favorite food? What do you remember about Germany? What do you dream of most? What is your father like?"

After a while, I asked him why so many questions.

He said, "I'm a student, remember?"

And I said, "Yes. A student of the Bible."

"A student is just someone who wants to learn about a subject," he said. And then he winked at me. "I'd like to become the world's leading expert on you."

The sun was nearly setting—which was a beautiful sight— before we took any note of time.

"I'm a terrible host," William said, running over to his

tent and fumbling with a can of biscuits, which he offered me, with some blackberry jam.

"Heidi will be worried."

We raced back to my aunt and uncle's house, this time riding the horse all the way up, the back way through the woods, and then the pasture, to the house. The lamp was lit on the back porch, and Heidi sat beside it, reading.

"I'm sorry to have her home so late."

"And I'm sorry, sister."

"Well, that makes three of us sorry," she said, "because I've been too caught up in the lives of the Bennett sisters to worry about you."

We all had a laugh about that. Heidi put on some water to boil for tea, and we sat on the porch together and drank it. As it was dark, we determined that William should sleep in the barn and head back to his camp in the morning.

"Good night to both of you." William rose. He nodded to Heidi, and then to me, but just as that day I knew he would follow me from the post office, I felt his eyes were saying more than good night.

Heidi and I got ready for bed. All these years of sharing a bed with her have taught me her sleeping habits, so I waited till I knew she was sound asleep. Then, by the light of the moon, I slipped back into my dress and out of our room. The floorboards creaked so that I thought Heidi would wake, but she didn't.

In a few moments I was on the porch and could see the barn. From somewhere in the distance an owl hooted. A light flickered at the barn door and then diminished. I rushed toward it in the near-darkness, running smack into William, who was dashing out to meet me. He caught me up in his arms and held me in the pale moonlight. His eyes shone and his body was rigid, like a marble statue. Then he kissed me. Not softly, which is the only way I've been kissed before, and then only on the cheek by family and friends. No. This was different. I can only describe it in one word: hunger.

Gee, thought Ellie. *That was helpful.*

* * * * *

The next morning Will was there to pick her up for church. In his layered T-shirts, green and brown, and stonewashed jeans, he looked like a model for J.Crew. Ellie was dressed in a chocolate-colored dress with simple lines that came just below the knee. She wore her hair straight as a board. Gold hoop earrings and a stack of bangle bracelets coordinated with metallic-gold gladiator sandals.

"Good morning." His smile was fresh and expectant when she opened the door. "You look nice."

"Thank you. You do too, or I'm sure you would if I were looking."

Will snorted. "You can look but don't touch."

Ellie rolled her eyes but grinned as he held Scarlett's door open for her. When she climbed in, she stayed on her side.

"Oh, now, that's just brutal." Will cocked his head at the empty space between them with sad puppy-dog eyes.

"No. It is necessary. I'm helping you and myself."

"Well, thanks for nothing."

"You're welcome."

Will started the car and they pulled away from the condo. "Did you sleep well?"

"Pretty well. I stayed up awhile reading my grandmother's diary."

"What's going on with that?"

"You don't want to know."

Will laughed. "Has she dumped my relative yet for Richie Rich Heinrichs?"

"No. Not exactly."

"So, what happened?"

"Last night they had their first kiss. It was beautiful and passionate and—"

"Oh."

"Yeah. That's what I thought. I may need to put the diary down for a while. Who knew translating an old lady's diary could lead someone into temptation?"

"I need to get you a copy of what I was reading last night. Put me right to sleep."

"What's that?"

"*The Last of the Mohicans.*"

"I thought that was like an American classic. Full of adventure."

"It is—both—but the good parts are stashed between long, boring descriptions. I hate to not finish it, but I don't know if I can make it through all of those pages."

They chatted about literature and movies all the way to the warehouse church. One thing Ellie had to admit was that, without the distraction of getting physical, she and Will were learning more about each other. Just when she thought she knew everything, a new story or random fact from his life would be unearthed. And he never tired of asking her questions.

"Hello there, Ellie, good to see you again." Sam opened the door for both of them to enter and shook Will's hand.

"How's it going, bro?"

"If I were any better, I'd be in heaven."

"You know it." Will fake-punched Sam in the arm.

As they made their way inside to find seats, Will explained that he and Sam had an inside joke with that little saying. "There was this old man who used to come here to church, and he would say that every time you saw him. He was one of the greeters. He said it like he meant it, but Sam and I thought it was hilarious. We used to always kid him about it."

"Where is he now?"

"He's doing better."

"You mean he died?"

Will unpacked his guitar. "Yeah, several months back. He's in heaven."

"Wow."

"But Sam is carrying on his tradition."

Ellie scanned the gathering people while Will conferred with someone about the music. The crowd was as diverse as the time before, and Ellie recognized many of the faces. McKenna was there, and the older businesslike couple, as well as the Hispanic family and the woman in the sari. The guy in the wheelchair was making his way to the front. Will stood beside her as the man prayed, opening the time of worship, then climbed onto the stage with his guitar. A team of singers, led by McKenna, lined up beside him. They sang a couple of fast, peppy songs. Then, slowing things down a bit, McKenna led with these words:

> *"This is the air I breathe*
> *This is the air I breathe*
> *Your holy presence living in me.*
> *This is my daily bread*
> *This is my daily bread*
> *Your very word spoken to me.*
> *And I, I'm desperate for You.*
> *And I, I'm lost without You."*[4]

---

4. "This Is the Air I Breathe," lyrics by unknown composer, popularized by Michael W. Smith.

For Ellie, it didn't matter where she was. It didn't matter what else happened in the service. It didn't even matter who else was there. A moment of clarity came to her, like a butterfly coming to rest on her shoulder, as she uttered the words from her own spirit: "*I'm lost without You.*"

It was as if everything about her life—good and bad—every choice she'd made, as well as every circumstance beyond her control, had come together to propel her toward this moment. It all converged. Everything—and nothing—suddenly made sense.

Chapter Twenty-Three

....

Dear Audrey,

Do you remember that time in fifth grade when you tried to evangelize Beecher and me? When you had been to some revival meeting and "got saved"? You were so excited you even brought your little Gideon Bible to school the next day. You talked to me about it in class—we were in Mrs. Sigman's—and then cornered Beecher on the playground. We both thought you were nuts.

Now, however, I'm not so sure you were (at least in that instance). ☺ I had an experience this morning in church that was pretty radical. It didn't happen by the book, which I guess is why I trust it. We were singing (Will was playing guitar), and while I listened to the words, it was like they became my prayer. I can't explain it, and you know I'm not into being overly spiritual about things. What happened to me can only be described in those terms, however. It was mystical.

The song was about God being as near to us and as vital as the air we breathe, or the food we eat. It dawned on me that I've never thought of Him that way. He's been more of a distant figure, like my real father, I guess (i.e., I know He exists, but I don't know Him personally). And then there was this line that really got to me. It said, "I'm lost without You." I started crying. I was completely undone.

By this point you are probably thinking I'm cuckoo for

Cocoa Puffs, so let me take it another step further. When the song was over, Will came down off the stage and sat by me. He asked me if I was okay, since I was being such a bawl bag. We left the service and walked outside. I told him everything I was feeling, and he said, "Would you like to trust Jesus personally, Ellie? To place everything you are in His hands?"

It was the most natural and easy thing I have ever done. Will and I prayed—in the parking lot! And I can't even remember what I said. All I know is there's a peace in my heart that I have never known. I told Will that so many things about my life—things I've seen in you, and even missing pieces about him and our relationship—fit together now. And the stuff that doesn't make sense, well, it's like I know everything's going to be okay because I've got Jesus with me. It's so different knowing Him personally than just knowing about Him.

Is this what happened to you in fifth grade, Audrey? No wonder you wanted to share it with me and Beecher. I'm sorry I thought you were nuts.

  E.

Elliementary, my dear Watson,

  Yes.

  Although it's different for everyone and I sometimes have to laugh at the memory of my experience—the evangelist at that revival had his hair shaved in the shape of a cross, for crying out loud—this is essentially what happened to me in fifth grade. I think of it like you said, and like that other (older) song. "I once was lost—but now am found."

  I am so happy for you.

  Your sister now on the deepest level, and BFF—

  A.

* * * * *

Ellie moved through the next few days in an atmosphere of wonder. To Will, she described the experience as "a veil being lifted," as if she had new eyes with which to see the world.

She had always thought of herself as a religious person—after all, she'd been raised to believe in God and to have a moral conscience. The whole relationship-with-Jesus-thing had never made sense to her. She'd assumed it was just a way of expressing one's religion—an Evangelical quirk. But now it was more. She belonged to Jesus. And He belonged to her.

If anything, this complicated Ellie's relationship with Will. While before she'd been able to appreciate his faith, and even learn from and be challenged by him, it was still *his*. Something he owned. She didn't have to be fully vested. And if it got to be too much for her, as it sometimes had, she could step back—at least emotionally. She could go along if Will needed to pray about something. She could even agree not to kiss if that was his conviction. But before, these were mostly his issues, and he was ultimately responsible.

Not anymore. As her spiritual eyes opened, Ellie saw more clearly the need for purity. It became her own conviction. Ironically, she also understood Will's heart more completely as well. With his tenacious pursuit of an authentic Christian life he became even more attractive to her. She longed for him even more than she had up to this point, and she sensed he felt the same. She didn't know where it all was going. But something was going to have to give.

* * * * *

On Wednesday of that week Ellie opened the Heinrichs Haus Tasting Room. "Just a practice run," she'd explained when she announced it to the cast that morning after play practice, inviting them down to Branson Landing for wine and cheese. Many of them worked the rest of the day in various jobs at The Shepherd of the Hills. She hoped at least a few might come down and see her that evening.

Will met Ellie at her condo at four thirty. He was freshly showered and casual in jeans, a V-neck T-shirt, and a button-down Oxford that he left untucked. His hair was still a little damp, accentuating its soft waves. Together with Dot, they walked the short distance to the tasting room, which boasted its new signage. Ellie unlocked the door and flipped on the lights—low industrial-style lighting inside and strands of naked bulbs draped in rows across the storefront. After they moved several bistro tables outside, the Heinrichs Haus tasting room looked as charming and inviting as an Italian trattoria.

While Dot snoozed on the mat by the door, Ellie went about preparing different party platters. Arranging buttery crackers, she cut wedges of Brie to go with her champagne and Merlot, and Bucheron for the Chardonnay. For the light reds and whites she had Jarlsberg and Kasseri, and for the dessert wines she would pair Mascarpone. Will lit candles on the small round tables inside and out and selected music for the sound system. Pretty soon Ella Fitzgerald was piping through the speakers.

The first person to arrive was Suzy. She brought a carload of friends from the College of the Ozarks—a shy-looking boy and two girlfriends. They all declared that they didn't drink wine, so Ellie introduced them to sparkling white muscadine juice. Carrying their elegant glasses, they took a table outside. Ellie brought them a platter of crackers with some Brie with hot pepper jelly.

Next came George Castleman with his wife. He turned to his wife and crooned, "I'd like to introduce you to my girlfriend." He presented her to Ellie in the slapstick manner of Ollie Stewart.

The short and spunky brunette elbowed him in the ribs. Then she stuck out her hand and shook Ellie's, saying, "I'm Terry. It's great to finally meet you."

Ellie laughed. "I feel the same. How do you put up with him?"

"It's a challenge, as I'm sure you're learning."

George huffed at them both. "Yes, you poor ladies have it rough with me."

Ellie served them a few different red wines, as they requested, and they sat down inside at a table near the counter, where they could chat with Will.

Along with passersby who were shopping Branson Landing, a few other people trickled in from the play—Eugene Johnston, Dillon Cody, and the guy who played Buck. They were all still dressed in their work attire and presented a hilarious picture as turn-of-the-century hillbillies against a backdrop of culture and class. Ellie and Will had fun serving them and spending time together in the different setting. They all visited for a couple of hours.

"This is wonderful," George's wife, Terry, commented. "What a great addition to Branson Landing."

Just about that time Dot growled and barked, shocking Ellie, who had never heard her sound so fierce. The dog then ran around behind the counter and cowered behind Will's legs, making a wet spot on the floor. He reached down to clean it and calm her.

Ellie snapped her head toward the door and saw Seth Young swagger in with Cristal Dunaway on his arm.

"Was that a dog barking in here?" was Seth's accusatory greeting.

"Yes." Will picked up Dot and held her in his arms. "You must have spooked her."

Cristal sneered at Will, but then her heavily made-up eyes got wider than frying pans. She lurched toward Dot. "That's my dog. I've been looking all over for her!"

Dot's upper lip curled over her teeth, but Cristal didn't heed the warning. "I can't believe you stole my dog. Come to Mama!" She put out her hand in a quick motion to grab Dot out of Will's hands, and Dot bit her. "Oh! You little jerk!" Cristal slapped the dog across the face.

Dot cried.

Ellie, who had been pouring wine at a corner table, strode across the room. "Get out of here!"

Seth tried to protest.

Cristal examined the teeth marks on her hand, visibly disappointed that there was no blood.

"I mean it. Get out." Ellie was seething.

Seth held up his hands. "Okay, okay. Chill."

"I'm not going anywhere without Princess." Cristal, who had regained her composure, put a hand on her hip. Her red lips pouted. "She was a gift from my daddy."

George and Terry Castleman rose to leave. They looked apologetically at Ellie, leaving a tip on the table, and the rest of the room cleared out behind them. Only Suzy and company were left outside.

"You just hit my dog in the face." Ellie enunciated her words as though Cristal were hard of hearing. "I didn't like you before, but now I'm really done with you. Don't ever come back here again."

"*Your* dog." Cristal smirked. "That's rich. How long have you had *your* dog, huh?"

Will stepped forward. "This dog was in very bad condition when it showed up on Ellie's doorstep. She made every effort to find the owner in the two weeks that followed. If she was yours—which I doubt— why didn't you check the papers, or the vet's offices? Ellie even put it on the radio, for crying out loud."

"Well, isn't that sweet? And so ethical. I'm glad to know she didn't just steal her, like she stole my part."

Seth sniggered, then coughed into his fist.

"It's obvious Dot doesn't want you. If you think you can prove she's your dog, bring it on. Take legal action. I'll fight you for her. But until then, get out." Ellie motioned toward the door.

Dot growled again, eyeing Cristal.

"You've not heard the end of this, Miss Heinrichs Haus!" Cristal turned on her heel and pranced out, dragging Seth behind her.

Chapter Twenty-Four
....

"'Miss Heinrichs Haus'? Are you kidding me?" Beecher tried to suppress a laugh, but Ellie could hear it coming out in little obnoxious bursts.

"I hear you, Beecher."

More laughter on the other end of the line.

"I can hear you laughing. Even though you're in Munich, you sound like you're next door."

"Ellie, you have to admit it's hilarious."

"I have to admit no such thing."

"Well, it *is* funny."

"I do not think a blond assassin coming into the tasting room on the arm of Seth Young with the intent to steal my dog is any laughing matter."

"But *you* are the one who stole *her* dog, remember?"

Ellie sighed loudly. "If Dot ever *were* her dog, which I *doubt*, then I *rescued* her by taking her in. She obviously fled from Cristal's abuse."

"You sound like a lawyer."

"Dot has made her choice, Beecher. And it stands."

An explosion of laughter ripped through the phone.

Ellie remained silent till Beecher contained himself. Then she said, "So you'll be bringing Opa and Mom?"

"I will. I'm going to sleep on your couch, if it's okay, so we can all stay together. Or do you want us to get a hotel?"

"Don't be ridiculous."

"Mom thinks we need to get there a little early so we can drop off our things at your house, and use the bathroom and stuff."

"Okay. I'll leave your tickets on the counter."

"How will we get in? Does Opa have a key?"

Beecher always thought of everything. "I don't think so. I'll leave one under the mat for you."

"How original."

"Be careful," Ellie warned. "I have an exceptionally good guard dog."

"I cannot wait to meet this champion of canine rights."

"I'm going to tell her to bite you." Ellie yawned.

"What time is it there?"

"Eleven thirty. I was about to go to bed."

"Sweet dreams, Miss Heinrichs Haus."

"Sweet dreams yourself."

* * * * *

Ellie took Dot out for the last time and then locked her front door and ascended the stairs. Curling up under the covers in her brother's boxers and a holey T-shirt, she reached for Elise's diary.

26 June 1887

I am simply bursting with the news: William asked me to marry him! We were sitting at Inspiration Point, looking out over all of the beauty God has made—the glorious hills rising up to meet the blue sky and the silvery water meandering down below. I said I had never seen a place so beautiful, and he smoothed the hair back from my face with his hand and whispered, "It's not half as beautiful as you."

Then he got down on one knee. He quoted the entire second chapter of Song of Solomon, beginning and ending with "Arise, my love, and come away with me." Then he said, "Elise Marie Falkenberg, will you please marry me?" Just like that! He said he wants to ask my father, and to do things "right," but that he wanted my answer first or there would be no point. He was shining and wonderful. And of course I told him yes. I am the happiest woman on earth.

I know it will all work out for good. I just have to figure out what step to take next. It is getting harder to keep my relationship with William a secret. And yet it is not something I want to share—yet—with anyone other than Heidi. I feel guilty hiding it from Mother, but the situation is complicated.

Since my father is away, Uncle Robert is our guardian. I believe he would listen to my mother and honor her wishes; however, I cannot be sure that she would allow me to spend time with a stranger. A stranger—who has asked for my hand in marriage! A stranger who is closer to me than my own soul.

Both my uncle and my mother are kind to me. Perhaps they would allow me to meet with William in public places like church, or have him in Uncle Robert's home. But I am selfish, I suppose. I don't want to give up my private times with him. I don't know that anyone but Heidi can understand my feelings. I cannot take the risk of being forbidden to see him— at least until I figure out what I am going to do.

28 June 1887

William and I have it all planned. When my papa returns to fetch us from Branson, I will wait till the moment is right, and then I will tell my parents about William. I know it will be a shock, but Heidi is on my side, and I pray my father, and the rest of the adults, will understand. I believe if I introduce them to William, any reservations will be dispelled. If my father gives his blessing, we will plan a wedding. If he does not, then we may elope. I pray it does not come to that. What a dreadful thing it would be to have to choose between the person you love and your family.

29 June 1887

Horror of horrors! My papa has been killed in a railroad accident! We found out by telegram today. The Baldknobbers caused it. Unspeakable sorrow...what will become of us all?

Here the page was stained with what must have been Elise's tears. Blotches of ink blurred the letters so they were hard to distinguish in places. Her handwriting, which to this point had been an elegant, flowing script, began to appear more clipped and choppy. Ellie turned each page with heightened caution, reading and translating with a growing sense of doom.

3 July 1887

I am back in Hermann now. The services to bury my papa were yesterday, and I feel numb. Words fail me to describe it. Dear, precious Papa. Can it be that I will never see you again this side of heaven?

My heart longs to hide itself in the haven of William How-itt. We barely got to say good-bye—how wrong I see it is now that I kept our love a secret from my family. He should have been here to share this sorrow, surely one of the deepest I will ever know, but it is my stupidity that made it impossible. And of course I cannot elope with him now—I cannot leave my mother and Heidi.

When we parted, he gave me an address: 1700 Wabansia,

Chicago, Illinois. "Write to me at this address," he said, pressing it into my hand. "I will come back for you. You let me know when the time is right, and I swear to you, I will be here." The taste of him is still on my lips. The scent of wood smoke in my nostrils. And most of all, the sound of his voice lingers in my ears.

7 July 1887

We received a letter in the mail from Branson. My uncle Robert's mill burned. All is lost.

17 July 1887

Richard Heinrichs came today. He renewed his offer of marriage and plans to support my mother and Heidi as well. When he left, I saw the first glimmer of hope in my mother's eyes since Papa died.

26 August 1887

My heart within me is sick and sad. I fear—no, it's more than mere fearing—I know I have made the wrong choice. But what else could I do with so many people depending on me? With lives I love hanging in the balance?

Perhaps one day I will believe what Ms. Barrett-Browning says: it is "better to have loved and lost than never to have loved at all." But today I cannot see it. Today love is a plague, a curse. For love found me in Branson, Missouri, when I was least expecting it. I wasn't looking. I never dreamed it would come looking for me. Me! A simple hill country girl! And for a brief, shining moment, all the world opened like a rose. Things I'd never imagined possible, heights of joy I'd never known, seemed all within my grasp when I held him in my arms.

I thought that love could last forever. But now, as suddenly as it bloomed, that rose lies dry and dead on the ground. And what's worst of all, I cut it down with my own hands. I know it's a sin, but I wish I could die too.

It's my wedding day.

Chapter Twenty-Five

·····················

It was opening night.

Ellie dried her hair with a large round brush, styling it smooth and straight. She wore a white button-down shirt, which would be easy to take off without messing up her hair, a pair of cutoff jean shorts, and the old-fashioned ankle boots that were part of her costume. The rest, a pink and blue calico dress, she would find waiting for her in the dressing room, along with a pink hair ribbon. Someone would be there to do her makeup.

Leaving the tickets Will had gotten her for Opa, Katherine, and Beecher on the counter, she bid Dot good-bye, slipped her key under the WILKOMMEN mat by the front door, and slid into the front seat of her BMW. Taking what was now a familiar shortcut, she arrived in plenty of time at The Shepherd of the Hills campus.

The dressing room, fronted by a faux general store, was bustling with activity. Suzy waved to Ellie, motioning for her to come and take a seat next to her for makeup. Stopping to chat with Cheryl Jech for a moment about her microphone headgear, Ellie made her way across the room to join her friend.

In Ellie's opinion Suzy's wholesome good looks were obscured by the pound of eye shadow and blush the makeup person had used. Ellie watched with dread as Suzy's lips were painted the color of a cherry bomb. Then the girl started on Ellie. By the time the makeup artist finished with her, Ellie felt like a clown, but she knew the bright colors on her eyes, cheeks, and lips would fade under the bright lights of the set. It was the way of live theater. This brought her some comfort.

Will had called earlier to talk and personally wish her good luck, which he did by telling her to "break a leg." It was an unspoken rule among theater types that one never said *good* luck, lest it cause *bad* luck. Instead, the appropriate phrase for a well-wisher was "break a leg." She and Will abided by this protocol even though they knew it was silly. It was a tradition.

Ellie could tell when they talked that Will was a little nervous, and she understood why. Besides the fact it was opening night for a new company of actors, The Shepherd of the Hills was hosting a conflagration of investors who had apparently come from all over to judge the prospects of investing in Branson property and businesses. Will had been on call with his boss for various public-relations activities, like taking them all to lunch that day. He was also responsible for a party after the play that would include the investors and members of the cast. This was a lot to ask of Will, Ellie thought. Sometimes she wondered if his boss had any idea what a director—and especially one of Will's caliber—actually did. At any rate, she'd be there serving juice and wine, compliments of Heinrichs Haus Winery. Beecher was going to help her.

The cast met in a pavilion on the far east end of the set, hidden by trees, as the audience gathered in the stands before the play. Only Chris, the guy who played Buck Thompson, was missing. He was in the pre-show, which as Ellie had seen before, included a humorous speech by Buck—rife with grammatical errors—and a bullfrog race.

Will's eyes sparkled as he gave last-minute instructions. The air around him seemed charged with intensity. "You guys will be awesome!" he encouraged. "You're totally ready for this. I have complete confidence in all of you!" Then he led them in a prayer:

"Thank You, Father, for the gifts You have given us, and for the opportunity to use those gifts and do something we all love as we minister to others. We believe this story has the power to transform lives, and so that is my prayer. May lives be changed through the telling of this redemption story. May Your blessing fall upon us tonight in order that we could be a blessing to the audience. In Jesus' name."

Ellie beamed. Excitement bubbled up within her. And joy. And a sense of purpose and peace. She winked at Will, and he smiled at her warmly.

Seth Young rolled his eyes.

* * * * *

As the first actors walked out onto the outdoor stage, Ellie and Suzy watched from the vantage point of the general store. Men dressed as backwoods hillbillies—as Ellie imagined some of her relatives had been in the time of Elise and William—assembled in front of Old Matt's mill. They pontificated about this and that, mostly revealing their different characters and setting up the story. Of course, there was a great buildup to the infamous contest of brute strength between Young Matt and Wash Gibbs.

When it came time for Sammy Lane to enter the scene, Ellie had a new experience that she would only be able to describe later as supernatural. A surge of something—power? animation? creativity?—came over her. There had always been an adrenaline rush as she took a stage, but this was altogether different. This was a gift of grace.

Ellie *became* Sammy. In the past, even up to the last few days of practice, there had been a disconnect. A hurdle Ellie could not seem to cross, even using all of the techniques she'd learned in college, and all of her previous acting experience. Try as she might, Sammy's character had somehow seemed shallow, one-sided, and flat, like a dime-store paper doll. Ellie chalked it up to the writing, what she called the low-brow literary quality of the script. But tonight—on *this* night—Sammy Lane came alive for her. It was as if, when Ellie walked onto the stage, she was walking into the pages of her grandmother's diary. The lines of reality blurred and then faded completely. She was living a part of her own history.

* * * * *

In the VIP section, a visiting investor named Jackson Jenkins leaned forward in his seat and adjusted his Gucci glasses. He was aware that Will Howard was a world-class director but hadn't expected even him to be able to draw this kind of performance from the raw material Jackson imagined was afforded in a place like Branson. However, the woman playing Sammy Lane was mesmerizing.

Jackson remained riveted to that spot until Ellie's scene closed, and then she exited, stage left. He whipped out the program he'd been furnished with earlier and searched its pages for her name. There were three Sammy Lanes who alternated nights, apparently, and they were all pictured in the program. But two of them were blond. This one—the dark-haired one—was unmistakable. Elise Heinrichs. He would have to meet her.

* * * * *

After the play, Ellie escaped the fate of most of the rest of the cast, which was to stand in a receiving line on the stage while members of the audience greeted them and asked them to autograph programs. She and Will had a brief moment together as they fled toward the conference center to prepare for the VIP reception. Stopping out of sight from the crowds, Will squeezed her hand.

"You were magnificent."

His eyes seemed to say so much more, and for a moment Ellie thought he was going to kiss her.

"Thank you. I am glad you were pleased."

"Pleased is not half of it. You gave the performance of a lifetime."

"Really?" Ellie grinned shyly.

"Surely you know."

"It *was* an amazing experience for me. I felt, I don't know, *anointed*." Her declaration was tentative. "Does that make sense?"

"I think it is perfectly accurate."

She hugged him, holding him tight and leaning her head against his chest. "Thank you, Will. For everything."

His breathing was heavy. She could feel his heart beating against her ear. "We better get up to the conference center, huh?"

"Yeah. Let's go."

When they got to the conference center, a building set off to itself, the caterers were set up with a lovely spread of finger foods. Long banquet-style tables draped in white organza were laden with shrimp cocktail, artisan cheeses with different breads and crackers, and an elaborate display of fruit that included pineapple, blueberries, grapes, oranges, cantaloupe, and kiwi. There was punch and a section for coffee, cleverly decorated with scattered beans, and a chocolate fondue fountain that boasted squares of angel food cake, marshmallows, pretzel rods, and strawberries.

Prominently positioned, which Ellie knew was because of Will, was a table covered in white and labeled HEINRICHS HAUS WINERY. Ellie went directly to it and pulled out the crate she had given him earlier. Feeling like she was now in character as Katherine, Ellie proceeded to set up a display with grapevines, wine and juice bottles, and decorative plastic grapes. She was just finishing the task when Beecher appeared with a box full of plastic wine glasses and napkins sporting the Heinrichs Haus logo. He set it down, then lifted Ellie off the ground in a hug.

"You were *wunderbar!*"

Ellie kissed him on the cheek. "Thank you. And thank you so much for being here."

They hugged again.

"Oh, Beecher. I'm so happy to see you!"

Will, who was assisting the caterer with a matter, walked over to join their brother-sister moment.

"This is Will Howard, Beecher." Ellie reached out to touch Will's arm. "And this is my brother, Beecher."

The two men exchanged a hearty handshake.

"I've heard so much about you," Will told Beecher.

"And I, you. It's good to meet you in person." Beecher regarded Will with an expression of respect. "Let me congratulate you on a job well done tonight. I think the performance surpassed what anyone in the audience might have been expecting."

"Thank you," Will said. "I'm so glad you could be here."

Just then Will's boss appeared at the entry, seemingly the head of an entourage. He motioned to Will.

"I look forward to visiting with you later." He clapped Beecher on the arm and smiled at Ellie as he walked away.

"Uh-huh." Beecher winked at Ellie. Then under his breath he said, "I have a few hundred questions for you, Mr. Howard."

She punched him softly in the ribs.

* * * * *

The reception was a bit of a whirlwind. It was bigger—in terms of attendance—than Ellie realized. Beyond The Shepherd of the Hills people, there was a host of Branson elite. As they came through the line for a sample of Heinrichs Haus wine or juice, she met Shoji Tabuchi, the famous Branson violinist, and his wife, Dorothy; the mayor of Branson and the director of the Branson Chamber of Commerce; the owners of Big Cedar Lodge; and several dignitaries from the College of the Ozarks. All of them complimented Ellie on her performance as Sammy Lane, except for the Tabuchis, who had performed in a show of their own at the same time as the play. The elaborately installed Shoji Tabuchi Theatre was right down the road. Ellie was able to tell them with complete honesty that theirs was her favorite show—besides *The Shepherd of the Hills,* of course—that she'd ever been to in Branson. It was only after the Tabuchis were well out of earshot that Beecher whispered, "Of course, the only other one you've seen, to my knowledge, is the one with the fake Michael Jackson."

"That one is actually quite good," Ellie whispered back. "And I'll have you know that I have also been to the Dixie Stampede."

Their surreptitious exchange was interrupted by the arrival at their table of a thirtysomething man in a gray suit and glasses. His green shirt provided a stylish splash of color and was complemented with a narrow, patterned navy-blue tie. His hair was short but slightly longer on top and gelled back with sideburns. He looked like he might have posed just the moment before for a Banana Republic ad in *The New Yorker* magazine.

"Hello," Ellie offered, "would you like to try our red or white wine? Or perhaps some juice?"

The man smiled and held out his hand. "Ellie Heinrichs?"

"That's me," she said, taking it.

"Monumental performance tonight. Totally blew me away."

Ellie retrieved her hand. "Thank you very much. How kind of you to say."

"And you are?" The man turned to Beecher, who put out his hand.

"Beecher Heinrichs, her brother."

They shook.

"I'm Jackson Jenkins. Nice to meet you both."

They nodded.

"What brings you to Branson?" Beecher poured the man a glass of white wine and handed it to him. "This is both of our favorite, by the way, a grape called *vidal*."

Jackson Jenkins took the glass Beecher offered him. "Thanks." He sipped it. "That's good stuff." He took another sip. "I'm in Branson as an investor. Just came down to look at some property."

"Where do you live?' Ellie asked.

"New York City."

"One of our best friends is in school there." Beecher cleared his throat. "She's in law school at NYU."

"Oh, really. I went to NYU," Jackson said. "Great school in a great town. I'm from there."

"What do you think of Branson?" Ellie asked.

"Hmm. Well, it's a friendly place. Beautiful country." Jackson's dark eyes flashed as he grinned. "I think it's safe to say I've never seen anything like it."

Beecher clearly got a kick out of that.

A line was forming behind Jackson, so he said, "I'd love to talk to you guys a little more and find out about your winery. Would that be okay?"

"Sure." Beecher took the business card Jackson offered.

"Could you possibly give me a call over the weekend? I have a few appointments, but it's pretty quiet till Monday. That's a really busy day, and then I fly out Tuesday."

"I'll call you in the morning," Beecher promised.

"Thanks. Good to meet you both."

* * * * *

The following morning at the condo Ellie made breakfast for her family. It was her first time to see Opa, as he'd been in bed when she and Beecher returned from The Shepherd of the Hills. Katherine had waited up after the play, hugging Ellie and telling her how amazing she'd been as Sammy. "We would have come to the reception, but Opa was not feeling well. I needed to get him home."

As she set a small pitcher of cream on the table, Ellie didn't want to think about why Opa looked so old and tired. It made no sense to her. Just that May at home he was robust and working in his garden. She'd had to work hard to keep up with him as they "waged war" upon the weeds. The Opa who sat at her table sipping coffee and picking at his peach-filled crepes was not the same man. He seemed a faded version of his former self.

"Opa, what's wrong with you?"

Beecher and Katherine exchanged a look that implied they were not entirely thrilled with Ellie's directness.

But Opa laughed. For a moment, the old light flickered in his eyes. "I don't know, Sunshine. I imagine I'm just old."

"Phooey." Ellie sniffed. "That's never kept you from eating fresh peach crepes before."

"I'm sorry. You're right about that, and I know they are delicious. But lately I seem to have no appetite."

"Have you been to the doctor?"

"You sound like your mother."

"Well?" Ellie persisted.

"No, I have not. You know I'm not very fond of doctors."

"Well, we are fond of you. And if you've lost your appetite, something is wrong. We need to find out what it is so you can get better."

Opa glanced at Katherine, and then back to Ellie, whose eyes were boring holes in his gaunt face. "I've held off your mother these last weeks, but now that you are joining her I suppose I should not argue." He looked to Beecher for help. "Any words for the defense, Counselor?"

"I'll take you myself on Monday."

Opa chuckled and shook his head. "Those were not exactly the kind of words I had in mind."

Chapter Twenty-Six

....

After breakfast, Beecher called Jackson Jenkins just as he had promised. They made plans to meet for lunch at Mel's Hard Luck Diner in The Grand Village, a quaint shopping center near the golf course condominium where Jackson was staying. Then Opa, Katherine, Beecher, and Ellie took a walk down Branson Landing.

It was a beautiful day. Sunshine poured out generously over Branson from a cloudless blue sky. The breeze floating upward from the adjacent lake was cedar-scented and cool. The trees lining the walkway of the Landing were full of singing birds. Opa commented on how the red bricks under their feet reminded him of the cobblestone streets in places they'd visited together in Europe.

They window-shopped awhile, then people-watched as they stretched their legs. When Ellie took them to the tasting room, everyone was impressed with how she had arranged things, from the furniture to the lighting, signage, and other décor. Katherine was especially pleased with the fixtures she and Ellie had selected together. They drank Lemon Pellegrinos out of the cooler, Opa sitting and resting on the couch, and Beecher took inventory of the tasting room's stock of wines and juice.

"You guys have done a great job setting this up," he said.

Katherine pointed with her bottle. "It's mostly Ellie."

Beecher ribbed her. "Branson hasn't turned out to be such a bad place after all, has it, little sister?"

Ellie shook her head. "Not nearly as bad as I thought." A smile broke over her face as she thought of Will and everything they'd shared. *Not bad at all.*

* * * * *

Mel's Hard Luck Diner was an all-American, retro-styled eating place famous for its hamburgers. It had a chrome sign with hot-pink neon letters, a soda fountain, red booths, and a black-and-white checker-board tile floor. It also boasted of singing waiters dressed in 1950s attire. Jackson and Beecher agreed that the latter was a feature they wanted to steer clear of, if at all possible.

Over good-sized burgers and piles of french fries, Jackson quizzed Beecher over viticulture and enology, finding him profoundly knowl-edgeable. He asked Beecher questions about Heinrichs Haus and what operations they had in New York, if any. Beecher expressed that while they were fairly well-known in the South, they didn't do a lot of business on the East Coast or up north, something he'd like to see change. They talked about possible collaboration. Jackson had hold-ings in the hospitality industry in New York as well as retail business. They both agreed to consider how they could work together to get Heinrichs Haus wines and juices into these venues.

"I like your wine," Jackson said. "And I like you—and your sister."

"Thank you." Beecher smiled. "We're kind of a package deal."

"She was astonishing in her role last night. I have to admit I was not expecting much. I never should have underestimated the local talent."

"Well, she is my sister, so it's hard to be objective, but I've always thought she had a gift for drama."

Jackson laughed. "Has she ever thought about trying to be bigger—I mean, going outside of Branson?"

It was Beecher's turn to laugh at the guy's naïveté. "Um, yeah. It's not exactly her dream to stay in Missouri."

"I didn't mean that insultingly. It's beautiful here. For some people, well, it's what they want. Like that Will Howard. He walked away from Hollywood to come here."

"I know. Crazy, right?"

"Different strokes for different folks." Jackson pushed back his empty plate.

"I don't think Ellie is like him. Her dream is to be on Broadway. She just hasn't gotten her chance yet." Beecher took a sip of his chocolate milk shake. "It's a long shot, you know. She has an agent, but so far nothing has happened."

Jackson's face brightened. "Beecher, I've got a friend in the business on Broadway. Let me make some calls—we'll see. Maybe he could get her an audition." He folded his napkin and set it on the table. "I'm not exactly an expert, but I do have taste. And I've not seen anybody as good as she was last night in a long time."

"That would be great."

"Don't tell her anything, in case it doesn't work out. But I'll make those calls and get back with you about it, okay?"

"Okay." Beecher shook his hand. "It's been very nice meeting with you."

"You too. I hope this is the beginning of a long, good relationship."

* * * * *

When Beecher returned to Ellie's condo, Opa was napping on the red couch. Dot was curled up beside him. They were both snoring. Dot's ears shot up, however, and she opened her eyes when Beecher's footfall made a board creak in the floor. Headed for a magazine on the table, he reached down to pet her. She growled. Beecher drew his hand back as if out of a fire.

"I think I'll just go back outside for a while." He tiptoed back down the stairs, put his shoes back on, and headed for the main thoroughfare of Branson Landing. He suspected he might be able to find his mother and sister in the vicinity of the J.Jill store, or possibly Coldwater Creek.

"Beech!"

"Over here!"

They were sitting under the awning of the Cold Slab Creamery. Katherine, chic as ever in her black sheath dress and Jackie Onassis sunglasses, waved to him to join them. Ellie was in a rattan-colored V-neck sweater and ivory Capri pants, with a wide-brimmed straw hat.

"You ladies are quite the picture of elegance." He kissed them both on their cheeks as he sat down.

"Want some ice cream?" Katherine offered.

"No thanks, I just had the all-American artery clogger—hamburger, french fries, and chocolate milk shake for dessert. I'm stuffed."

"Isn't that place good?" Ellie swallowed a spoonful of strawberries and cream. "I love it there."

"It is. It was fun."

"How did the meeting go?" Katherine set down what remained of her dulce de leche, and Beecher took it up.

"Really good. I think Mr. Jenkins is pretty taken with our products—and possibly with you, Ellie."

Ellie stopped in the middle of a bite. "Wha—?"

"He went on and on about your performance as Sammy. He was very impressed."

"That's nice."

"Anyway, we'll see what comes of it all. I'm supposed to be checking on some things for him, crunching some numbers. He's got ties that might help us expand our business on the East Coast."

"That would be great." Katherine took out a compact and powdered her nose, then reapplied some Bordeaux-colored lipstick.

"Yeah, and he mentioned something that might be interesting—I mean, as a side job, if I move back to the States."

"What's that?" Ellie asked.

"Viticulture consulting. Apparently there's a niche market for some of that. Even in New York."

"Sounds interesting."

"Just don't give away any of our trade secrets." Katherine smiled and patted him on the arm.

Beecher eyed the large bags that surrounded their table. "Were you guys done shopping?"

Ellie grinned at him. "We've only just begun."

Beecher carried their shopping bags back to Ellie's condo alone. This time, instead of going anywhere near Dot, the snoring bulldog, he set the bags down in the kitchen and slid into Ellie's desk seat, opening her computer. Typing in his password, he deleted five or six junk e-mails before opening the one he was looking for.

Dear Bumble Beech,

I am excited about your visit. It will be good to have a little piece of home come to me, even if it is flying onward to Munich.

What do you want to do while you are here? It's nice that you have seen all of the touristy sights already, so we don't have to worry about them (unless you want to go back, of course). I've been thinking of all of the places I would like to share with you—there's a little park near my apartment where I love to sit and read, and a bakery where I get these little pastries I think you would like. Then of course there's my favorite bookstore, and coffee shop, and a theater that shows independent films.

And I'll have to take you to the Southern-fried restaurant. It's such an anomaly here that it is simply a must.

Is there anything you want me to cook for you while you are here?

Anything else you can think of that will make you happy?

If you'll humor me, I want us to go to the soup kitchen. Just once, at least, so you can see what it's like.

Looking forward to seeing you,

A.

P.S. I'll pick you up at the airport, but you have to tell me when.

Beecher suddenly became aware that he was grinning ear to ear. He shot a look toward the couch, glad that no one was there—awake— to see him. Hitting REPLY, he gave in to another impulse.

Audrey,

I am grinning ridiculously after reading your e-mail, like Alice's Cheshire Cat. And so it seems that all I need to make me happy is—I'll say it—a word from you.

I'll be at La Guardia at 7:00 p.m. on Tuesday—Flight 1025.

Warmly,

Beecher

Chapter Twenty-Seven

....

Ellie's performance Saturday night was at least as good as Friday, according to the observations of her esteemed director. She was on a roll. But what excited her more was the fact that she was going to be baptized—by that director—in the presence of her family. It was a spur-of-the-moment decision that felt eternally right.

On Sunday morning they all went to church with her and Will, everyone except Opa, who stayed home to rest. Afterward, they went back to the condo and picked him up and then headed out toward Table Rock Lake and Will's cabin. He'd invited them all out for lunch.

Before eating, however, the little group assembled at the water's edge. Will had placed a row of three ladder-back chairs on an even spot in the grass for Opa, Katherine, and Beecher, and as they were seated, he led Ellie out into the water. The lake was as smooth as glass and cool—not cold. Ellie found it refreshing even as it soaked into her jeans. The white button-down she wore as a jacket over her red tank top billowed around her as she went deeper. It was not quite as deep for Will, who was taller, but Ellie was about waist high. A squirrel skittered up an oak tree. Across the way, a fish jumped, causing a ripple effect upon the surface of the water.

Holding her hand tightly, Will turned to face her. He smiled and Ellie read in his face the expression of total joy, complete satisfaction. She felt his face was a mirror for her own soul.

He whispered, "Are you ready?"

She nodded, feeling the tears glistening in her eyes.

"Ellie asked me if we could do this today, and though it's a little unconventional, I agree with her that it is God's perfect timing." Will addressed the threesome on the shore. "You are her family, the people who love her the most and the ones she loves and trusts completely. It is fitting and right that you be the ones to share this sacred moment in her spiritual journey."

He faced Ellie again. "Ellie Heinrichs, do you believe Jesus is the Son of God and that He died on the cross to save you?"

"Yes."

"Have you accepted Him as Lord of your life—past, present, and future?"

"I have."

"Is it your desire to follow Him in believer's baptism, as a symbol of your faith in Jesus and your commitment to follow Him all the days of your life?"

"It is."

"Then it is my privilege to baptize you, my sister in Christ, in the name of the Father, the Son, and the Holy Spirit."

Gripping Will's arm, Ellie grabbed her nose to hold it. As he plunged her underneath the water, he said, "Buried with Christ in baptism unto death..."

And then, as she came up to the surface, Will's voice again: "Raised to walk in newness of life."

From his place on the edge of the lake, Opa started clapping.

* * * * *

Ellie's heart swelled with thankfulness. She hugged Will—still out in the water—and the warmth of their bodies joined like two points of light coming together to form a radiant beam. They climbed out of the lake, clothes completely soaked, and together with Ellie's family headed for the cabin.

Will dried off quickly and changed his clothes while Ellie went for the shower. While Katherine and Opa sat on the back porch in wicker rockers, Beecher helped Will get the grill started. Soon Ellie joined them, bringing with her the steaks Will had marinated overnight.

"Did you put the potatoes in the oven?" Will asked as he took the steaks from the platter, transferring them to the grill.

"I did—before I got in the shower."

"Awesome. Thanks."

"Is there anything else I need to do?"

Will contemplated. "Not right now. I've got the salad all ready and the stuff for the potatoes. We just need to remember to put in the bread when it's time."

"How long does it need?"

"I'd say about fifteen minutes."

"Okay. Let me know when the steaks are about fifteen minutes out."

As Will had set the table that morning, there was nothing else for Ellie to do. She eased into one of the cushioned chairs on the other side of Opa and put her feet up on the ottoman.

"Well, Sunshine, you seem pretty at home here."

Ellie colored slightly. "I guess it is a pretty comfortable place."

"That it is. I like it very much. Will is quite the landscape artist."

"It's so peaceful," Katherine said. "You'd never imagine you were just a few minutes away from Branson."

"Isn't that the truth." Ellie ruffled her hair, which was not yet dry.

"Was the water cold?"

"No, actually, it was about right."

"Table Rock is a beautiful lake."

"I was baptized in a lake also," Opa said.

Katherine lifted a graceful brow. "You never told me that."

"Or me, either," Ellie added.

"It wasn't actually a lake. It was the pond near our house." Opa chuckled.

"Ew," Ellie said.

"It wasn't bad. Especially for a little boy who played with bullfrogs."

"Tell us about it," Katherine urged.

"I had been through confirmation, which to me was no empty ritual. I had a true experience like Ellie found here. When it came time to be baptized, though, I got the idea I didn't want to be sprinkled. I asked to be baptized in the pond, and my parents humored me. We did it at the annual church picnic."

Ellie slapped her knee. "Opa, you never cease to amaze me!"

"Why did you let me be sprinkled?" Katherine asked.

"That was your choice. I don't think God cares how it's done, since it's not the water that makes you clean, anyway." Opa's eyes crinkled around the edges, and he drew his fist to his chest. "It's what happens in your heart."

* * * * *

Will called them inside, placing a steak on each plate around his large dining table.

"Oh no, I forgot about the bread," Ellie told him. "You never told me—"

"That's okay. I got it on."

"I love these pewter plates!" Katherine said admiringly.

They passed a large bowl of mixed salad greens, and after that the bread and potatoes. Will had butter on the table, some homemade vinaigrette, and a mixture of sour cream and sharp cheddar cheese for the potatoes that looked delicious.

"That's clever," Beecher commented. "Do you cook a lot?"

"Not really. I have about three meals I do well, and this is one of them," Will admitted.

"Well, thank you for having us," Opa said. "This is quite a treat."

* * * * *

After the meal, they all moved to help clean up, but Will would not allow it. "I can do this. You all relax."

"I hate to admit this, but I am very tired." Opa's face was gray and worn.

Will offered, "Would you like to lie down here?"

"That's very kind. But, if it's okay with you, Katherine, I think I need to go back to Ellie's." He motioned for the door.

Ellie grabbed her bag from a hook by the door. "Why don't I take you back, Opa?"

"But what about Will?" Katherine asked.

"He's got some fun plans for you and Beecher that I don't want you to miss. I can do it anytime." Ellie took Opa by the hand. "You guys stay here, and Will's going to bring you home on the boat."

"Cool!" Beecher's response.

"Okay," said Katherine, "sounds wonderful to me."

* * * * *

Opa fell asleep in the car as Ellie maneuvered their way back to Branson Landing. She was completely comfortable driving the side roads now and marveled at how much stress it saved her. *Without these shortcuts, I could never live in Branson*, she mused. *How could anyone?*

Rousing Opa slightly after she pulled into the garage, she helped him into the house and up the stairs. She turned back the bed in the guest room, where he'd been sleeping, and he crawled in, as though just short of collapsing. He seemed to shrink as the bed swallowed him. Ellie thought his face looked ashen. Kissing his cold cheek, she tucked in the covers around him. He was already snoring.

After taking Dot out for a good long walk, Ellie returned to the condo feeling tired herself. The weekend had been wonderful, with the play opening and all of her family being there. But it had also been taxing. Knowing it would be a good while before the boaters showed up, she decided to take a little nap of her own.

As Ellie headed toward her bedroom, she stopped. Like a breeze stirs up leaves into a dance with an unseen partner, her spirit was stirred in another direction. She turned and walked to the door of the guest room.

Opa had shifted in the bed from the way she left him. Now he was facing the far wall, away from the door, and with the covers wound around him he looked like two big uneven lumps of sugar. Ellie's heart warmed when she saw him. She remembered seeing him this way many times, when as a child she would wake up very early in the morning. Some days he would take a nap with her in the afternoons. Other times she and Beecher had padded into his room in the night when they heard a scary noise.

Silently, she crept over to the bed. Without pulling back the covers, she lay down on top of them and inched toward Opa. His silver hair was mussed in the back and he smelled fresh, like Dial soap. She faced the wall like he was and drew up close to his back, snuggling in behind him. She laid her head on his pillow, and the tip of her nose touched the rugged lines carved into the back of his neck. Bending her legs to match his, she gently wrapped her arm around him, just above his waist. His breathing was a bit more labored than usual, it seemed, but it was even. He found her hand with his rough one and laced her fingers through his, placing it on his chest. She could feel the steady, reassuring beat of his heart.

Ellie and Opa slept like this for over an hour. When she woke, she didn't want to speak or move for fear of disturbing him, but he surprised her by speaking first—or rather, singing softly.

> *"You are my Sunshine, my little Sunshine.*
> *You make me happy when skies are gray.*
> *I think you know, dear, how much I love you.*
> *Please don't ever go too far away."*

The tears streamed down Ellie's face even as she laughed. Opa had modified the words of the song to fit his liking long ago and sung this version to her and Beecher every night, as children, as far back as she could remember.

"There's a lot of Heinrichs family philosophy in that little song," she said, still holding on to him from behind.

"You are right, Sunshine. It says almost everything that is really important."

She gave him a little squeeze. "Do you know, Opa, that you are also *my* Sunshine? And Mother's and Beecher's?"

"I do know that. As I hope and believe you all know that you are mine." Opa's voice was raspy, not far above a whisper.

"You've always done a good job of showing us. I've never had to wonder how my Opa felt about me."

He cleared his throat. "Now that you have Jesus, Sunshine, there is really only one other thing that matters."

"What's that?' Ellie whispered in his ear, rising up on one elbow.

"Write it on your heart that those you love are what really matters. Being together and loving—that's what life is all about."

Ellie pressed her cheek to his weathered one, finding his was also wet with tears.

"I've had Jesus, and been loving you, your mom, and Beecher for a long time. I am a most blessed man."

Chapter Twenty-Eight

....

In the time it took to go by boat from Will's dock on Table Rock Lake to Lake Taneycomo, and the White River Catfish Co. restaurant at Branson Landing, Beecher decided that he liked Will. It had been building, the feeling that this was a cool person who might be worthy to date his sister. Will's artistic background and accomplishments in his field were impressive to Beecher, who measured a man in large part by his brain. Then there was the issue—not always to be trusted—of Ellie's affection for Will, the apparent happiness he brought her, the things in common they obviously shared.

Furthermore, Beecher liked how Will treated Ellie at the cabin; his honor toward her and her family at the baptism, their obvious companionship over lunch, the gentle tone of his voice when he spoke her name. He also lacked the weirdness Beecher usually associated with Protestant Christianity.

The deciding factor for Beecher, however, followed the moment when, unexpectedly, his cell phone rang when they were out in the middle of the lake. Will slowed the boat to a crawl so Beecher could talk.

"Hello, Beecher?"

"This is Beecher."

"Hey, this is Jackson Jenkins. I wanted to let you know that I talked to my friend who's involved in the theater in New York."

"Wow, that was quick."

"Yeah, well, I have some really good news. He's preparing to direct a revival of Tennessee Williams's *Streetcar Named Desire*. If Ellie is interested, he's willing to give her an audition."

"You're kidding! That's awesome!"

"Could she go to New York next week?"

"I can't speak for her, but for a chance like this, I imagine so."

"I need to let him know."

"I'll see her in a few minutes. I'm out on the lake right now." Beecher looked at his watch. "Let me talk to her and have her call you tonight. Will that be okay?"

"That's fine."

"Is this number good?"

"Yeah. She can call me back at this number."

"Thanks, man."

Beecher eyed his mother, then Will. He traced his index finger along the side of his loafer. "Wow."

"What was that all about?" Katherine peered at him with eyes as clear as the water.

"That was Jackson Jenkins."

"The New York investor you met with?"

"Yes."

Katherine made a face. "What did he want, calling you on a Sunday out here on the lake?"

"It was about Ellie."

Will blinked, as though just registering the conversation with Beecher's latest sentence.

"What about Ellie?" Katherine asked.

"Well, you know, he was at the play the other night, and he's apparently into theater. He was impressed with Ellie's acting. He said something about it, but I wasn't expecting anything to come of it—"

"Come of what? What did he want, Beecher?" Katherine leaned forward.

"He wants Ellie to go to New York." Beecher glanced back and forth from his mother's face to Will's. "He got her an audition with a director friend of his on Broadway."

Katherine's mouth dropped open, and she clapped a French-manicured hand over it.

"Jenkins talks like the guy's the next Elia Kazan." Beecher laughed nervously, and the sound scattered, disappearing into a heavy silence.

Will looked out at the lake.

For a moment nobody spoke, and then Will said, "Well, that's wonderful. She's so deserving."

Katherine searched both of their faces. "Do you think she will want to go? I mean, things are going so well for her here."

"She has to go." Will set his chin toward the wind and picked up speed. "It's her dream."

As they docked the boat at White River, Beecher called Ellie and Opa to let them know they were there. He, Will, and Katherine got a round table on the deck outside, directly on the water, and waited for the twosome to walk down Branson Landing and join them. A server came with iced teas, hush puppies, and coleslaw. It wasn't long before Opa and Ellie appeared.

"You guys look refreshed." Katherine scooted over so Opa could take the seat next to her, and Ellie sat down between Will and Beecher.

"We had a good nap."

"Yes, we did." Ellie winked at Opa. "How was the trip on the boat?"

"It was lovely." Katherine patted her windblown hair. "Quite an amazing experience. Will is a very good tour guide."

"They were excellent passengers."

"I'm surprised Beecher let you drive." Ellie smiled at Will.

"He had an important phone call."

Ellie turned to Beecher with a bemused look. He sensed that she disapproved of his taking a call when he should have been getting to know Will.

"You took a call on the boat?"

"Well, yes. It was Jackson Jenkins."

"Who?"

"You remember—Jackson Jenkins, whom we met at the reception?"

"Oh, yeah. What on earth did he want?"

Katherine, Will, and Beecher all looked at each other and then back at Ellie.

"You guys all resemble cats who have just eaten canaries. What's the deal?"

Beecher's mouth broadened into a huge grin. "He wants you to come to New York. He set up an audition for you with a friend of his on Broadway."

Ellie's eyes widened. Her face turned from white to pink to crimson. She swallowed hard. Then she said, "No way."

Will patted her leg. "It's true."

"Are you kidding me? Mom—is he lying?" She shot a look at Beecher.

"No—he's not. It's true."

Ellie fanned her face with her hand. "Oh, my goodness. I can't believe this. I don't know what to say." She was beginning to hyperventilate.

"I think you need to call him and say you'll be there." Will smiled at her reassuringly.

"But what about the play here?" Ellie suddenly remembered *The Shepherd of the Hills* and her commitment to the role of Sammy.

But Will shook his head. "Ellie, this is your dream. We can take care of things here. This is too good of an opportunity for you to pass it up."

"Wow." Ellie remained in a state of shock for the entire meal.

* * * * *

Beecher drove Katherine and Opa home to Hermann later that night. It was decided they should leave Branson Sunday night, rather than waiting till morning, because of Opa's impending doctor visit. After calling first thing in the morning, Katherine was able to get him in for a ten o'clock appointment at their family doctor in St. Louis.

There was so much to do at the winery that Katherine stayed in Hermann while Beecher drove Opa in to St. Louis. Doctor Rippy did a thorough exam, finding nothing wrong, though she did order a round of blood work. Back in the lab, the person who drew blood had to stick Opa three times, which almost made Beecher sick to his stomach. He was glad when it was all over.

"I'll call you if there are any abnormal results." Doctor Rippy patted Opa's back as they left.

"I told them there was nothing wrong with me." He winked at her. "No news is good news."

For lunch, Beecher took Opa to a German restaurant they both liked in south St. Louis. The exterior was dark wood, and it had a chalet façade, complete with white shutters and scalloped roof shingles.

"It's like walking into a cuckoo clock," Opa commented as Beecher held open one of the double doors.

Once seated, Opa ordered stroganoff. Beecher had schnitzel. A server in a blue and red dirndl brought them coffee. They shared a hot apple strudel with ice cream for dessert. Their conversation was light, mostly about Munich and law and Opa's garden.

At one point Opa said, seemingly out of the blue, "I am proud of you, Beecher. You are a good man." For a moment their eyes locked, and then Opa finished off the strudel.

On the drive home, Opa fell asleep. Beecher stole glances at him as he struggled to keep his speed sub-Autobahn on the Missouri freeway. It was hard in Katherine's Lexus. He noticed that it was true, what everyone had always said. Opa's profile was the same as his own. Just older. The high forehead sagged a little and the skin over his cheekbones was not as tight. The square jaw was less defined now than it had been at Beecher's age.

Opa's lips, slightly parted, let out a little whistle as he breathed.

Beecher felt an uncharacteristic warmth spread all over his body.

"If I am a good man, Opa," he thought aloud, "it's because of you."

Chapter Twenty-Nine

....

Audrey DuPree sat with her legs crossed in an uncomfortable chair at the end of the concourse, watching people. Beecher's flight from St. Louis was on time and she was glad for many reasons, not the least of which was that La Guardia was getting a bit creepy. She'd already been hit on by two guys.

Of course, she was ridiculously overdressed. Banking on Beecher's usual haute couture, she'd chosen her most expensive outfit, a dress recently purchased at Bloomingdale's when her parents visited New York. Her mother had insisted she needed it for their evenings at the theater, and it fit Audrey like a glove. It was iridescent Aztec blue, crinkled silk chiffon, with a crossover neckline, pleated bodice, Empire waist, and flowing, split-front draping. It came just to her knee, and with it she wore black wrap-around, high-heeled sandals. Her arms, legs, and neck were bare. The dress needed no hose or jewelry.

Her naturally curly hair flowed loose in fancy ringlets just past her shoulders, and wispy bangs framed her lovely white face. Her makeup was understated and elegant, which made her pouting red lips seem extravagant. She fiddled with her bangs and looked up at the clock. With her luck, this would be the one time in his life Beecher Heinrichs donned sweatpants or some other completely logical, casual outfit people wore in order to be comfortable on airplanes.

The musician in dreadlocks who was standing a few feet away struck up a new song on his guitar, sounding like Jack Johnson.

Audrey caught something in the lyrics about bubbles and toes. A group of passengers began to emerge from the corridor in front of her. There was a bedraggled mother with two little kids and an old Laotian man who used a cane. Next came a soldier in camouflage fatigues, apparently on leave. Then she saw Beecher. He was wearing a flax-colored linen suit.

For just a moment Audrey watched him scan the waiting crowd.

"Beecher!" She stood, waving, and his eyes lit up—unmistakably—as he saw her. He hurried over, setting down his Louis Vuitton bag, and threw his arms around her and hugged her, picking her several inches up off the floor.

"Audrey. It's great to see you." He set her down and stepped back, examining first her face and then her dress. "You look amazing."

"Thanks." Audrey blushed in spite of herself. She glanced down at her shoes, then back up at Beecher through a veil of dark eyelashes. "So do you."

They chatted about the flight from St. Louis as they made their way down a few levels, via escalators, to baggage claim. They stood amongst a cross section of modern humanity and waited. Beecher's matching suitcase was soon spit out onto the revolving belt, and he grabbed it as soon as it came close by. Then they went outside to hail a taxi.

It was eight thirty by the time they made it to Audrey's apartment in Greenwich Village. Lugging his suitcase and carry-on bag up five flights of stairs, Beecher deposited them in Audrey's foyer so he could look around.

"I love your apartment," he said. "So contemporary. Such clean lines."

"It was furnished already, but I like it too. Something different."

"Who did the painting?" Beecher pointed to the abstract expressionist piece that covered one of Audrey's whole dining-room walls.

"A friend of mine in law school. He gave it to me."

"Do you understand it?"

Audrey giggled. "No."

"I don't either."

"The guy is really into Jackson Pollock. He's his hero."

Beecher nodded. "He was a fascinating artist. Did you—"

"See the movie?" Audrey finished his sentence. "Yes. Not before, but I rented it after Ellie told me to. It was great."

"Yeah. It was."

"Are you hungry, Beecher? Did you want to go out, or are you tired? What do you want to do?"

"I don't know. I could go either way."

"Well, you pick. We can go out, or order in, or whatever you want."

"Let's go out. You look too pretty to stay in."

* * * * *

Audrey suggested Ai Fiori, Michael White's new Italian place in the Setai Hotel on Fifth Avenue. They took another taxi to get there. Once inside they were seated by a middle-aged hostess at an intimate corner table. It had crisp white linens and a candle glowed in the center. A blind man played soft music on an ebony grand piano.

"This is probably not very elegant, but I'm going to order pizza," Beecher said after perusing the menu.

"The pizzas are the best thing."

"Want to share one with me?"

"Sure. I like the one with artichoke hearts and sun-dried tomatoes." Audrey leaned across the table to show Beecher the right one on his menu.

"Amy's Aphrodisiac." He read the name aloud, raising an eyebrow.

Audrey narrowed her eyes. "I don't get it for the name."

"Sure, sure."

"You are so immature."

He grinned at her and then set down his menu. "Audrey's Aphrodisiac it is."

"Beecher!"

The waiter appeared to take their order.

"We're going to share an Amy's," Audrey told him.

He nodded and took their menus.

"So, tell me all about Ellie's opening night. I called to wish her luck before, but I haven't talked to her yet about how it went."

"She was outstanding—just unbelievable. You'd never imagine, or I wouldn't, that a person could do what she did with that role. I mean, that night she turned this little hillbilly story into high art."

"Really?" Audrey said. "Good for her."

"It was something."

"Do you think Will Howitt has something to do with it?"

Beecher snorted. "Uh, yeah. I'd say."

"What's he like? I mean, your impression. Because Ellie obviously—"

"Is crazy about him."

"Yeah. And I've been worried about that. For her sake, you know. I hate not being there to gather my own impression."

The waiter filled their water glasses.

"To be honest, I came home for that as much as opening night. From my vantage point in Munich, things seemed to be getting pretty serious."

"Do you think they are?"

"I do. And you know how I usually hate all of Ellie's boyfriends."

"Yes." Audrey snickered.

"I don't feel that way about Will. He is definitely different."

Now Audrey was shocked. "I've thought that from what she has told me, but hearing you say it—that's major."

"He's very kind to her. Honoring. And he's smart, at least—not like that idiot Seth Young."

Audrey rolled her eyes. "Did you see him in the play? Can you believe he showed up there?"

"Yes. I saw him. His part is ridiculous—he doesn't even have to act."

"Did he see you?"

"No."

"What else about Will?"

"I can't believe Ellie hasn't called you."

"What do you mean? They're not getting married, are they?"

Beecher gave her the look he usually reserved for people he thought were idiots.

Audrey was unfazed. "Well, spit it out!"

"Okay, this is all tied in with why I liked him so much." Beecher took a sip of his water. "We met this guy from New York in Branson, and it's a long story, but he has a Broadway connection and he offered Ellie an audition."

Audrey's eyes gleamed with joy. "No kidding! That's wonderful!"

"See—that's exactly what Will said." Beecher paused. "And that's when I knew I liked him."

"Ah. He passed the friendship test."

"Yep."

The waiter came back with a steaming round plate covered in pizza and set it in the center of the table. He gave Audrey and Beecher both smaller white plates and offered fresh Parmesan and fresh cracked pepper. Audrey authorized both. Then, using her fork, she took a piece of pizza.

Beecher followed. "This pizza is as beautiful as its name."

Audrey chomped into her piece, ignoring his comment.

The crust was as thin as paper and perfectly crunchy. Instead of a tomato-based sauce, White used pesto, and then covered that with spinach leaves and arugula, yellow bell peppers, sun-dried tomatoes, artichoke hearts, red onions, avocado, and farm cheeses. This was placed in the oven and top-broiled—till everything was roasted but still crisp and fresh. It exploded with colorful flavor.

"Heaven on a plate." Audrey went for her second piece.

After the pizza was gone, Beecher ordered a piece of amaretto cheesecake, which they shared for dessert. Then they had decaf coffee. It was midnight before they returned to Audrey's apartment. After tossing her shoes into her bedroom, Audrey retrieved linens from the closet at the end of the hall. Returning to the living room, she and Beecher began to stretch sheets over the couch where he was going to crash.

"I wish I didn't have to go to work tomorrow."

"Me too." Beecher consulted his watch. "You're going to be tired."

"I don't have to go in till nine o'clock, so it's not so bad." She tossed him a pillow, which he placed at one end of the couch. "I did get off for Thursday and Friday, though."

"That's great. And I've got that meeting tomorrow anyway, so we'll get our business tended to and then do some playing before I have to leave."

"'Night, Beech." She held out her fist to punch his softly.

"'Night, Audrey."

* * * * *

The next morning Audrey moved as silently as possible around the apartment. She knew Beecher had to be beat, after flying in from Munich, then going straight to Branson, making the trip to St. Louis with his Opa from Hermann, and then flying to New York and staying up late with her the night before. She remembered him as a heavy sleeper anyway, from all of the times she'd spent the night with Ellie growing up. Their giggling, dancing to music, and other antics had never seemed to faze him. That sort of fortitude, she thought, would serve him well on her couch.

Hiding out in her bedroom, Audrey dressed in a lime-colored suit that was seam-detailed. The cotton and spandex jacket had oversized buttons and long sleeves, which she pushed up. She also turned up the collar. Gathering her hair into a ponytail, she twisted small sections of it back, creating a chic bun at the back of her head, just above the collar. She used several bobby pins to tame her rebellious curls and a few more to hold back her bangs. Again, she wore no jewelry.

She sneaked past a sleeping Beecher, who had stripped down to his boxers and V-neck undershirt before he went to bed on the couch. Audrey swallowed hard. His chest was visible over the top of the quilt. It rippled with muscle under the shirt, and he had chest hair, which Audrey had always found sexy.

His feet were sticking out of the blanket Audrey provided him—her grandmother's butterfly quilt—and her eyes lingered for a moment on his toes. He had the ugliest feet of anyone she'd ever met. It wasn't really his feet, though, it was *the toe*. The second digit on each of Beecher's two feet. They looked like toes and a half, with the upper part hooked so that the joint looked like a little knob, and the toenail curled insidiously under it.

The toe was a genetically inherited atrocity that had apparently plagued the Heinrichs family for generations. Audrey and Ellie had teased Beecher about it mercilessly as children, and she'd even heard Katherine say how thankful she was that *the toe* skipped her, passing directly from Opa to Beecher. For Beecher's part, he took it all in stride, usually responding to their teasing by touching them with the toe or making some remark about it being his one imperfection. Opa would join him, saying, "They are just jealous of us, Beecher. The toe is obviously a mark of genius."

Feeling like a kid again, Audrey dug down in her purse. She crept stealthily over to where Beecher was sleeping and squatted on the rug beside his feet. She took out her hot pink nail polish and began to paint the nail of each hideous toe, starting with the one on the left foot and then moving to the right. Beecher stirred once, and Audrey nearly dropped the brush, but then he settled down and she was able to finish. It was a masterpiece.

Checking to make sure Beecher was sound asleep, Audrey replaced the polish and got out her phone to take a picture. Then she tiptoed out of the apartment, shutting the door and locking it behind her. She would send the picture to Ellie while she was on the subway.

Chapter Thirty

....

"Will, you have got to see this!"

Ellie held up the phone from where she was cooking in the kitchen. Will set down the magazine he was reading beside the chair and walked up to the bar. He took the phone from Ellie.

"Is that Beecher's foot?"

"Yes! Audrey did it to him in his sleep. Isn't that hilarious?"

Will smiled, feeling a male's sympathy for Beecher. "The tortured toe. He's going to be surprised when he wakes up."

"I'm sure he was. The picture was from this morning."

Ellie drained the pappardelle, which was al dente, and folded it into the pork ragù she'd been slow-cooking for hours.

"That smells wonderful."

"Thanks. It's a new recipe I found in Williams-Sonoma. I hope it's good."

Will opened the Heinrichs Haus Chianti Ellie had set out and poured them each a glass. He sat down at the bar, facing her. Using braising tongs, Ellie dished up the hearty ragù in white pasta bowls and rounded the bar to join him.

"I'd like to propose a toast."

Ellie lifted her glass. "Okay."

"To you and your new adventure. I believe this is going to be a big break for you, Ellie."

They clinked their glasses together, and each took a sip of the Chianti.

Ellie set her glass down tentatively. "I should really be toasting you, you know."

"Why's that?"

"For giving me the wings to fly away from here."

A shadow passed through Will's eyes, but he smiled at her. "It's your dream. What else could I do?"

"Well, for starters, you could make me finish out my contract with *The Shepherd*."

"I wouldn't stand in the way of anyone's dream—much less yours."

"I know. And it's wonderful of you." She traced the rim of her glass with the tip of her index finger.

"That's not to say it's easy. I'm going to miss you terribly—in the play and around here."

Ellie's chest tightened. She took a deep breath. "I'm going to miss you too."

As they ate, Ellie watched Will's jaw move up and down. She liked the way it connected underneath the skin just behind his cheekbone... that, and almost everything else about him. She hoped Jackson Jenkins didn't have the wrong idea. Ellie appreciated his recommendation—immensely. In a very real sense, he had given her the chance of a lifetime. Even René Schay hadn't been able to get her an audition on Broadway. But every time she talked to Jackson—he'd called twice now—she got an eerie feeling. Maybe *eerie* wasn't the word, because he didn't scare her at all. It was just a feeling that he might expect more to come out of their association than business dealings with Heinrichs Haus and an audition for the theater. A feeling that he was interested in her. Hoping she was wrong, she hadn't shared that feeling with anybody. Not Katherine, Audrey, or Beecher, and certainly not Will.

"Ellie?"

Will's voice startled her out of her reverie.

"Did you ever finish your great-great-grandmother's diary? You haven't said much about it in a while."

Ellie set down her fork. "I did."

"Well, how did it end?"

"It was horrible. I guess that's why I haven't talked about it. I hated the ending."

"Don't keep me in suspense. Tell me about it."

"Did you like that?" Ellie pointed to his empty bowl.

"It was delicious. You can try out new recipes on me anytime."

Ellie smiled, plopping down from her bar stool.

Will followed, clearing the bar and going to the kitchen to stack their dishes in the sink. "Can I get you anything?"

"No thanks, but you can come and sit by me."

They walked together over to the red couch and sat down. Will sank into the end, and Ellie scooted close to him, taking his arm and placing it around her shoulders. He smiled at the gesture.

"Her father—my great-great-great-grandpa—died in a rail accident that involved the Baldknobbers."

"No way!"

"Yes. And then the diary is sketchy on details, but it seems she was forced to marry Richard Heinrichs."

"Your great-great-grandfather."

"Yes."

"Why was she forced?" Will's eyes were penetrating with interest.

"Well, it raises all kinds of feminist issues with me, but I think she felt she had no other choice. Her nearest male relative, her uncle Robert, probably would have taken them in, as he was rich."

"He's the one she was visiting in Branson, with the mill."

"Right. But the mill burned."

"Whoa. Baldknobbers?" Will raised his eyebrows.

"The diary didn't say, so I don't know."

"But it wiped him out financially."

"Yes. Her father had just died, and then that happened. They were three destitute women—her mother, sister, Heidi, and Elise—and along came Richard Heinrichs with a marriage offer."

"Hmm. Do you feel like he took advantage of her situation?"

Ellie shook her head. "There's nothing in the diary to indicate that. He was clearly interested before William Howard ever came into her life, and as far as I can tell, he may have never known that William existed."

"So he truly loved her."

"I think so. And I believe taking care of her mother and sister was simply an expression of that."

"He sounds like a good man."

"I believe he was. But that didn't make him the right man for her."

"It must have been so hard for her to make that choice."

"In the diary she seems suicidal."

"Wow." Will let that sink in before he asked, "And what about William? Is there anything to indicate what happened to him?"

"He told her he would wait—he would come back for her. But I assume he never heard from her again."

"Man, that is sad."

"Yeah, I know. Makes me sick to think about it."

She leaned over on his shoulder, and Will rubbed her arm. "Well, at least we know one good thing that came out of all of it."

"What's that?" Ellie turned her face toward him.

"You."

* * * * *

That night after Will left, Ellie called Audrey to make arrangements. They didn't talk long, since she knew Audrey was busy. She'd gotten a text from Beecher while he was at the Guggenheim, and Audrey sent her a picture of them together on the steps of the Museum of Modern Art, where a Matisse exhibit was in town. Apparently they'd also been to an early performance at the Philharmonic and were now out to dinner at Tavern on the Green. When Ellie told her what time she was flying in to New York, Audrey said she'd just stay at the airport after she went in with Beecher to see him off on Saturday.

"There's some big new to-do at Delta La Guardia Terminal D. I've been reading about it in the *Times*. Something like thirteen new posh eateries are setting up shop."

"Oh yeah, I saw that too. Dom DeMarco Jr. is going out there, and Jason Denton and Pat La Frieda."

"And Lee Hanson and Riad Nasr. They're opening a new French Bistro."

"So you don't mind waiting around there for me? That's a two-hour difference."

"I'll have French food and a good book. What more could one need?"

"Just another Heinrichs invasion, I guess."

"Gotta love that."

"Okay, see you Saturday then. Tell Beecher I love him."

"She said she loves you," Ellie heard Audrey say to Beecher.

"I love her too," Beecher's voice replied. Faint jazz was in the background.

"We both love you too, Eliminator."

"Ellie-minator?"

"Sorry. That was a bad one."

"You're slipping." Ellie thought of something better. "How about Ellie-gant?"

Chapter Thirty-One

....

When Beecher awoke the next morning, the first thing he did was check his hooked toes. The trained eye still might detect a faint stain of hot pink, as there was a tiny bit of residue Audrey's acetone had left behind, but more or less the evidence of her previous vandalism was gone, and no new defamation had occurred—as of yet—in its place. The wolf in sheep's clothing who had done the damage to his toes was in the kitchen with her back to him as she stared into the refrigerator. Her dark ringlets were a tangled mess stuffed into a clippie at the back of her head, and she wore purple polka-dot satin pajamas that covered every inch of her skin. She was singing "Can You Feel the Love Tonight?" from *The Lion King*, a Broadway production she planned to drag him to on this—his last night in New York City.

"I'm feeling some love this morning." Beecher stood and stretched, his back a little achy.

Audrey placed the milk and a carton of eggs on the counter beside the fridge, keeping her back to him. "Poor Beechy. I told you I would sleep on the couch last night, but you always have to be so chivalrous."

He padded into the kitchen. "What's for breakfast?"

"Omelets. Does that sound good?" She shut the refrigerator with her foot, her hands full of butter, cheese, and a carton of mushrooms. Her black-framed glasses were askew.

"Sounds great. But can you help me pop my back first?"

"Sure."

Audrey set down the items and followed him back over to the

rug, where he lay down on his belly. Coming alongside him on her knees, she said, "Ready?"

"Yep."

She straddled his back and then fell forward, arms tucked in front of her, with all of her weight.

"Humpf."

"I didn't hear any pop."

"Do it again."

This time Audrey fell on him with considerably more force, and his spine cracked like so many knuckles. She lay there on top of him, squirming.

"That's awesome." Beecher turned his face to the side. "Now scratch."

Audrey climbed off his back and sat beside him, scratching his back over his T-shirt with her squarely filed nails. "You will never find a wife to put up with you," she declared.

"Why not?"

"Because your mother and sister have spoiled you rotten."

Beecher rolled his eyes in ecstasy. "Let's not forget about you."

"And here I sit carrying on the tradition." Audrey began karate-chop action on his back.

"What's with your pajamas?"

"I beg your pardon?" She chopped a little harder.

"I mean, they're pretty, but aren't you hot?"

"No. I'm cold-natured." She stopped chopping altogether.

Beecher did a push-up and held himself suspended in the air. Their faces were almost touching. "You don't have to sleep in a burqa, you know." He tweaked her glasses with his nose.

Audrey crossed her arms. "What's that supposed to mean?"

"I mean, it's summer. Why are you wearing those long-sleeved, long-legged pajamas?" He did another push-up.

Audrey pelted herself against him, knocking him over. She

started to tickle him and, amidst his protests of laughter, said, "I'll wear what I want to wear. You got that, buster?"

He grabbed her wrists. "Whatcha going to do now?"

She kicked at him with her feet.

"Come on, tough girl. Is that all you've got?"

"Let me go, Beaster."

"Beaster?"

"That's right. You're a beast."

He let go of her wrists. "Get into that kitchen and cook us some breakfast, then, little woman."

"Oh. If I was big enough, I'd show you a thing or two." Audrey punched him in the gut, drawing back her fist and rubbing it.

"But you're not. You and Ellie both think you're so big, but you'll always be my little sisters." Beecher jumped to his feet and held out his hand to pull her up.

She took it, grudgingly.

* * * * *

While Audrey cooked, Beecher took a quick shower and got dressed in black cargo shorts and two layered T-shirts, black under gray. He decided to wear tennis shoes since they would probably do lots of walking. During their breakfast of garden omelets and cracked wheat toast, he and Audrey planned their day.

"What do you want to do, Beecher?"

"After all of those museums yesterday, nothing intellectual. I want to see your soup kitchen, sit on a bench at your park, buy pastries at your bakery, and eat at your Southern-fried restaurant."

"Those are all good answers."

"Oh yes, and I long to see *The Lion King* on Broadway so I can truly feel the love tonight."

"I'll have you know that those tickets sell out in advance, and you're lucky I had the forethought to get some for the time you are here."

"A great relief it is." Beecher toasted her with his orange juice. "In your debt I will remain."

"You sound like Yoda." Audrey slid off her bar stool and took her dishes to the sink, starting to clean up.

"I'll do the dishes," Beecher offered. "You go get ready."

In thirty minutes Audrey was back in white long shorts and a romantic pink top. The top was actually a set—a cardigan with a sleeveless shell of cotton and rayon. Fastening with a hook and eye, it had chiffon rosettes and rhinestone details all down the front. Her hair, a thick sheet of black satin, looked like it had been ironed. The smell of ripe strawberries was in the air.

"How'd you get your hair straight like that?" Beecher looked up from the magazine he was reading in her cube-shaped chair.

Audrey rolled her eyes. "It's called a straightener."

"Oh, well, it looks nice."

"Thanks."

"I like it curly too, though."

"Thanks."

He extricated himself from the chair. "Ready to go?"

"You betcha."

They climbed down the stairs that led them out of the building.

"Where to first?"

"The soup kitchen, I think. We need to get there before lunch unless you want to work it."

"I'm game for whatever."

"Let's just go by there. And I can show you my school."

"Cool."

They walked down Charles Street till it came to Greenwich, then turned up it and walked to Greenwich Square.

Chuck Filson was already at the soup kitchen, poring over recipes, and he waved Audrey in when he saw her at the door. "Miz Audrey! Great to see you!"

"Hi, Chuck."

They walked over to where he was sitting at one of the cafeteria-style tables.

"I wanted to introduce you to my friend, Beecher Heinrichs."

Beecher stuck out his hand, and Chuck shook it firmly.

"Pleased to meet you. Chuck Filson."

"This is quite a place you have here."

"Thank you. We're a part of Manna Ministries. Audrey can tell you—we feed about two hundred people a day."

"Wow."

"What's on the menu for lunch?" Audrey asked him.

"I'm looking at some good ol' chicken noodle." Chuck grinned, and his black eyes glinted.

"That sounds good." Beecher smiled back.

"Have you got plenty of help?"

"I think so today, Miz Audrey. 'Course, you are always welcome."

"No, if you don't need us, we're going to do some things in the city. I'll be back before too long, though."

"Thanks for coming by."

"It was nice to meet you, sir."

"Nice to meet you too, Beecher."

They left Greenwich Square and traveled back down Greenwich till they reached the Avenue of the Americas. Then they walked down it till it crossed Third Street, which would take them to NYU.

"Don't you love urban walking?"

"I do," said Audrey.

"I practically walk or ride my bike everywhere in Munich."

"Do you have a car?"

"Yes, but I leave it parked all of the time, unless I'm going to the airport or driving somewhere else out of town."

They arrived at NYU, which was a mass of beautiful and stately buildings. Audrey took him to the Bobst library, and Beecher was impressed.

"I can't believe you'd want to drop out of such a school," he whispered as they passed the front desk.

"My heart is in the soup kitchen."

"But what about your head?"

* * * * *

After NYU, they took the subway to Brooklyn for lunch at the infamous Pies 'N' Thighs, where Beecher met Caroline, the waitress Audrey had told him about who had a "great story."

Then it was back to the area near NYU and Audrey's apartment for a rest on the benches of Washington Square Park.

Audrey showed Beecher her favorite spot, which was near the small lake with the black swans. She led him to the bench where she liked to sit and think, and they sat on it together.

"You didn't tell me much about your meeting Wednesday."

"There's not much to tell." Beecher stretched his legs out in front of him. "It was with a partner in our firm who runs the New York office. I talked to her about possibly relocating here."

Audrey gasped. "Not much to tell? That's not much to tell?"

Beecher laughed.

"What did she say?"

"She was interested. We've actually been talking about it back and forth for a while."

"Does Ellie know?"

"Not really—I didn't want to get my family's hopes up till I decided."

"And have you?"

"It's looking that way."

"What made up your mind?"

"I don't know, really. It's just this growing feeling I've had of home-sickness. I don't want to go all the way to Hermann, at least not yet, but I'm ready to come back to the States."

"I see." Audrey looked out at the water. "Well, that's great. Your mom, Opa, Ellie—everybody will be so happy."

Beecher folded his hands in his lap. "That's part of it right there. Opa."

"I heard he's not feeling well."

"He's not getting any younger, and I hate to be so far away."

Audrey nodded. "I know what you mean."

"Did you know Ellie got baptized?"

"Yeah. She told me. I think it's great." She crossed her legs, clasping her hands together around her knee.

"Me too."

"You do?"

"Yeah. Why wouldn't I? You think I'm a heathen?" Beecher grinned.

"No, but we've never talked much about spiritual things."

"Except when you tried to proselytize me."

Audrey made a face. "That didn't go over too well."

"Nope." Beecher laughed.

"At least I cared about your immortal soul."

"That's something."

"Then you went through that phase of quoting Richard Dawkins and watching *Religulous*."

"I still like it, and Christopher Hitchens."

"But you're a Christian."

"Yep. When it comes down to it, my philosophy is more along the lines of Tim Allen's *Santa Clause*."

Audrey stared at him like he was crazy. "You've got to be joking. I hate those movies."

"Hate them? How can you hate them?"

"They are mindless trash. I hate them with bloody passion."

"Such violent speech. And seemingly ironic from the lips of someone who likes Disney musicals." Beecher grinned.

"That is a different matter entirely. *The Santa Clause* is nowhere in the realm of *The Lion King.*"

"Touché."

"So, what on earth are you talking about with the whole Santa Claus thing? I object. I'll have you know that faith in God is a lot more than some mushy, feel-good fairy tale. It takes guts." Audrey kicked at the ground with her toe.

"Precisely. That's what Opa said too, after he took me to see *The Santa Clause.*"

"Will you quit talking in riddles?"

Beecher laughed. "I know the movie is corny, but I was a little kid. Anyway, there's this line I'll never forget. A little boy is trying to explain to a psychologist why he believes in Santa Claus. The man says you shouldn't believe in someone you can't see—that 'seeing is believing.' And the little boy says, 'No. That's where you're wrong. Believing is seeing.'"

Audrey stopped kicking and pondered that.

"When we left the theater, Opa talked to me about that line on the way home. He compared it to faith. I've never forgotten it."

"Hmm." Audrey smiled thoughtfully. "Objection withdrawn. That is a good one."

"So *The Santa Clause*—at least Opa's interpretation of it—has helped me to stay on the straight and narrow."

"I'm glad." Audrey wiggled her foot up and down. "Someone needs to."

"My faith is also partly your fault, you know."

"What does that mean?"

"Well, I can argue with lots of things, but I cannot doubt your faith."

Audrey was startled. "That's ridiculous."

"No. It isn't. There's something different about you—always has been."

She gazed directly into his eyes. "That's kind of you to say, but faith has to be personal. My faith can't get you into heaven."

"I know that, Audrey." He pulled her over and mussed her hair. "I've got faith of my own. I'm just saying you've helped me. Helped me—sometimes—not to give up."

Audrey stood and offered her hand to Beecher. He took it. As he rose from the bench, he didn't let go. "Want to take a little walk around the lake?"

"You've helped me, too, you know." Audrey didn't look at Beecher. Her eyes were on her feet.

"How?"

"By talking to me about all of the school stuff."

"Oh, yeah."

"I think I've come to a decision."

"You're going to tell your dad?"

"I think I am."

Beecher nodded, pensive.

"Beecher?" Audrey stopped then and faced him.

He held on to her hand.

"Do you think I'm letting my heart rule my head?"

Beecher's blue eyes were kind. "Maybe."

She groaned and stuck out her tongue at him.

"But I didn't say there's anything wrong with that."

Audrey started walking again. "You'd never do it."

"I might."

"When? How?"

"I guess if I knew it was right."

* * * * *

Later that evening, while Audrey was in the shower, Beecher went out to pick up Chinese at a little place called Nanking in Greenwich Village. He thought she looked strange when he returned, but he didn't say anything. She finished getting ready in her room while he showered. By the time he was dressed in pinstripes and a French blue shirt, she seemed her normal self. She was ravishing in a champagne silk skirt and matching jacket with a faux-jewel pull-through brooch. Her hair was gathered up. They stood at the bar in her kitchen and ate moo goo gai pan quickly as they were in a hurry to get to Broadway and *The Lion King*.

Beecher was surprised by how much he liked the musical. Being with Audrey released him to feel—and act—like a child again. He didn't know if it was their shared history, or if it was just her. She was so innocent, even though she was wise enough to be a hundred years old.

Back at the apartment, Audrey went straight to bed because it was so late. Beecher was tired too, so he curled up in his place on the couch. Not long after he'd settled down, he heard a noise. It sounded like Audrey was crying. Beecher turned on the lamp so he could find his way down the hall and tapped at Audrey's bedroom door.

There was no answer. The sound quieted.

"Audrey?"

Sniff.

He tapped on the door again.

"Come in."

Beecher opened the door and saw Audrey sitting on the edge of her bed, facing away from the door and toward her one window. Her hair was sticking out in every direction, like streamers on the bow of a fancy gift. Light from the nearby buildings streamed in through her sheer curtains, illuminating her purple polka-dot pajamas. The bars on the window cast vertical stripes on Audrey's silhouette.

"Are you all right?"

She leaned over, like the Tower of Pisa, and crashed down onto her pillow. She started to sob.

Beecher, on an impulse, jumped into her bed. The covers were wadded between them, and he pulled them up on Audrey's side so she wouldn't be cold. Then he lay down behind her, bending his elbow and propping his head up with his left hand. With his other hand, he stroked Audrey's wet cheek.

"Audrey? Can you tell me what's wrong?"

More sobbing.

He smoothed her hair as best he could. "Audrey? Are you okay?"

"It's Atticus. He hates me." Audrey's hand found the tissues on her bed table, and she blew her nose.

"Not possible," Beecher said to the back of her head.

"He was so disappointed. I could hear it in his voice." Audrey blew her nose again.

"When did you call him?"

"Before the play."

Her confession gave way to another round of sobbing. So that was why she seemed strange when he came in with the Chinese! "Why didn't you tell me? We didn't have to go—"

"Yez, we did! I wasn't going to have you biss *The Lion King.*"

Beecher laughed softly. As if. "Oh, Audrey, it will be okay. Atticus will come around."

Without saying anything else, Audrey reached behind her back and found Beecher's hand. She pulled it to her, wrapping his arm around her waist.

Beecher lay there still and staring, somewhat stunned.

After some time, he heard a slight *whiffle* noise. Audrey was snoring.

He could have tried to move his arm—to leave her—but Beecher decided against it. He laid his head down beside hers on the pillow, smelling her strawberry shampoo, and went to sleep.

Chapter Thirty-Two

....

When Audrey woke the next morning, Beecher's arm was in the same place she had put it around her waist, his strong, lean fingers laced through hers. His breathing was heavy. She could feel it—warm and wonderful—on the back of her neck. Why did he have to be leaving today?

Audrey closed her eyes. For a fleeting moment she worried what he might think when he awoke. Would it be awkward? Probably so. Maybe she should get up. Then again, maybe she should pretend to be asleep and let him awaken. Then he'd have to deal with the awkwardness. It might be fun. In fact, she could even tease him about taking advantage of her in her fragile state. He'd probably be embarrassed. But better him than her.

After all, she couldn't believe she was lying in bed with Beecher. He had been so kind, so tender the night before. It was a side of him she'd never seen. Of course, she couldn't remember another time when she'd been vulnerable to him like that. Sure, Beecher was her friend— the brother kind of friend who sticks up for you and even sticks with you. But not the kind of friend who holds you while you cry. Had it all been a dream?

Beecher stirred. Audrey was afraid to speak or move so she lay there, still. He gently untwined their fingers.

He's getting up, she thought. *He's glad I'm still asleep so he doesn't have to face the embarrassment. I wonder if he'll pretend it didn't happen—*

Audrey's mental dialogue was broken by the gentle sweep of Beecher's fingertips across her back. He scratched her back, up and down and then across, over her purple polka-dot pajamas from her shoulders to her waist. All the while she could feel him breathing, though it was not as heavy as when he was asleep. Audrey was still afraid to move. It was as if they were under a spell that she feared might be broken.

Beecher nudged her over onto her belly, spreading her arms out to her sides. Then he sat up beside her, not saying a word. Starting with her neck, he massaged the taut cords on either side till they became putty. Next he worked his way down to her shoulder blades, concentrating on the knots that had formed underneath each one. It was as if his hands had sensors that were drawn to individual spots—heat sensors that located pain and eradicated it, made it fade into nothingness.

Audrey felt that something broken in her had been restored. "You know, you're really good at that."

Beecher patted her on the back and then made a circular motion with his hands.

She turned her face on the pillow and faced him. "Thanks."

He looked at her for a long moment, as if he wanted to say something but thought better of it. Then his face broke into a mischievous smile. "Wait till I tell Ellie that you lured me into your bed."

"You wouldn't."

"Oh, yes, I would."

"She won't believe you."

"Of course she will. I'm her blood."

"You are also evil, and she knows it." Audrey rose and whapped Beecher over the head with her pillow.

"First you take advantage of my innocence in the night, and then you assault me." Beecher feigned offense.

Audrey reared her pillow again, but this time he caught it midair. "Not so fast."

Audrey struggled to free the pillow from his grasp.

"Is this how you repay my kindness?"

"What do you expect?" Audrey cocked her head to one side.

"I expect..." Beecher set down the pillow and got up from the bed. "I expect I need to brush my teeth."

Audrey snorted. "You truly are crazy."

While Beecher went to the bathroom, Audrey put on her glasses and made her bed. Then, as soon as he was out, she took her turn, though she didn't brush her teeth. She didn't see any sense in it before breakfast. She walked down the hall and into the kitchen where Beecher was preparing fruit. She popped three blueberries into her mouth, followed by a ripe strawberry. He had set out the yogurt and granola she picked up at the whole foods store before he arrived. The plan seemed to be parfaits.

"I can't believe I'm leaving today."

"Me neither." She sat down on a bar stool to watch.

"Thanks for having me. You've been the hostess with the mostest."

"He says as he prepares his own breakfast."

"And yours. I hope you like parfaits."

"These are my ingredients after all."

He handed her a spoon and a stemmed glass layered with vanilla yogurt, fruit, walnuts, and granola. It was quite pretty. She took a bite. Beecher stood across the bar from her assembling his own parfait in a mixing bowl.

"Why did you brush your teeth?" Audrey licked her spoon.

Beecher stirred everything in his bowl together.

"I mean, if you were going to eat, why did you brush your teeth first?"

He looked up at her, then back down at his bowl. "I can't answer that question."

Audrey laughed. "Sure you can."

"Nope. I decline to answer." He took a bite.

"You're so weird."

Beecher grinned at her wickedly. "You'd really think I was weird if I told you why I wanted to brush my teeth." He took another bite of his yogurt mess.

"I already do, so you have nothing to lose."

"I'm not so sure about that."

Audrey set down her glass and spoon. "You are the most exasperating man, Beecher Heinrichs."

Beecher set down his bowl then. In a swift motion he came around the bar and whisked Audrey out of her chair. Carrying her over to the sliding glass door that led to the balcony, he said, "You should not have said that." Then he slid the door open with his foot, maneuvering "the toe" around the handle.

* * * * *

The morning was lovely. Sun glinted off the trees and buildings, and the city was bursting with life. A flag blew in the distance, rippling with color. The air was pleasantly cool, and the scent of jasmine floated on the breeze from an urban flower garden below.

"What are you going to do—throw me over?" Audrey beat her fist gently against his chest.

"No, I'm going to answer your question."

"What question? About your teeth? Put me down before you hurt your back."

Beecher gazed into Audrey's eyes with a mixture of humor, longing, and tenderness. And then he did the last thing she ever expected him to do in a million years. Drawing her closer in his arms, he bent his head toward her face and kissed her on the lips.

Audrey's ears burned. Her head was spinning. When the kiss was over, Beecher released her, and she stood, unsteadily, on her feet. He reached out to touch her arm, and they both laughed.

"Did you just kiss me?"

"Guilty as charged."

"What on earth?"

Beecher squeezed his eyes shut, and then forced them open, looking straight at her. His voice came out like a bullfrog. "I'm in love with you, Audrey."

Audrey crashed back into the ironwork chair she kept on her balcony, and it made a raking sound against the floor. Her glasses fell crooked on her nose. She sat looking up at him through one of the lenses.

"Beecher, you can't be serious."

A grin played around his lips. "I know." His laugh was somewhat rueful. "And I'm sorry to put you in a bad position. But there it is. I can't help it." He shifted his bare feet.

Audrey looked out to the street below them, seeming to size up his words. It was as if the truth revealed itself to her very gradually. "You are serious, aren't you?"

Beecher nodded, and she rose to her feet. Her hands were on her hips. Nobody spoke.

Then Audrey said, "All I can say is, it's about time." She lifted her arms and encircled his neck.

He put his hands around her waist, eyeing her intently. "What in the world do you mean by that?"

"I mean, I've been in love with you for as long as I can remember."

They kissed again, more passionately this time. And they didn't let up till a man hooted and hollered at them from a sidewalk across the way.

Chapter Thirty-Three
....

Ellie's plane touched down at La Guardia at approximately four o'clock on Saturday. After leaving Dot with her ears back at Will's cabin, saying a tearful good-bye to Will at the Springfield airport, puddle-jumping to St. Louis, and then flying through a thunderstorm in the Northeast, the image of Audrey jumping up and down and waving as Ellie deboarded her plane was a sight for sore eyes. She ran into her friend's arms, feeling provincial, shaky, and exhausted all at once. They walked the length of the long corridor arm in arm, able to avoid baggage claim because Ellie brought only a carry-on. Audrey, seasoned with experience, hailed them a taxi.

By the time they reached Audrey's apartment in The Village, Audrey was brought up to speed on the particulars of Ellie's association with Jackson Jenkins and the instructions she had for meeting his friend for the audition. For her part, Audrey told Ellie about her time with Beecher—what all they had done, the fun they had, how she thought Beecher was doing, etc.

Ellie loved Audrey's apartment. The building, with its brick façade and quaint elevator—which Audrey said didn't work half the time— fit neatly into her vision of a charming New York life. She also loved the efficiency of Audrey's small space and the artistic irony of putting ultramodern furnishings in an individual apartment, tucked within such a nonmodern, cozy building. It was imaginative and bold, like Audrey. And like she envisioned herself becoming as an actress in New York.

Audrey poured her a glass of water and told her to sit down. "I'm glad you like my apartment; I'm glad you're finally here; I love everything you're saying and how you get me and my place. But I have to tell you something. I've been dying to tell you since you got off the plane."

Ellie sat down as Audrey instructed her, and they faced one another on the couch.

"Well, what is it? I'm in dire suspense."

"Ellie. You're just going to die."

Audrey's eyes were dazzling with intensity. In that moment Ellie thought her friend was more beautiful than she had ever been before. What in the world could it be?

"Tell me! Spit it out!"

"I don't know where to start."

"Audrey, I am going to kill you."

Her friend leaned forward. Ellie noticed that her lily-white neck was broken out in red blotches. She finally squealed, "Beecher kissed me!"

Ellie's eyes popped out as her jaw hit the floor. "Oh. My. Goodness."

"He said he loves me—he's *in* love with me—*me*, Ellie. *Me!*" Audrey bounced up and down.

Ellie's eyes filled with tears till they brimmed over and ran down her face. She reached out for Audrey's hands and squeezed them. "I don't know what to say. Audrey—my Audrey! Tell me everything!"

* * * * *

Ellie and Audrey stayed in that whole evening talking about Beecher, Will, their families, law school, acting, and life. During their powwow, Ellie told Audrey more about her encounter with God in Branson and how He was healing the area of her heart that longed for a father. Audrey confessed that she had located a few Andrew McMurrays in New York, and they agreed to pray together about how to proceed.

Ellie and Audrey only moved to change into their pajamas and answer the door after the pizza delivery guy came. At about 1:00 a.m. they broke out the cheesecake Audrey had in her freezer. By one thirty it was sufficiently thawed to be devoured with two forks. They paired it with a second pot of Old-fashioned Country Turtle coffee, staying true to their tradition.

* * * * *

After sleeping half of Sunday, Ellie and Andrey managed to get dressed up for an early dinner at Ma Peche. Then they headed to Village Vanguard for some jazz, where saxophonist Ravi Coltrane was performing.

* * * * *

Monday morning after Audrey left for work, Ellie called the number Jackson had given her for Corbin Oliver, his friend who was directing on Broadway.

"Mr. Oliver?"

"That's me."

"Hi. This is Ellie Heinrichs."

"Who?"

"Um, Ellie Heinrichs."

"I don't know any Ellie Heinrichs."

"Oh. Well, sir, I got your number from Jackson Jenkins. He told me to call you about an audition."

"Okay, yeah. Are you in New York?"

"I am."

"How soon can you get here?"

"Where are you, sir?"

"I'm in the basement of the Eugene O'Neill Theatre."

"Is that on Broadway?"

"Where did Jackson find you?"

"In Branson, Missouri, sir."

"The Eugene O'Neill Theatre is on West Forty-ninth between Broadway and Eighth."

"I can be there in half an hour."

"Okay. I'll see you at nine thirty out front."

Ellie threw on her makeup and pulled her hair back from her face. Donning black Capri leggings and a white poet's shirt with black ballerina slippers, she hurried to the subway. After a jolting ride on a graffiti-decorated train, Ellie jumped off, slipping through the crowd, and took the stairs two at a time. Popping up out of the ground like a prairie dog, she ran toward the Eugene O'Neill Theatre, arriving there breathless. As Corbin Oliver was standing under the awning smoking, she didn't have time to be nervous.

Mr. Oliver was younger than she expected. Skinny, with spiky yellow hair and cool glasses, he looked like he was under thirty. He wore a black T-shirt and distressed jeans with Converse sneakers. He threw down his cigarette butt as she approached.

"Mr. Oliver?"

"Yeah."

"I'm Ellie Heinrichs." She stuck out her hand.

He grinned but didn't take it. "Come on in."

The lights were on in the theater, which seated about eleven hundred guests. Ellie thought that it looked like an old-fashioned opera house, the kind you'd see in the movies. It had tiers of red seats and gilded boxes with ornate trim. For all of her worldliness, Ellie felt like a backward country mouse in the home of a city cat. She had the feeling she was about to be swallowed whole.

"Go ahead, get up on the stage." Corbin Oliver sat down in the aisle seat, three rows back.

The curtain was drawn, so Ellie had only the few feet in front of it on which to move. She stood there in the center looking out at him.

"Do you know the play we're doing?"

"*Streetcar.*"

"That's correct. I want you to pretend you're Blanche, and you just came to town."

Although his instructions were a complete surprise, Ellie was prepared to obey them. She'd starred as Blanche her senior year in a St. Louis production of the play. And Tennessee Williams was her favorite. She still knew all of the lines by heart.

When she finished that scene, Oliver moved her on to the big confrontation with Stanley, which he read from his chair. It was rather awkward to play the scene without getting physical. Ellie wondered if he was even taking her seriously. Why wasn't anyone else there? A stand-in for Stanley at least, so she could adequately demonstrate Blanche's struggle?

Corbin Oliver showed no visible signs that he liked her or not as she did her audition. His gray eyes were like steel. Ellie couldn't help but think of Will and the contrast between their personalities, their styles. *You're not in Branson anymore,* a voice inside her head said. *This is what you wanted.*

"Well, Ellie." Mr. Oliver stood to his feet and offered her a hand.

She took it and made the leap off the stage, feeling more than a little awkward.

"Thank you for coming. You're a good sport."

She didn't know whether he was serious or mocking her. Or both.

"Thank you for letting me audition."

He motioned with his arm for her to lead the way out, which she did, taking mental notes as she walked up the aisle so she could describe it to Will. She didn't expect to step one foot back in this theater again unless she was a ticket-holder. And she didn't think

LOVE FINDS YOU IN BRANSON, MISSOURI

she wanted to purchase a ticket for Corbin Oliver's production of *Streetcar*.

"It was nice to meet you, Mr. Oliver." Ellie's manners trumped her honesty in this case.

"Yes, it was."

She couldn't bring herself to ask if he'd be in touch.

"I have your number in my phone, I believe." He took it from his pocket and scrolled through, confirming.

"Okay. Well, have a nice day."

"Thanks. You too."

Ellie made for the door.

* * * * *

"It was so humiliating!" Ellie ducked into the nearest café, a place called Bling, and called Will.

"What do you mean?"

"It was awful. I made a fool of myself."

"I hardly believe that."

"It's true."

"What did you do? What did the director say?"

"He wasn't very nice either. He made me feel like an idiot." Hot tears stung her cheeks. "I think he was there only to humor Mr. Jenkins. He must owe him something. The audition was a farce."

"Oh, babe, I'm sorry. I wish I could be there with you right now."

"Me too."

"Where is Audrey?"

"She's at work at the law office. I'll text her in a minute. We're supposed to meet for lunch, but I'm not hungry."

"Go with her though, okay? Don't go home and hibernate."

"That's what I feel like doing."

Will laughed lightly. "Me too. Dot and I are both kind of pathetic with you gone."

This brought a smile to Ellie's face.

"If work didn't force me to get out this morning," Will continued, "we'd probably be on the couch right now eating potato chips."

Ellie laughed at the thought. "She does love her chips."

"Yes, she does."

"Will?" A pause. "I miss you."

"I'm glad. I have this fear of a new director sweeping you off your feet."

Ellie wiped her eyes on her sleeve. "I don't think that's happening."

"Well, it's his loss."

"Thank you."

"For what?"

"For you."

* * * * *

Ellie and Audrey met for lunch at The Plaza Food Hall, a fancy food court nestled into the basement of the hotel, formerly the laundry facilities. Drowning her sorrows in sushi, Ellie began to perk up over a Grasshopper, which was Audrey's dessert treat from the Curly Cake. A mud-dark cake topped with an assertive green dollop of frosting, the Grasshopper, along with some strong coffee, was just what the doctor ordered. Audrey soon had Ellie laughing as she told of the latest antics Ray had assigned her to at Juvenile Hall.

"Have you talked to Beecher today?" Audrey asked.

"No. He said to let him know about the audition so I guess I will, and I need to call Mom and Opa too."

"What do you want to do tonight?"

"Not a play. Definitely not a play."

Audrey's eyes lit up. "I heard there's this awesome jazz band playing at the Rose Theatre. Like an eighty-five-year-old drummer named Roy Haynes is teamed with Wynton Marsalis and Danilo Perez. Are you interested in that?"

"I don't know. Are you?"

"I'm always interested in jazz, but it's your call."

"Honestly, I think I need something else tonight. A place to put my mind."

"How about a movie?"

"Sounds good to me. Let's do it." Ellie threw her napkin over the remaining crumbs of Grasshopper.

"I'll meet you back at the apartment after work."

"Okay."

Rising from her seat, Audrey eyed Ellie suspiciously. "What are you going to do? You're not going to mope, are you?"

Ellie, noncommittal, simply looked at her.

"Oh, brother." Audrey tugged at Ellie's arm. "Come on. At least walk with me out into the daylight."

Chapter Thirty-Four
....

After Audrey finally stopped fussing over her, leaving late to return to work, Ellie wandered across the street and into Central Park. She hated zoos, so she bypassed the Central Park Zoo, walking up East Drive till she found an empty bench near the Conservatory Pond. She called Beecher.

"Ell's Bells."

"Not you too."

"It gets to be addicting."

Ellie crossed her legs. "Oh, I've heard about your little aud-iction."

Beecher laughed at that. "She told you, huh."

"I'm so happy. Really, I can't believe my luck. In that department, at least."

"Did you suspect?"

"No. I mean, I used to hope, but it didn't seem likely."

"I didn't suspect it either. How could I have been so blind all these years?"

"Better late than never."

Beecher's voice had a schoolboy quality. "Does she really, you know—"

"Love you?"

Beecher cleared his throat.

"Um, yes. She's so happy, she's giddy. And you better not hurt her."

"I don't ever want to."

"Well, I trust you know what you're doing."

"What about you? Have you had your audition?"

"I had it this morning."

"Well? How did it go?"

"Horrible."

"Huh-uh. It didn't. How could it?"

"It just did." Ellie scraped at the fingernail polish on her right thumb.

"How do you know? Did you mess up or fall down or something?"

"No. It was the director. I think he hated me."

"Ellie, that's irrational. If you can't even say anything you did wrong—"

"It was just a feeling I got. Like his mind was made up before I did anything. I think it was only a joke—like he did it to humor Jackson Jenkins."

Beecher was pensive. "Still, surely Jenkins wouldn't set up something totally worthless."

"Maybe he didn't realize it, but it seems so."

"Have you heard anything definite?"

"I'm not expecting to hear anything."

"Give it a day or two."

The next person Ellie called was her mother. Her response and advice were the same as Beecher's; it was as if they shared a brain. When she asked to talk to Opa, he was sleeping, which Ellie found odd for the middle of the day. He was apparently still not feeling well.

Ellie watched people for a while and then joined a small group for a guided tour called Amble Through the Ramble, following an enthusiastic park guide over streams, under arches, and through the woods along a maze of pathways that led through the secluded area. The exercise was good for her. Afterward she headed back to Audrey's for a good, hot shower.

When she got out of the shower, she put on Audrey's robe that hung on the back of the bathroom door. It was ankle-long on Audrey but came to Ellie's knee.

She checked her phone to see if Will had called. Instead, there was a message from Corbin Oliver that said simply, "Please call me back at this number."

Her heart beat rapidly. She dialed the number, and he answered.

"Ellie?"

"Yes, sir."

"If you want the part of Stella, it's yours."

Ellie choked, dumbfounded. "Stella?"

"It's a good part."

"I know! I know! I just—"

"I want you to stand as a backup for Blanche too; we've got Emily Jordan in there, but you never know."

"Oh my goodness, I don't know what to say."

Corbin Oliver remained silent, which didn't help her at all. Then he said calmly, "So, we'll see you tomorrow at practice."

"Thank you, Mr. Oliver. Thank you so much!"

"Ten a.m."

"Okay! I'll be there."

He hung up.

Ellie stared at the phone as if it were a frog that might jump out of her hands. Then she lifted it to her lips and kissed it, squealing for joy. She whirled around, dancing out of the bathroom and down the hall into the front room.

Audrey was coming in the door.

"I got a part!"

Her friend dropped her bag, pulling off her shoes. Her face broke into a fabulous smile.

"I'm going to be Stella!"

Then Audrey put on a Brando face, complete with drooping eye-lids, and flexed the muscles in her neck. She screamed, "Stellaaah!"

Pitching her shoes down the hall toward her bedroom, she ran into Ellie's arms and gave her a big bear hug. "Yippee! I'm so happy for you!"

"I'm in shock. I can't believe it."

Ellie called to share the news with Will first, then Beecher and her mother and Opa. They were all very happy for her, and Beecher said he told her so. She and Audrey celebrated that night with Antonio Banderas and a spicy Indian dinner at Banjara in the East Village.

＊ ＊ ＊ ＊ ＊

The next several days were a flurry of activity. Ellie had no time to make a trip home. Using money from her savings, she bought a few clothes to get her by. Audrey was happy to have her in the apartment, even though some days they barely saw each other. Ellie became educated by total immersion in the theater culture of New York City. She ate, drank, and slept *Streetcar Named Desire*. Corbin Oliver demanded nothing less.

Because she spent so much time with them, Ellie made friends with several others in the cast. She got along well with Chris, the guy who played Stanley, Stella's husband. He was a former model with gritty good looks. He was also gay. Will had been relieved to hear this, as Oliver was pushing Ellie to play out the animal attraction that fueled Stanley and Stella's relationship, and it put her into situations that he said sounded, to him, quite risqué.

She also liked the man who played Mitch. His name was Steve, and he was big-hearted, rather like his character. Ellie was comforted by his presence. Her stand-in, Jane, was great. It surprised her how accepting they'd all been toward a girl from Missouri.

The biggest surprise had been how well she got along with Emily Jordan, the Broadway star cast as Blanche DuBois. Miss Jordan was a striking redhead whose natural good looks had to be dulled by the makeup and hair artists lest she appear too glamorous. Her eyes were an astounding blue-green—like unpolished turquoise—and her figure was thin, wispy. She almost seemed like an apparition as she sashayed across the stage. She brought an otherworldly quality to Blanche that Ellie found delicious. This was a woman she could learn from.

Other than the actors in the play and Audrey, the only person Ellie saw in New York was Jackson Jenkins. She'd written an e-mail to thank him for the reference and subsequent audition out of courtesy. After that, he had shown up at a play practice to watch, then offered to take her to dinner.

In the leggings and silk batik tunic she'd worn to practice, Ellie felt severely underdressed for the upscale Italian place he suggested in Tribeca. Scalini Fedeli was infinitely romantic, and Ellie wondered why Jackson Jenkins would choose to take her *there*. The average main course price was sixty dollars. Trying to be conservative, she ordered Tuna Milanese with arugula, cucumber, and tarragon salad. Jackson had the peppered rib venison chop with port and balsamic vinegar sauce, which he said was out of this world.

Dressed in black Armani with a light blue shirt and Lanvin blue silk tie, Jackson was gorgeous and charming. The conversation was sophisticated, touching on opera and art. He told her how he knew Corbin Oliver. The director was the younger brother of his college roommate, and Jackson gave him a place to stay when he first moved to New York.

"I guess you could say we're like family."

"That's like Audrey and me."

Jackson gave his credit card to the waiter. "Who's Audrey?"

"She's my best friend from home. I'm staying at her apartment. She's in law school at NYU."

"Oh."

"In fact, I need to be getting back. She'll be looking for me."

"Did you call her?"

"I did, but I told her I wouldn't be late."

They rode the subway to Tribeca, but Jackson insisted on getting a taxi to Audrey's apartment. When they arrived, he walked her to the door of the building.

"Thank you for dinner," Ellie said. She fidgeted.

His dark eyes were inquisitive, but he didn't ask anything. He nodded. "You're welcome."

"Well, I'll see you around."

He grabbed her arm gently as she turned for the door. "Is it— okay if I call you?"

"Um, sure." But as she spoke the words, a siren went off in her head.

"Okay then. See you."

"'Bye!" She bolted through the foyer and up the stairs, not waiting for the elevator.

* * * * *

When she got inside, Ellie immediately knew something was wrong. The door thudded behind her. Her flustered emotions regarding Jackson Jenkins turned to fear as she glimpsed Audrey's face. It was wax. Audrey's coal-black eyes were red-rimmed. Setting the phone down on the coffee table, she rose from the couch and crossed the room to take Ellie by the hand, leading her to sit down. Audrey's hand was icy and sweaty at the same time. They faced each other, in the same position as the night Ellie arrived and Audrey told her about Beecher.

"Ellie, something has happened."

Ellie braced herself as fear crept up her spine like a hairy spider. Audrey squeezed her hand till it hurt. A single tear escaped one of Audrey's eyes and cut a rivulet down her pale cheek.

"Opa is dead."

Chapter Thirty-Five

....

Ellie, Beecher, and Katherine, along with Katherine's brother, Garry, sat in the front row of folding chairs provided by Hermann Funeral Home. Will and Audrey stood behind them. Opa's casket, which at his request was the cheapest available and a color called Spartan Silver, was only a few feet in front of them. Ellie's hands were folded in her lap. But if she stuck out her arm, the casket holding Opa's body would be barely beyond her reach.

On top of the casket was a spray of red roses. Dozens of them cascaded over the sides, suffused with greenery and baby's breath, along with ribboned banners that read FATHER and GRANDFATHER in silver glittered letters. Other flower arrangements were spread about the base. These were from friends and well-wishers, most of whom were not present at the small, private service held only—again per Opa's request—beside the grave.

"No pomp and circumstance for me," Opa once said in regard to his funeral plans. And those wishes were honored, as best as they could be, by his loved ones. The only extravagance was a set of bagpipes played by a man named MacGregor in traditional Highland dress. This was insisted upon by Garry. He and Opa had been to Scotland together once and were privy to a town parade in Ben Nevis. Opa said he liked the bagpipes. Ellie figured this was Garry's way of honoring that memory.

As music from the pipes resonated through the air, Ellie felt Will's hand resting on her shoulder. It was warm and soft. A contrast to her heart, which was cold—flat and dull—like the drone of the pipes, which underscored the melody of "Amazing Grace" that wafted on the air above it.

In that moment a single yellow swallowtail came into view, floating down under the funeral home's canopy of bright blue and landing on the silver casket. For a time it hovered over the roses, and then, as if hearing a distant call in its own language, it moved on, taking flight.

Ellie watched it soar past the headstones of the cemetery and into the sky. Soon it became a tiny speck against the great blue backdrop of the heavens.

The piper held the last note out long and full, and Ellie closed her eyes and listened. An inner voice reminded her of the lyrics. *"I once was lost, but now am found...was blind but now I..."* Ellie exhaled as she pondered the last word. *See.*

* * * * *

After the service, they all returned to the house, where Ruth, Katherine's assistant at the winery, was overseeing a spread of food. Visitors came in a steady stream. Ellie tried to help her mother by receiving them and listening to their stories of Opa, though she really felt like going to bed. Her head pounded, and her soul ached. It was hard to even be in the house, because all of Opa's favorite places were empty.

When things were finally quiet, and Katherine herself was lying down in her bedroom, Ellie went for a walk with Will. They ended up beside the pond. Sitting on a rock where she and Opa had fished a thousand times, she told Will how bereft she felt. How dry and barren and wasted. And then she started to cry.

* * * * *

Will didn't tell her it would all work together for good. He didn't say there was a reason for everything or that Opa's passing was part of God's sovereign will. He simply sat beside her and held her, letting the tears soak his shirt. He stroked her hair. He stayed in that one position on the rock without moving till his whole body ached, and then he stayed there longer. He stayed until Ellie was ready.

After her tears were spent, they walked together back to the house, where she crawled in bed with her mother. Will sat down in the living room, reading and praying and waiting for Audrey, who had kindly invited him to stay the night at the DuPrees'.

* * * * *

Meanwhile, Audrey and Beecher were on the front porch. They huddled together in the porch swing, holding hands and watching the sunset over the Missouri River. A whippoorwill chirruped in the distance. Crickets played their leg violins. Audrey's midnight-blue dress rustled to the rhythm of the swing. Her feet barely touched the ground, clad in black peep-toe sandals. Beecher's tie was loosened, and his jacket was thrown over the arm of the white wicker rocker by the front door.

His face was red from crying. His eyes, usually so clear and bright, were bloodshot and tired from jet lag. The porch swing swayed gently, as if marking the notes of a lullaby. He slumped, as if his last reserves of energy ebbed away even as the sun dropped lower and lower, leaving the sky a dark, royal purple.

Audrey loosened her hand from his grip and scooted to the far end of the swing. Then, putting her arm around his broad shoulders, she tugged him over so he could lay his head in her lap. Keeping her arm around him and holding him close, she stroked his cheek with her other hand and curled his hair around her tiny fingers. He closed his eyes and more tears came. She wiped them away one by one.

Audrey and Beecher stayed like this for a long time. The stars came out and, with them, a bright three-quarter moon. His breathing became even, the tears stopped, and she thought perhaps he'd fallen asleep. She leaned her head against the swing and closed her eyes, still cradling his head on her lap. She had no idea how much time passed this way.

Then he reached for her hand and brought it to his lips. Sliding out of the swing, he dropped to his knees in front of her. "Audrey," he said, breaking the silence, "I want you to marry me."

Dazed, she leaned forward in the moonlight to inspect his face. Placing her hands on his shoulders, she caressed the back of his neck and then dug into his shoulders, loosening knots of muscle with her delicate fingertips. "You're not lucid, Beecher. You're under extreme duress."

He pulled her down from the swing and onto his lap so their noses were nearly touching. She tucked his head into the soft pillow of her neck and hugged him like a child, excusing his irrational behavior.

He kissed her on the neck, then spoke into her ear. Audrey tingled all over.

Beecher's voice was muffled by her hair, but she could hear him whisper, "I mean it." There was urgency in his words.

Now it was Audrey's turn to cry. Maybe he was delirious, and maybe the offer would be rescinded after a good night's sleep. She wouldn't hold it against him. But just in case this was really happening, Audrey wanted to feel it—completely. She could always remember it later as a beautiful dream.

"I would love to marry you, Beecher."

He leaned into her then, putting his arms around her and

enfolding her in a tight embrace. "I love you, and I need you, Audrey. I don't want to live another moment apart."

She shook her head and smiled at him. "We don't have to."

"I want to seize the day."

Just like their first kiss on her New York balcony, this really was happening. Beecher had proposed, and Audrey had accepted. They held each other for a long moment in the moonlight. Then she stood, and he rose with her, keeping her close.

Her voice was that of a lover and a friend. "I don't want to leave, but you need to sleep."

He turned her toward him, cupping her cheek in his hand, and kissed her gently on the lips. Once…twice…three times.

Audrey led Beecher inside the house to his room and kissed him again at the door. "I'll be back in the morning."

He kissed her eyes, her nose, her lips.

"Good night, Beecher."

"Good night, Audrey."

Chapter Thirty-Six

....

It was the best of times; it was the worst of times. The best because Audrey and Beecher were getting married, which was a dream come true for Ellie on so many levels. But even such boundless joy was darkly overshadowed by the overwhelming loss of Opa. Time seemed insignificant, and the weeks that followed were a blur. Ellie stayed home in Hermann for four days, returning to New York with Audrey only at the insistence of her mother and Beecher. It was that or lose her part in the play.

Once she was back in New York, she poured herself into her role, glad for the respite of being another person and having another life outside the void of facing life without Opa. Sometimes as herself, Ellie felt the void would swallow her up. Playing the part of Stella helped her escape. Working was all she could do to keep going, to survive. That, and running. She became very familiar with the running trails of Central Park. By not answering her phone unless it was Will, her family, or Audrey, she also managed to avoid Jackson Jenkins.

On opening night everyone came. Beecher, Katherine, and Will flew to New York together, along with the DuPrees. They all booked rooms at the Washington Square Hotel, not far from New York University and Audrey's apartment. Jackson, who had contacted Beecher, sent flowers and also expressed his condolences about Opa. He planned to join the group from Missouri on the third row, center stage, and Ellie hoped he would absorb the fact that she and Will were a couple.

Thirty minutes before the lights went down in the house, Corbin Oliver came to the door of the room where Ellie was dressing. His eyes were wild, and there was a deep crease in his forehead. His spiky hair was wet with sweat.

"There's been an emergency." Oliver was breathless. "Emily Jordan cannot perform."

Ellie turned her head to one side, knowing she could not have heard him right.

"What?"

"Her son was in a serious accident. She's on her way to Mount Sinai right now."

The director's words began to sink in.

"You want me to play Blanche? Tonight?"

"You have to, or we're sunk. Can you do it?"

Ellie's mind raced. "Who will be Stella?"

"Jane can do it. She's your alternate, Ellie; I already told her." Oliver's voice was developing an edge.

"I'm sorry. This is just so sudden." Ellie looked the director in the eyes. "Of course I'll do it. Let me get ready."

She rushed to Emily's dressing room, where a costume designer was waiting. Ellie was much taller than Emily, and they had to be creative to make things work. When she walked on stage as Blanche, however, Ellie lost herself in the character. Channeling all of the pain she'd experienced in the past month from losing Opa, she gave the performance of her life.

The theater critics raved about the girl from Missouri. "Branson Beauty Haunts Broadway as Blanche," the headline in the theater section of the *New York Times* the next day proclaimed. Even Corbin Oliver was not short on praise. The celebration of Ellie's success seemed to do them all—especially Katherine, Beecher, and herself—good. She knew Opa would be proud.

As she and Will said good-bye at the airport, Ellie didn't want to let him go. "I don't know when I'll ever come home now, Will."

"You've got all of New York at your feet." He smiled, but his eyes were wistful.

"Could you ever come to New York City? I mean, to stay—and be with me if I was here?"

"I am so proud of you, Ellie. And you must know how I long to be with you." Will looked away for a moment and then back into her eyes. His voice was gentle, yet firm. "But I belong in Branson. I know that's where God wants me to be."

He held her for a long time, crushing her to him, before they said good-bye. As Ellie watched him walk away, a piece of her heart went with him. Something had changed. It was as if the universe had shifted. And she didn't know if it would ever be the same for her and Will again.

* * * * *

Ellie remained in the role of Blanche, continuing to get great reviews. Emily Jordan's son recovered, and because of Emily's star power Corbin began to alternate their performances so that part of the time Ellie went back to being Stella. To the critics, it seemed Ellie could do no wrong. She was their new darling, a precarious position to be in, she knew, but a wave she planned to ride as long as possible.

Jackson Jenkins was persistent. As much as Ellie hated to admit it, her contact with Will had slowed down, and she felt them moving apart, as though their geography was redefining their emotional boundaries. Since the weekend of opening night, they had not been able to find their footing with one another. The implications of it all made her uneasy. Ironically, Jackson seemed to speed things up in proportion. There were roses in her dressing room before every performance and invitations to fashionable events. A reporter from the New York City *Wire* magazine snapped a picture of them leaving Madison Square Garden after a concert, and they were featured in the society section as New York's new "Power Couple." Most of the time Ellie was too distracted—and depressed over Opa—to give it much thought. Jackson was a nice and undemanding friend.

One Sunday afternoon Jackson took her for a carriage ride in Central Park. For once, he was dressed in jeans with a pummeled gray T-shirt. He wore a washed cord shirt the color of a persimmon for a jacket, and copper-colored leather basketball sneakers that were scuffed, like antiques. Ellie was in a dress Katherine ordered her from Sundance, a lacy silk-cotton number in gunmetal that was ironically dubbed "Elysian Fields."

The ride took them past the Dakota, where John Lennon once lived and died, the Wollman Rink, through the Mall, and ended at the Sheep Meadow. At the Sheep Meadow, Jackson paid a seemingly random guy for a kite and handed it to Ellie to fly. She was surprised at how effortlessly it glided on the wind. The colors were vibrant and the shape exotic, like the ones she imagined the children flying in Khaled Hosseini's book.

After a time, the wind died down, so Ellie began to reel in the kite. Something on the tail caught the light of the sun just right and it sparkled, shooting out rays of blinding fire. When it came in closer, Ellie realized there was a ring tied to the kite's tail—a platinum ring with a very large diamond.

She turned it over in her hand and looked at Jackson, who was beaming. There was no hint of fear in his eyes, just confidence. And excitement. He was a good person—a good friend, even. But Ellie had no design on marrying him. If she married, and it had become a big "if," the only life she imagined was with Will. But Will would never be a New Yorker. And for now Ellie's dreams were here. Did that mean God had sent her Jackson? Was she crazy to turn down a millionaire's offer? The ring shimmered and glowed like the bright lights of New York.

"Jackson, I cannot accept this."

The stars in his eyes flickered slightly.

"It's beautiful—amazing. And I am very honored. But it would be wrong of me to take it. I can't."

He grabbed ahold of her hand. "Ellie, you are a fascinating woman. No one has captured my interest like you do. Please consider it."

Ellie shook her head, pressing the ring firmly into his palm. "No."

* * * * *

At the next performance of *A Streetcar Named Desire* Ellie got a standing ovation. Jackson, who miraculously didn't hate her, was in the front row leading the charge. As he stood smiling at her, exultant in her success, Ellie prayed. She bowed, looking out over the crowd as though searching for God's will. "What is Your will? Your will, Lord? Your *Will*," she murmured.

She could not wait for the curtain to go down but ran off the stage and into her dressing room. The scent of roses filled her nostrils as she closed the door behind her. Almost immediately the knocking began.

"Ellie!"

"Miss Heinrichs!"

"May we have a word with you?"

Ellie picked up her phone and dialed Will. It was nearly midnight, but he answered on the first ring.

"Hey there. What are you doing?" His voice sounded sleepy, and she could hear someone snoring in the background.

"Who is snoring?"

"You mean you don't recognize her?" The snoring grew louder and more obnoxious.

It was Dot! Ellie sighed with relief then cringed at her own absurdity. "Thank goodness Cristal hasn't sued you for custody."

"Oh, Cristal's cooled down quite a bit since you left town. She comes to practice with Seth and acts all sugary sweet. I think she's got new designs on the part of Sammy."

"Well, maybe she wouldn't run out on you, like I did."

"I'm not that desperate for a new Sammy yet. Suzy's coming along."

"That's good."

"Ellie, honey, what are you doing?"

"I'm calling you."

"Are you on stage?"

Ellie laughed. "No. I just ran off."

"Why would you do that? You don't want to disappoint your public."

"I don't care about my public."

"Ellie, have you lost your mind?"

"No. Just my heart."

Will sounded more wide awake now. "What do you mean?"

"Will, I mean that I love you. Do you love me?"

His voice sounded anguished. "You told me not to say that unless I was ready to put a ring on your finger."

"Well, do you love me or not?"

"Ellie, I can't hold you back. I won't do that. It would never work."

"Will, you haven't. In fact, you let me go so easily that I, well, I don't know. I've been confused. And with Opa, everything's been kind of a fog. But I'm gaining clarity. And I have to know right now. Do you love me?"

Will sighed heavily into the phone. "Ellie, I love you more than anything or anyone besides Jesus."

A warmth spread over Ellie from the top of her head to the tip of her toes. There it was. She could see it. She could finally *see* God's *Will*.

"I'm coming home."

Chapter Thirty-Seven
....

The vineyards were resplendent with color. It was harvesttime, and the air was cool and kissed with the sweet fragrance of grapes. At the end of the rows under a bower in the center stood Sam and behind him a crowd of guests on chairs draped with white organza. Ellie recognized most of the cast of *The Shepherd of the Hills*, as well as many friends from Hermann. Even Jackson Jenkins was there with his new girlfriend.

On one side of Sam was Beecher, a Greek god in his black tux and tails, and Will was on the other in matching attire. He was the only man who could possibly have been more handsome than Ellie's brother. Ellie could hardly believe she was going to go home with Will, and make her home with Dot in their cabin, and live happily ever after in Branson. God had given her more than she ever could have imagined!

There were two aisles defined by the spaces for walking on either side of the very middle row of grapes. On Beecher's side, about thirty yards back, stood Audrey. Her hair was up, except for the curling tendrils that framed her face, and she wore a gown of pure silk and her grandmother's Victorian lace veil. Mr. Dupree was with her, short and balding, but distinguished in his tuxedo. He patted the tiny manicured hand that was slipped through his arm.

On the other side of the row of grapes, facing Will, Ellie stood with her mother. Katherine had never looked more beautiful than she did today, Ellie thought, and her heart swelled with pride. Katherine looked like a swan in her white chiffon—the epitome of gracefulness. Because of her love, and Opa's, Ellie had made it to this day. She didn't leave anything important behind in New York, except perhaps the enigmatic Andrew McMurray. But that was another story, for another time. What really mattered were the people around her here—at home—and the memories she had of Opa, whom she'd see again in heaven.

Ellie wore a beaded satin gown with scalloped neckline and an impossibly long train. In her hands she carried Opa's handkerchief, and the diary of her great-great-grandmother Elise. She didn't believe in ghosts. But in her spirit she sensed they were both smiling on this day. What an amazing surprise it had been to receive, as a wedding gift from Will's mother, a bundle of old letters and papers wrapped in brown paper and still tied together with string. Along with a check for five hundred dollars "to go toward the wedding," there was a note that said: *Thought you might enjoy putting together this puzzle of family history.* Apparently she'd found it in a recent move to Florida. Will's mother regretted she could not attend the wedding.

As McKenna sang a cappella, Ellie nodded to Audrey. Simultaneously, they walked down their respective aisles, Audrey stepping lightly while she clung to Mr. Dupree's arm, and Ellie and Katherine moving slowly, holding hands. The brides were given away. Sam said a few beautiful words, none of which Ellie would remember. She meant her vows. They all did. Will slipped a simple gold band onto her finger to complement her great-great-grandmother's ruby solitaire, now a valuable antique. But what Ellie was waiting for was the kiss.

* * * * *

William Daniel Howitt
1700 Wabansia, Chicago, Illinois
28 September 1887

Dear Mr. Howitt,

Thank you for your heartfelt condolences at the loss of my father. I regret he was not able to make your acquaintance, as your friendship will always remain very dear to me.

I hope you are well. I will not be able to write to you again as my family's circumstances have been greatly altered since the death of my father. I pray you will forgive me.

I am enclosing your gift of the ruby solitaire, though I treasure the gesture, and your kindness, more than you can ever know. I trust such a rare piece of jewelry will return to you safely and that, in years to come, you may find a perfect home for it as God wills.

Sincerely,

Mrs. Elise Falkenberg Heinrichs

15 May 1891

Dear Daniel,

Congratulations on receiving your Doctorate of Theology. My little sister Ann and I are most proud and rejoice with you in your new post at the college.

Your old chum,

Theodore Proctor

Bishop, Chicago Diocese

20 September 1892
Chicago Tribune
Society Page

Dr. William (Daniel) Howitt of the University of Chicago, and wife, Ann, daughter of meat-packing magnate Paul Proctor, welcome twin boys, Branson Peter and Paul David.

25 July 1893
Chicago Tribune
Obituaries

Ann Proctor Howitt and infant daughter, Elise. Complications of childbirth. Services at St. Mark's Episcopal Church, Saturday noon.

7 April 1910

Dearest Father,
In these hills of my namesake I have come alive both as an artist and a human being. I wish you could see the hill people the way I do, for it is among them that I have found my true beloved. I am staying in a cabin owned by her parents, Old Matt and Aunt Mollie, who have extended such warm country hospitality to me that I feel almost as if they are family.
I plan to paint my darling and bring her portrait home so you can see how beautiful she is. But like these hills, her

beauty goes so much deeper than the surface. I hope I am able to capture that with my brush.

Your loving Son,
Branson

25 October 1915

Father,

Out of respect, I have tried to follow your plan for me, but I see now I was wrong. I cannot stay in the old country studying dead artists anymore when my heart is in Missouri with my love. I know you will disown me, and I am sorry it has to be this way, but you leave me with no alternative. I pray you may someday have a change of heart, but, until then, goodbye, Father.

I love you.
Branson

2 March 1926

Dear Doc Howard,

I wanted to thank you for all you have done for me. Young Matt and I are so excited about going to Chicago to college. What a grand adventure! We know it is your letter of recommendation that got us accepted, and on full scholarships, no less! We cannot wait to bring what we learn back to Branson to benefit the land and lives of the people we hold so dear.

Even more importantly, however, I must thank you for

your spiritual guidance in my life. It is no exaggeration to say that through you, as the Shepherd of the Hills I love so much, I have learned to trust in the true Shepherd of our Souls. For it is through your kindness, and your personal story of redemption and restoration with your son, God rest his soul, and of course your enduring friendship with my in-laws, that I have understood the love of Jesus. I thank the Lord every day that He brought you back to Branson. He truly does work all things together for good, doesn't He—in His time. May He continue to bless you as you feed and care for His sheep!

Your daughter in the faith,
Sammy Lane Matthews

P.S. Congratulations on your new cabin and property on the lake! I plan to ride my horse over there for a visit soon.

Author's Note

....

Love Finds You in Branson, Missouri, is particularly close to my heart because I live not far from Branson. Researching and writing the novel brought back many good memories of childhood vacations there with my family. Also, the landscape is much like my home, and I love the mountains, rivers, and wildlife that surround the town.

Although I started with an outline or map for this story, like most of my travels, the map didn't last long. My characters seemed to have unexpected places they needed to go, so I jumped on board for the ride! From Missouri to New York to Germany and back again, it was a beautiful journey for me, affirming the truth that God's love *really can* find you—wherever you are.

The main themes of *Love Finds You in Branson, Missouri*—God's lavish grace and a family's love—are the themes of my life. I feel very blessed to share them with you. If you'd like to share your journey with me, drop me an e-mail at gfaulkenberry@hotmail.com, or check out my profile on Facebook.

About the Author

....

 Gwen Ford Faulkenberry lives and writes in the Ozark Mountains of Arkansas. She is married to Stone, and they have three children—Grace, Harper, and Adelaide. In addition to mothering and writing, Gwen teaches English at Arkansas Tech University—Ozark Campus. She is the author of *Love Finds You in Romeo, Colorado*, and three devotional books—*A Beautiful Life, A Beautiful Day,* and *Jesus, Be Near Me.*

Love Finds You in
Martha's Vineyard, Massachusetts
by Melody Carlson
ISBN: 978-1-60936-110-5

Love Finds You in
Prince Edward Island, Canada
by Susan Page Davis
ISBN: 978-1-60936-109-9

Love Finds You in Groom, Texas
by Janice Hanna
ISBN: 978-1-60936-006-1

Love Finds You in Amana, Iowa
by Melanie Dobson
ISBN: 978-1-60936-135-8

Love Finds You in
Lancaster County, Pennsylvania
by Annalisa Daughety
ISBN: 978-1-60936-212-6

Love Finds You in
Sundance, Wyoming
by Miralee Ferrell
ISBN: 978-1-60936-277-5

COMING SOON

Love Finds You on
Christmas Morning
by Debby Mayne and Trish Perry
ISBN: 978-1-60936-193-8

Love Finds You in
Nazareth, Pennsylvania
by Melanie Dobson
ISBN: 978-1-60936-194-5

Love Finds You in
Sunset Beach, Hawaii
by Robin Jones Gunn
ISBN: 978-1-60936-028-3

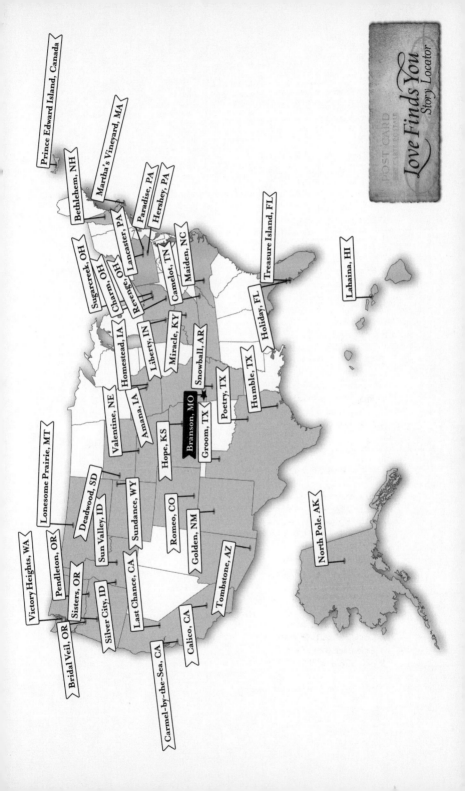